JUST KILLINGS

For Martin
from
Maggie

Enjoy !

JUST
KILLINGS

MAGGIE FEELEY

POOLBEG
CRIMSON

Published 2022 by Crimson
an imprint of Poolbeg Press Ltd
123 Grange Hill, Baldoyle
Dublin 13, Ireland
www.poolbeg.com
Email: info@poolbeg.com

© Poolbeg Press Ltd. 2022, copyright for editing, typesetting, layout, design, ebook

* A catalogue record for this book is available from the British Library.

ISBN 978178199-488-7

www.poolbeg.com

About the Author

Maggie Feeley is the author of *Murder in the Academy*, the first Alice Fox mystery (published by Poolbeg, 2021). She has worked as a social researcher and educator in Ireland and is an activist on issues of gender, sexuality and equality. She was born in Roscommon, Ireland, and spent much of her life in Belfast. She now lives in Dublin with her wife Ann – except for the past seven months when they have been in Catalonia where the third Alice Fox mystery takes place.

For Anaïs, Tamaris, Corbin and Zaga – may you be well loved and learn about kindness.

Prologue

Wicklow Mountains

March 2014

Francis Twomey shuffled from the small bathroom in his slippered feet. The most minimal bodily process took him an inordinate amount of time now and every effort was exhausting. It was just after noon and, on the radio that was perched on top of a small wooden bookcase, the earlier current affairs programme had been replaced by some irritating popular music. He made a deprecating sucking noise between his tongue and teeth and pressed the knob that quieted the din instantly. The silence brought immediate relief.

Taking hold of the arms of the chair, he reversed his stiff frame onto the frayed cushion that afforded him a little comfort. This seat in which he spent his days faced out onto the field behind the cottage and he was momentarily back in An Cuan watching a small boy lead the cattle down to graze in the lower meadow.

Outside he heard a car door slam. He hadn't heard the vehicle approach but at this time it could only be the new volunteer that Meals on Wheels had phoned to forewarn him about. Callers to Brother Francis were few and far between these days.

Now that there was a promise of food, he felt his appetite sharpen and sat up a little more erectly to greet the incomer.

"Hello there!" he called out as cheerfully as he could, when he heard the front door push open.

1

Belfast

March 2014

Mary O'Brien arranged the fresh spring flowers on the main altar of St Oliver's Chapel with a practised sense of dignity and respect. The smell of incense and candlewax lingered in the air and she breathed deeply to get the full sense of it. She had lived in this Belfast parish all her days and every significant happening in her family had been marked in this place – births, marriages, deaths and everything in between.

The chapel didn't play such a big role in life these days, she ruminated, as she tinkered with the flowers. Her own children rarely went to Mass and never to Confession. They snorted with laughter if she ever suggested it. It used to be you had to get in early to Mass in order to get a seat. On Sundays and Holy Days they would be three deep standing at the back and side-aisles and out into the porch. Now, the congregation at the 10 o'clock morning Mass was a handful of grey-haired people, and their walking-aids were parked precariously in the central aisle beside their pews. It's a wonder, she thought, that there weren't more accidents because it was like a slalom run getting up to the altar rails to receive Communion. Of course, there was also an occasional sprinkling of young nuns from Asia or Africa that, in the absence of local vocations, were shipped in to the nearby convent to look after the older sisters. They didn't mingle much and always seemed to be in a dreadful hurry to get back to their duties. Where would it all end, she sometimes tried to figure out. It was unsettling to think that there soon would be no need at all for a big chapel like this one, to say nothing of all the larger churches. She felt oppressed by the inevitability of it all. No doubt St Oliver's would be turned into apartments like that enormous property up the road that used to house orphans and women and girls who got pregnant outside of marriage. Back in the day, the convent and its laundry had been a thriving concern in the area. By all accounts, the nuns had made a pretty penny out of that development but it hadn't made joining the order any more attractive to the local young ones.

Mary examined her flower arrangements with satisfaction and rubbed a damp cloth across the edge of the marble altar to pick up any detritus she had left behind. It was then that out of the corner of her eye she noticed an amber light over one of the confessionals down in the body of the chapel. It struck her as unusual as the light signalled that a priest was inside, available for Confession, but they only had Confessions on a Friday evening now and even then there were very few in attendance. She went down the few steps from the altar, turned respectfully back towards the tabernacle and genuflected. Then she made her way through the altar rails and walked towards the confession box at the top of the left-hand side aisle to turn out the light. Money was always an issue and the parish priest, Canon Murphy, regularly impressed on her that wasting resources was unacceptable. She felt virtuous now to be saving St Oliver's precious pennies.

The wood-panelled confession box had a door in the centre, behind which the priest sat when hearing the sins of those who came to confess, to be absolved and given their penance. This forfeit usually amounted to a few short prayers that had to be recited so that the deal was complete. Mary saw it as a fair bargain and still liked the idea of having what her mother had called "*a clean slate*", when all your sins and misdemeanours were cancelled out. Probably for ventilation, the upper third of the central door was open fretwork, covered on the inside by a purple curtain to ensure discretion. On either side of the priest's position were cubicles with small sliding partitions where the penitents knelt and whispered their sins to the priest. When one person was done, the priest slid the partition across and opened the one opposite. Mary remembered queuing for Confession on a Friday evening as a child, when there would be row upon row of people silently waiting their turn. Back then the sound of the partitions sliding back and forth was what kept the queue in motion. As children they had always wondered what kept some people so much longer than others. Were they really dreadful sinners and what might they have done? Their childish imaginations were well exercised with such speculation.

Mary approached the solid wooden structure casually, vaguely aware of an unpleasant odour. She opened the door of the priest's section and held back the curtain in order to reach in and extinguish the light. Immediately she caught a glimpse of a black jacket sleeve and voiced a hasty apology. "I'm so sorry, Father. I had no idea…" Then she held her breath and her hand clamped over her mouth as she struggled to make sense of what she saw. Momentarily she thought it might be a practical joke of some kind. But no. Something here really did not smell too good and the mouth in the face she saw was a bloody mess, gaping widely and filled with something very messy indeed. There was a sheet of paper, with something typed on it, pinned to the front of the person's clothing. She let the curtain fall, looked around futilely for some source of support and became quite breathless with panic.

She moved towards the sacristy where she had left her coat and her bag which contained her mobile phone.

She took the phone into her shaking hand, dialled 999 and waited. Like an episode of something on the telly, the reply came: "Emergency. Which service do you require?"

She tried to pull herself together. "I think I may have found a dead body in St Oliver's Chapel," she said, aware of how ludicrous this sounded. "In the confession box. I think the person might have been murdered."

The voice told her to move to a place of safety and stay on the line.

"I am safe," she said. "I am in the sacristy and there is no one else here."

She was told that the police and ambulance service would be there in minutes and that she should stay on the line until they arrived. The woman kept her chatting and she calmed down a little. She explained that she had just been doing the flowers and had no idea what had happened or when.

In what seemed no time at all, Mary heard sirens and then heavy footsteps on the tiled floor of the chapel porch. She moved out of the sacristy so that she could show them what she had found.

2

Two male uniformed police officers, followed by an ambulance crew, were making their way up the central aisle of St Oliver's, looking a little awkward and distinctly out of place.

Mary, waiting at the altar rail, found the weapons the policemen carried somewhat shocking in the context of the church. As she waited for them, standing on the step leading down from the altar rails, she thought fleetingly that she was like a hostess welcoming guests for afternoon tea. Instead, when they reached her, she pointed towards the confessional, announcing quietly, "He's in there".

She had left the door ajar earlier when she fled from the horror within and now, with a gloved hand, the officer cautiously edged it open as if it might be booby-trapped. He inspected the scene with some deliberation and then turned towards the ambulance crew, shaking his head.

"Nothing for you here, lads. This one is long past saving. It's the mortuary wagon we'll be needing here. Unless ..." He turned to Mary with a questioning look.

She dismissed him, saying, "No, no. I don't need anything. I'm not hurt. I'm just a wee bit shocked but I'll make a pot of tea now and I'll be fine."

The older policeman turned to his fellow officer and issued a series of directions. "We'll need to tape this off as an immediate crime scene, Bert. Tape the outside as well and then take up your post at the door and only admit Murder Squad, Pathology and Forensics on production of ID. I'll phone through now to the station and get all that sorted and get us some more uniforms to help cover all the exits. Then I'll take a statement from this lady here and make contact with the church authorities."

With that he turned to Mary and asked her if there was somewhere they could talk.

"The sacristy, sir."

He told her to wait there for him and he would be with her shortly.

She withdrew to the sacristy and put on the kettle. Waiting for it to boil, she wondered if she should phone across to the parochial house and let Canon Murphy know what was happening. It was lunchtime and he would be having his meal and then his afternoon nap. Contacting him would be the right thing to do but she hesitated to act without first checking with someone. The police were in charge now and she would wait to talk to the officer before acting on her instincts. Best if they made those awkward decisions.

More than half of Mary's life had been lived in the context of the Northern Ireland Troubles, when violent and deadly actions had taken place on a daily basis. Her community still did not fully identify with the newly packaged police force and she felt that cultural clash now as she waited. She was out of her comfort zone being on her own with a uniformed policeman, never mind that she had just found a dead body. She made a pot of tea and sat down to wait.

The police service of the northern six counties had been totally overhauled in 2001 when the RUC – the Royal Ulster Constabulary – became the Police Service of Northern Ireland – PSNI (known locally as "the Pizznees"). The reforms aimed to bring greater community balance to the force where there was only a small percentage of recruits from the Catholic community. The RUC had been seen as partial towards the Protestant Unionist community for decades and hostile to nationalists. When moves were made to reform the force, serving RUC officers had been offered generous retirement deals to vacate their posts and a 50/50 recruitment policy was given ten years to equalise the community make-up of the new police force. By 2011 the results were a 60/30 split of those perceived to come from the Protestant and

Catholic faiths. Loyalist and Unionist representatives said it was time to end blatant discrimination against non-Catholics who wanted to join up. Nationalists claimed that the policy was positive discrimination designed to end sectarianism in policing and should be continued until parity was achieved. The controversial policy was stopped ten years after its introduction and, in the three years between then and now, little progress had been made in bringing the equality objective forward.

Mary had registered that neither of the two policemen had known how to behave in a Catholic church and that didn't surprise her one bit.

In the sacristy, she told the PSNI officer all that she could about the few moments that led to her dreadful discovery. He asked her if she had noticed anything out of the ordinary. She replied that she had already told him that the light over the confession box signalling that it was in use on Wednesday morning was unusual. That was what had made her go there. She had wanted to save the parish the additional expense of having lights left on unnecessarily. Look where that had got her.

When the canon finally arrived over, in response to the call from the police, he looked at her as if she was the one responsible for disturbing the afternoon routine that he guarded so preciously. She felt peeved and disgruntled and now apparently she had to wait for the detectives to arrive and tell her story all over again. For such a small slice of her time, telling and retelling it was taking up an awful lot of her day. When would she get some lunch, she wondered ... but who, apart from her, was going to give any thought to that?

3

Detective Inspector Caroline Paton, head of the Belfast Murder Squad, had just sat down in Alice Fox's living room when her phone rang. She was dressed for work in a well-cut, charcoal-grey trouser suit and a pale-blue shirt blouse. Her shoulder-length chestnut hair was tucked behind her ears, showing a pair of jade-green stud earrings that matched her eyes. As usual, she had kicked her shoes off as she came through the door and had thrown herself onto the comfortable sofa. She rolled her eyes now and knew in her bones that this wasn't a routine call. Her colleagues knew better than to disturb her lunch with something that was less than extremely serious.

Alice stopped pouring their coffee and waited for Caroline to finish on the phone.

It ended with her saying, "OK, I'm on my way. I'm

just in Botanic so ten minutes at most." Already getting to her feet, she looked apologetically at Alice. "I was really looking forward to a peaceful break but we have a fresh murder up Ormeau Road and I need to get there pronto."

She swiftly gathered her belongings and, as she left, touched her fingers to her lips and blew Alice a kiss.

"Who knows when I'll see you, Alice Fox! I'll call you when I get a minute." And she was gone, taking the stairs to the ground floor at a gallop.

Alice smiled as she heard the car engine rev enthusiastically outside and turned to her coffee and tuna salad with just a little less appetite than before.

Alice was in many ways, in appearance at least, the epitome of the all-American woman – slender and blonde with a tan that never really faded completely. Underneath that gentle exterior she was flexible and muscular and carried her strength, like her sharp, critical mind, with quiet confidence. She exuded fitness. Where Caroline struggled to get to the gym a few days a week, Alice ran the length of the Lagan towpath every morning, often before the sun had managed to rise.

Since she had arrived in Ireland for the academic year in 2013 a lot of unexpected things had happened in Alice's life. She was on a university exchange programme between Belfast City College's Department of Peace and Reconciliation, known locally as DePRec, and City University New York. At the beginning of the term in August, she had taken up the one-year post-doc position. An ex-detective turned academic, she had completed a doctorate in CUNY on the topic of restorative justice. The project was both personal and academic in that the catalyst had been the sudden death of her police sergeant father in an encounter with a drugged-up teenage joyrider. Alice and some of her family had participated in a restorative-justice dialogue with the young man who was by then incarcerated in a bleak detention centre. The upshot was life-changing for her. She had left the police force and gone on a learning journey to try to understand the roots of those tumultuous events in some kind of meaningful and useful way. Over ten years later, she considered herself to be still looking for answers although perhaps the questions had changed since she had first framed them. Now, in Belfast, she divided her time between college work in DePRec and a community-based placement in the EXIT youth project in West Belfast. Her deskwork took place either in her college office in the *Titanic* Quarter or at home in the Botanic area where she had settled happily into a rhythm of life that suited her very well.

The Botanic area was the ideal location for her to have the abundance of exercise that she craved in her life. As well as her daily run along the Lagan towpath, she swam in the Queen's University Physical Education Centre and cycled around the city between DePRec, home and the EXIT group. She regularly practised Tae Kwon Do, a skill that she was now sharing with the young people in her EXIT study group. During the Christmas break she had walked in the Wicklow Hills and now, under the loving guidance of DI Caroline Paton, she was discovering the impressive scope for hiking in the Mourne Mountains. There was no absence of opportunities for keeping fit.

Her liaison with Caroline had surprised them both. Neither had been really looking for an intimate relationship but nonetheless they now found themselves exploring this new and very satisfying territory. The unromantic context of their initial meeting had been the gruesome murder of a DePRec colleague which was discovered after the Christmas break, over two months ago now. The proximity of the killing to Alice's life had drawn her back into the business of detection and she had, in her characteristic unobtrusive manner, made an invaluable contribution to solving that case.

Once Alice and Caroline had got together there had been some soul-searching, mostly for Caroline, about how open their relationship should be. Alice had no issues with being openly gay although she didn't make a big deal about her sexuality and was discreet by nature. In the aftermath of her father's death her long-term relationship with a guy had floundered under the pressure of all the changes she was going through, both personally and in terms of her worldview. A gaping chasm had opened up between them and by the time Alice had graduated and decided to move into postgraduate studies there was nothing left to salvage. Little by little, she had become more consciously feminist in her views and had a few short but happy intimate relationships, mostly with women. Time was her biggest restraint but, since she had finished her PhD, she now had more opportunities to relax and become more outward-looking.

She understood that it was a different story for Caro who would move cautiously about introducing any distracting factors into her steady connections with her Murder Squad colleagues, or anyone else for that matter. Northern Ireland had great equality legislation but organisations like the police force moved slowly in terms of the practice of becoming less misogynistic and more open to diversity.

There was also the personal issue of their divergent views on justice and policing, and so far that too had taken its place on the list of deferred conversations. Perhaps as a way of avoiding these issues, they had decided to take things slowly and without articulating the obvious fact that Alice's stay in Ireland was time-limited. And, anyway, who knew what would happen when the academic term finished?

Since they had worked together on the DePRec killing, Alice had immersed herself in her academic and community work but had been irresistibly drawn to the company of the senior police officer. In as much as she could explain the attraction, she had been drawn to

Caroline for her direct and often droll manner. She exuded a powerful drive and was razor-sharp professionally. At the same time, with her peers and in her personal life she managed to be kind and irreverent and very entertaining. She was both very serious and at times entirely and shamelessly silly.

As they exchanged observations about each other one morning over breakfast in bed, Caroline confessed that she had fallen almost immediately under the spell of Alice's "understated charisma".

"What might that mean in plain English?" Alice had prodded her mischievously between the ribs with her forefinger.

"Well, I suppose it means you have a kind of reserve that makes you fascinating. You don't reveal yourself too easily. You are happy to stand back and avoid the limelight and that paradoxically attracts attention to you. Well, it attracted my attention to you." She paused and held Alice's open, amused gaze. "And ... leaving aside your brilliant mind just for the moment ..." here she feigned serious reflection, "your bodily confidence, the way you move so melodically through the world, well, it's just captivating for a humble police officer from Northern Ireland. My resistance to your charms plummeted to zero once the work was out of the way. Or maybe even a bit before that, if I am to be entirely honest."

And these reflections had stopped there as the need

for analysis was overtaken by the irrepressible urge to act on those attractions.

As the weeks passed and they were each flushed with pleasure at just how much they could delight in the other, there was increasingly an unspoken consciousness of the timescale that limited their future. The swallows that were getting ready to leave on their migratory journey when Alice arrived the previous August were already on the return trip towards the cool Irish summer. March was well under way and Alice was due to return to the States in just over five months. Both women were holding off on that conversation for now but it was lurking in the background and would soon demand attention ... but not just yet.

Alice pulled herself out of that train of thought, finished her lunch and gathered the things she would need for the EXIT programme later. She and Hugo, the youth worker with the group, had put together a self-defence course. It included a martial arts session from Alice to build the young people's bodily confidence and then a group discussion that looked at how to avoid or manage conflict in relationships through peaceful means. In the gap between the two parts, Hugo usually treated Alice to fish and chips in a nearby, small, family-run Italian café where he was a regular customer. It was only right, he said, that the project acknowledged her voluntary contribution and it was his way of making sure she had enough stamina to cycle home after her labours.

Hugo and Alice rubbed along well together and both they and the group of eight young adults enjoyed the challenge of the work they were doing. Many of the young people had already been convicted in the Northern Ireland criminal justice system and had spent time in juvenile or adult incarceration. Some were engaged with Hugo in restorative-justice encounters with their perceived victims, although where the root responsibility lay for their alleged crimes was often not entirely clear-cut. To address that quandary, as a group, they were currently planning meetings with a range of public representatives. In these gatherings they would ask for explanations of the systemic wrongs they felt the social structures perpetrated on them and their families. These promised to be lively encounters.

As she glanced out the window at the early spring sunshine, Alice felt the relief that came with the promise of longer days and lighter evenings. This year had been intended to help her transition to a new phase in her academic career. She had a book proposal to complete and funding to chase but, for now, life in Belfast was enough and she was loath to plan anything that would disturb that easy contentment.

4

Detective Sergeant Bill Burrows and Detective Constable Ian McVeigh of the Belfast Murder Squad waited in the car outside the chapel for the DI to arrive. Burrows was in his fifties and more than a little grey around the temples. He wasn't big into exercise and had an expanding waistline that stretched his shirt buttons to their limits. By contrast, McVeigh was in his early thirties and a sharp dresser. He kept himself fit doing weights training whenever work and family demands allowed. He was enthusiastic about his detection work and planned to seize whatever career opportunities came his way. Being selected for the highly competitive post in the Murder Squad had given him a great boost and he gave it his all, taking every opportunity to learn from his older colleague.

There was a local station nearby and the uniformed

officers from there had already done a good job of taping off a traffic lane on the road outside the chapel to allow the incoming personnel to park with ease.

Burrows and McVeigh had been briefed by a local officer and then returned to the car to try and have their lunch before things got really busy. The two men were comfortable in each other's company and both were finishing their sandwiches and listening to the lunchtime news on the radio when their boss arrived. They rapidly swept away the crumbs from their laps and stood out on the pavement.

They greeted her with a respectful "Ma'am", and she asked for an update. The three had an easy but professional relationship and the men knew that when a new case was in question Paton was focused on that to the exclusion of all else.

Burrows gave a brief report. "Shortly after twelve-thirty, a woman doing the flowers on the altar noticed a light on outside a confession box. It is supposed to signal that a priest is *in situ* and available to hear confessions but the woman knew this was not the case and went to turn off the light. Apparently she had been told by the parish priest to save electricity. When she opened the door and pulled back the curtain to locate the light switch, she discovered a body. She did not know the victim so we are probably not looking at someone from this parish. She only touched the door handle and the curtain and immediately backed off." Burrows paused to allow a young uniformed officer carrying a large roll of tape to pass and then continued. "She called in to emergency services at twelve thirty-eight and is waiting inside to talk to us. Mary O'Brien is her name. She lives locally and regularly does odd jobs around the chapel. A couple of times now she has let the uniforms know that she needs to have her lunch at some point."

Caroline smiled. "Who have we got on the job so far?" she asked over her shoulder as she flashed her badge at the uniformed officer at the door of the chapel and ducked under the yellow-and-black tape.

Burrows and McVeigh followed in her wake, listing the colleagues that had already arrived.

"Dr Boylan arrived just a few moments before you, ma'am, and the forensics team is on its way. It will be Tim Bryson leading. We worked with him on the DePRec case back in January." McVeigh was pleased to be catching up again with his college buddy but didn't mention the connection. DI Paton wasn't interested in superfluous detail that had no bearing on the facts of an inquiry.

Inside the gothic entrance, a number of people were already putting on protective clothing. The three Murder Squad detectives joined in the process, slipping the disposable hooded white jumpsuits over their clothes and the matching booties over their footwear. There were holy-water fonts on either side of the inner doors and a number of looming statues on the high window ledges in the porch. These gave the detectives a distinct, ironic sense of being kept under surveillance while they got geared up to approach the murder scene. Caroline thought that if the perpetrator had come in or out this way, the scene was already well contaminated by those in attendance. Perhaps the locals had thought of that but anyway there was no point in making a fuss at this point.

"We'll view the scene first and then we'll talk to Mrs O'Brien and the person in charge in the parish. We need to take ownership of the scene from them and all that entails. What is the name of the senior cleric?"

"Canon Murphy, ma'am," said Burrows.

'Well, at least we're not going to be stopping Sunday Mass." She gave a characteristic wry look at her colleagues. "Are we all set, guys? Let's see what we've got."

They opened the double wooden doors, with an adrenalin push, and headed inside.

5

Entering the main body of the chapel, it wasn't hard to identify the precise location of the murder. The area around a wooden structure at the top of the left-hand side aisle had been taped off, indicating the immediate scene of the crime. A passageway and door off to the right had also been designated as being of interest by the presence of more crime-scene tape. Caroline was relieved that the potential entrance and exit had been sealed for scrutiny. A uniform officer was posted at this point to deter anyone straying into the area until it was meticulously swept and recorded by forensics.

Already a sizeable group of people dressed in protective clothing were busy in the immediate vicinity of the wooden confessional. The pathologist Cynthia Boylan and her assistant were standing by behind the tape, as someone was setting up a series of strong spotlights on adjustable stands. Boylan's junior was assembling his camera equipment, ready to record the elements of the scene relating to the actual body. Others were investigating the detail of the wider location that might be necessary when and if a case finally came to court. A band of uniformed officers was searching the entire area of the church, bagging finds and placing numbered markers at points of possible interest. A series of heavy-duty plastic stepping-stones had been strategically placed around the confessional to preserve the surface. There was a ragged hum of activity that was doubtless alien to the sombre array of saints that overlooked them from sunlit stained-glass windows behind the main altar.

As the Murder Squad made their way up the central aisle, the lights in the whole church were switched on, presumably to make the business of locating and recording evidence easier. The dramatic impact of this change to the setting was like walking from night into day and revealed that the interior of the chapel was much larger than was previously apparent. An elaborately carved wooden pulpit rose from amongst the seats at the top left-hand side. Here was where sermons were delivered and the faithful kept on track.

The three detectives paused momentarily and took their bearings again in the newly lit nave of what was now exposed as a slightly down-at-heel place of worship.

The arrival of the Murder Squad made a tangible impression on those already present at the scene. As the chief investigating officer, Caroline Paton commanded attention and had authority and priority in viewing the scene. The local officers who were facilitating the incoming specialists deferred immediately to her. They stopped what they were doing and waited for the order to proceed.

"Carry on!" She waved impatiently at them to keep going. Then she spoke directly to the pathologist. "We'll be there with you in a moment, Cynthia, and then you can get started."

Caroline had hesitated as she moved through a gap between two rows of seats that would access the side aisle. She had noted an elderly, portly man dressed in a dark suit and wearing a white dog collar standing proprietorially on the altar. From his position, caught in the light from the windows behind, he looked a little like a caricature. He was red-faced and scowling and looking horrified by the drama developing before him. Although nothing was audible, she thought he might well have been hissing.

"Canon Murphy, I presume," she said as she approached. "I am Detective Inspector Caroline Paton."

He looked down on the detectives and drew his lips into an irritated pucker.

"I am the parish priest here in St Oliver's," he announced a little pompously. "I am the person in charge of everything that happens on church property." He paused then, resting his joined hands on his stomach and perhaps thinking that this might not be the role to assert in these unusual circumstances.

Caroline quickly relieved him of his responsibilities. "I am afraid we will be taking over this crime scene for the immediate future until we have gathered any evidence that is available." He raised his eyebrows as if to object but she deftly cut him off. "When my detectives and I have had a chance to inspect the scene, I will need to ask you to accompany them to view the remains so we can establish if the deceased is a member of your congregation."

The canon hesitated at this suggestion and then reluctantly appeared to accept the unpleasant task as his duty. He signalled his compliance and Caroline continued to outline her requirements.

"Might I ask you also to ensure that any activities planned for the church, in the next twenty-four hours at least, are cancelled. As senior officer, it is my responsibility to make sure that no part of the area is contaminated by people who may unwittingly disturb a piece of evidence." Having made her point, she continued in a more kindly tone. "I understand that you live nearby, Canon Murphy. Can I ask you to withdraw now and trust me to make sure that your premises are treated respectfully? My investigators will call on you as soon as we need you."

She left him no room to argue with this option and, turning, made her way back to the location of the body.

Burrows approached the elderly cleric and asked

him to show him the way to the parochial house, thus diplomatically escorting him off the premises.

With their rights securely established, Caroline and McVeigh turned their attention to the confessional which was now surrounded by a number of strong freestanding spotlights, giving the impression of a carefully prepared set, ready for filming to begin.

They approached the confessional and edged the door further open. Under the glare of the standing spotlights, the gruesome reality of their latest murder case was starkly revealed. The victim was seated in the confession box, facing outwards. He was in his sixties with grey, slightly wavy hair that retained some signs of his more youthful colour. He had jet-black eyebrows that were raised in an expression of alarm. Most demanding of the viewer's attention was the mouth. It gaped rudely, reluctant to accommodate something composed of bloodied flesh that had been inserted and was only partially contained within the mouth cavity. Superfluous matter hung garishly around the area, concealing the lips and leaving an impression of someone caught in a shocking act of gluttony. The pale-blue eyes were open, staring and horrified.

The man was dressed in a black suit of a style often worn by members of the clergy. A surprisingly pristine-white dog collar was visible above a large sheet of white paper pinned to the man's chest with a sizeable nappy pin. There was some printed text on the paper but it wasn't possible to read it because the man's arms were folded upwards at the elbows and crossed so that each hand rested on the opposing shoulder. The feet, clad in muddy black-laced shoes, were touching at the heels and pointing outwards so that the knees and upper legs fell open. The crotch of his stretched, black trousers was stained as if he had wet himself. There was a discernible and sickening aroma of some bodily fluid and something like alcohol trapped in the enclosed space.

Caroline looked carefully at the corpse before her and the way it had been staged. "There's a lot going on here," she muttered quietly to herself then turned to those waiting to get to work on the latest puzzle they had been set. "Do your damnedest, guys," she said. "Tomorrow morning for the autopsy, Cynthia? I'll let you know later which of us to expect to join you. As soon as George has some pictures he can upload them to the shared drive. That will give us something to work on." And to the rest of the white-clad investigative staff she said, "It looks as if there are lots of messages left for us with this one so we must make sure not to miss anything. Let's get to work."

Her words were like the starting pistol at a race and everyone immediately became immersed in their own part of the forensic-evidence collection.

Caroline and her team withdrew to the quieter area of the altar. Behind the carved wooden railing and raised by several steps, they viewed the scene. The taped-off passageway to their left led to a side door and the marks on the tiled floor suggested this was indeed the route that had been taken by whoever had transported the body to its final resting place. At their elevated level they could see another route taped off to their right that must lead from the altar to the sacristy where Mary O'Brien waited impatiently.

"I'll have a word with Mrs O'Brien and you have a look at what's on the other side of that side door. Is there any sign of forced entry or information to be gleaned about how the victim got here? At least it has been dry overnight so that's in our favour. We won't have lost any evidence to the rain." She paused to consider the facts. "It looks as if the killing and arrangement of the remains may have been done elsewhere. Otherwise we'd have more mess here or signs of cleaning up ... Let's hold all that in mind anyway."

Burrows and McVeigh were attentively following Paton's line of thinking. All three were comfortable with each other's approach to a new case and knew from experience that the DI's initial instincts were always sound.

"You two have a first talk with the canon. Ian, your insider etiquette will be useful."

They all nodded, affirming her understanding of the complexities of local cultural politics. The police force had not historically been well-disposed to Catholicism and, while some deep trenches of bigotry still remained, the Murder Squad led by DI Caroline Paton would never be found guilty in that regard.

Ian McVeigh wasn't religious now but had been brought up in a Catholic family and this wouldn't be the first time his cultural savvy had been useful to the team. Initially, he had sometimes thought of himself as the token Catholic on the squad but he had never sensed the smallest hint of discrimination from his two immediate colleagues. His experience of the wider police force was not so flawless but he had learned that these were matters that mostly remained elusive, hard to verify and so far were usually best disregarded.

"See if anything out of the ordinary has been happening recently," Caroline said. "He has agreed to help with identifying the remains when Cynthia has had a chance to tidy things up a bit. If he doesn't know the victim, what does he think about the possible identity of the cuckoo in his nest? See what he's got to say on the matter." She paused to see if they were in agreement. "OK. Good. I'll call into the local station when I'm finished here and sort out the niceties of an escort for the body and I'll get the door-to-door started ASAP. If we're lucky maybe someone saw the delivery take place. We can meet up back at base this evening and agree a plan of action."

DS Burrow's expression indicated that he wanted to add something.

"Yes, Burrows?"

"I'm imagining the press will love this one, ma'am. Any thoughts about how we want to control the message?"

Ian McVeigh was nodding vigorously. "There'll be no chance of keeping a lid on this ... this is a very tight community where news travels fast." He had family in the area and understood the territory.

"You're right, of course. I'll phone the Super from the car and get an initial press statement ready for him first thing when I get back. We'll try and push the full press conference back to tomorrow afternoon at the earliest when we'll have a better idea what we're at. We can't assume this is a member of the clergy. It may be some staged kind of anti-clerical statement. Maybe the canon will give us a name or we'll hear from Cynthia that there is some ID on the body. Then things will become more straightforward in terms of what we're dealing with."

The Belfast Murder Squad dealt with in and around twenty murders each year and had access to support staff from local branches when this was necessary. All three of the core team preferred it this way. The more staff on a case the easier it was to lose both track of where they were in an investigation and the momentum needed to keep on top of the twists and turns each case took. As an elite team, they had an excellent record of solving cases and had established a rhythm of work that suited them all.

McVeigh was married with a first child which meant his sleep pattern was interrupted most nights. He had fast-tracked through the graduate programme and was quietly ambitious. Burrows was older and, like Paton, had begun his career in the RUC and then remained to become part of the new police service. Making that decision in itself was indicative of an interest in a more open and inclusive organisation and Burrows was fully committed to the PSNI goals. He had witnessed the darker days in the force when it wouldn't have been possible to claim the organisation was fair in its dealings with the whole community. Burrows was a gentle family man whose grown-up children had flown the coop. He and his wife Myrtle were avid gardeners and with the advent of spring they were already busy outdoors when the weather permitted. McVeigh could tell when the gardening season had begun by the amount of soil under his colleague's nails. "Burrows by name and Burrows by nature," Myrtle would say when he embarked on digging a new flowerbed. It was true. He loved excavating and puzzle-solving and was equally happy tinkering with small bits of DIY or labouring over a complicated thousand-piece jigsaw. His approach to detective work was no different. He was adept at following a trail of evidence until it fully gave up its secrets and he relished that patient burrowing into each new case.

As they rang the doorbell of the parochial house, both men harnessed all their resources for this new inquiry. A slim, grey-haired woman answered the door allowing an unpleasant, lingering smell of cooking to emerge. She was wearing a flowery apron on which she was wiping her greasy hands. When they held out their PSNI ID, she winced slightly and looked away.

"Canon Murphy is expecting you. Please follow me."

6

Alice and Hugo took their usual Wednesday table in the chipper on the Glen Road, around the corner from the EXIT project. It was automatically reserved for them each week and there was always a small pot of wild flowers on the table. Nonna Anna, the eldest of the Fusco family members, was a romantic and hopeful that Alice and Hugo would become a couple. Hugo, in his late forties, was divorced and had a teenage son, and she thought that the attractive American would be the perfect match for him. Hugo had been of the same mind for a while but now realised that they would continue as close friends and colleagues and that would do well enough.

The Fuscos came to Ireland from southern Italy back in the middle of the previous century when there was an influx of Italian families that set up businesses right across the island. They specialised in fish and chips, pizza and homemade ice cream and most flourished and settled into their chosen communities. Domenico and Anna started the café in 1956 and called it Mario's after Domenico's grandfather. They were both just thirty then and worked hard to build both a family and a business. Anna, now known to everyone as Nonna – Grandmother – was eighty-eight and still pottering around chatting to customers and directing the younger family members who kept the business going. Dom had died of a massive heart attack ten years earlier and his widow still wore black as a sign of her loss.

After her Tae Kwon Do session with the group, Alice was always hungry and allowed herself the indulgence of the generous helping of fried fish that was the norm in Mario's. Since their first visit there back in January, Nonna had made Alice a special green salad every Wednesday and she joked with Hugo that if he would forgo some of his chips his romantic possibilities might be more hopeful. Tonight, as they ate, they were discussing the unusual absence of Jed from today's session. He was rarely missing and, if he was, there was always an explanation sent along with one of the others or he texted Hugo in advance. Jed was working on his literacy skills and had mastered a few useful text messages that he delighted in using. Gary, another group member, spent a few hours a week working one-to-one with Jed and the rest of the group were very encouraging and supportive of this. They all felt that they had been wronged by the system in a number of ways and admired any actions to redress those injustices.

"I think if he's not in this evening's session I'll call to the house afterwards and make sure all is well there." Hugo always held off interfering in the group members' private lives until he was invited but he balanced that alongside his sense of their vulnerability and tried to strike a sensible balance.

He was tinkering with his food more than eating it and Alice recognised this as measure of his concern. He was an inveterate eater.

"There's just him and his mother and they are very close. Brenda's mother, Jed's gran, lives in Dublin and has only been in their lives since Jed was eleven or so. Before that they were on their own." He seemed contented to have made a decision and tucked into his remaining food with something more like his usual appetite.

Alice recognised all too well the family story of people who are dealt a more difficult hand in life. With the young people she worked with in Lowell, Massachusetts, she had seen it all and knew that the brute luck of the family you are born into can determine your whole life trajectory. Despite her father's tragic death, she realised her own privilege and the support her family were for one another. They didn't have the financial issues most of these kids had and they all got a sound educational base to build on or not as they chose. She was closest, in age and every other way, to her sister Sam and they talked several times a week.

With the time difference between Lowell and Belfast it was usually when Alice was getting ready to sleep and Sam was just finishing work. She had a brother too but they were not on the same wavelength about many things. There was a family loyalty and he would weigh in if she needed him but they had moved miles apart in their view of the world. Red thought Alice was wasting her time with disadvantaged young people. He thought people made their own prosperity in life and if they failed they had only themselves to blame. He was a firefighter in their hometown, married with three kids and was struggling to understand them as they became restless teenagers who no longer thought he was infallible. Roberta, Alice's mom, had become more involved in her local community since her husband died but mostly she lived for her children and grandchildren. She delighted in baking for any available family member and watching them eat her creations. She was the personification of the saying that food is love.

"Maybe you'd come along with me to Jed's?" Hugo broke into Alice's thoughts. "He lives down the Road in the Divis Tower and you could head on home from there."

He didn't often ask her to do extra things and she knew on instinct that he had some good reason for this request.

"Sure," she said without hesitation. "I'm always open to exploring new horizons." She bestowed her one-sided smile on him and without further elaboration he knew she had understood.

7

Brenda Clinton had gone to the Wednesday meeting of survivors of clerical and institutional abuse directly from her cleaning job in an office block at the back of the Belfast City Hall. She and her son Jed lived in the Divis Tower block on the lower Falls Road and so she was easily able to walk to and from work in the city centre. The survivors' group met in the premises of Amnesty International on the Ormeau Road and she could get there on the bus in less than ten minutes if she was lucky. In any case, nobody minded if she was late and she had always felt accepted and welcomed in that place.

The group was meeting this week to discuss the newly established Historical Institutional Abuse Inquiry that had begun its work in January that year. Although she had only started to attend recently, the survivors' group had been meeting for years and was encouraged by the successes of similar groups south of the border. As long ago as 1999, those in the twenty-six counties had already seen a State apology by the Taoiseach for wrongs done to children taken into State care. More recently in the previous year there had been another State apology in the South to the women who had been treated abusively in the Magdalene laundries. A comprehensive inquiry into the Irish Industrial Schools and a redress scheme were put into place which had seen people's stories discussed openly in the media. In many ways this had galvanised public outrage and support but, listening at a distance, those in the North had felt left behind and less cared about by the authorities there. Northern survivors were angry that their rights to be heard and get justice were constantly overshadowed by the bickering of the local political parties. Sinn Féin, the Alliance Party and Amnesty International were consistent advocates for survivors' rights but progress was slow and it just all felt like more layers of abuse pouring down on the survivors who had the added misfortune to live in the North.

Sometimes it seemed to Brenda as if there was a hierarchy too amongst victims that determined who was able to access their rights and who wasn't. The enquiry that had just begun didn't cover everyone. Victims of clerical abuse in the North were outside the remit of the Historical Institutional Abuse Inquiry as were former residents of Magdalene Laundry-type residential settings, if they were aged eighteen or over at the time. It was these omissions that were being talked about most in the survivors' meetings around this time and Brenda had a personal interest in the arguments being made. She had never spoken in the meetings, as she didn't have the confidence or the education to be comfortable voicing her views in public. She had strong feelings and often wished she could just raise her hand and add her voice to the others in the room but that never happened. She knew she would struggle to find the right words and, even though she knew how she felt, each time she failed to respond to the urge to speak out she berated herself for being such a coward. She knew that this was not very helpful behaviour for herself or anyone else but, for now, being present was the best she could do. At the age of thirty-nine, decades after her own abuse, she knew she had finally found a place where she fitted in and that was enough progress for the moment.

Brenda shook off this distracting thread of ideas. The man next to her was passing on the attendance sheet and she signed her name carefully and added her email address. She rarely wrote anything as her writing wasn't the best but she could read enough to get the gist of emails the group sent out and identify the dates and times for meetings.

She passed the clipboard to the older woman who had arrived after her, complaining about the delays in the traffic on the road.

"There's some kind of a blockage up the road," she grumbled. "The traffic is well and truly jammed up."

Talk in the room had turned to the topic of the Kincora Boys' Home. It came up at the meeting nearly every week. The man from Amnesty said the point was that the British Government had been colluding for decades in the cover-up in relation to the East Belfast Care Home. Back in 1981 three senior members of staff had been jailed for abusing eleven boys there. But, he said, they were quite certain there was more abuse that never came out and that British Intelligence Services were involved in blocking the original police investigation into a paedophile ring at Kincora. Amnesty International had always claimed that visitors to Kincora, to access the young boys, had included members of the military, politicians and civil servants. They alleged that a cover-up had been managed by the Ministry of Defence and MI5.

Brenda felt her blood boil. Something snapped in her head and before she realised what was happening she was on her feet. "Excuse me, mister. What you're saying is making me so angry I feel as if I will burst." She looked around as if for guidance about what to say next but then continued. "What can the likes of us do if the ones with all the power are stopping the truth from coming out? They've been doing it for years and years. Those government and army ones are protecting people that buggered wee boys who had no families to look out for them. They don't care a damn about the truth or what is right. They are just covering their backs and protecting their own cronies. And the Catholic Church is just as bad. I know that story personally, believe me. But for those abused by the clergy – we are not even included in the inquiry."

She found all eyes were on her. People were nodding in agreement and she thought she saw the man next to her wipe away a tear with the back of his hand. She felt that she must have made some sense if people were reacting as they were. She took a deep breath and continued.

"I'm finished now – I'm running out of words – but I hope that all the work you people are doing won't stop until we are all getting our fair share of the justice. You have to speak up for those of us that are too frightened or ground down to be able to do it. I suppose what I mean is thank you and keep it up!"

And then there was spontaneous applause from all sides of the room.

Brenda realised she had said what others were thinking and she flushed with pride that she had risen above her fear. She felt as if she had won a small victory against the enemy that kept her silent and it felt very satisfying.

The man from Amnesty was answering her. He was talking about the need to keep on fighting against oppression even in small ways, like writing letters or speaking to neighbours and friends so that the word spread. Brenda knew he was right. Each time you spoke your truth you added a little bit to the fight against the ones who tried to block the facts from getting out. She had said as much the other day when she had told her Jed a little of her own mother's story. She knew he wasn't sure what to do with the information but he was a good lad and he would work it out.

The man beside her tapped her gently on the hand and whispered, "Thanks, Brenda".

She realised he must have read her name off the clipboard when she was signing her name and contact info. She smiled at him and tuned back into the ongoing discussion while at the same time enjoying the deeply satisfying feeling of having found her voice.

8

After a lively group discussion about relationship management, Alice and Hugo locked up the EXIT project and set off on their bikes for the Divis Tower. No one in the group had heard from Jed and they were more convinced now that calling to see him was a good course of action. It was just after eight o'clock when they left and now completely dark. In a few weeks the clocks would change and extend the reach of the bright evenings but for now they were glad of the well-lit streets and the car headlights to illuminate their path. It was marginally downhill all the way to the Divis Tower and they were there in not much more than fifteen minutes.

"Jed is on the tenth floor," said Hugo, pressing the call button on the lift. "At least the lift's working. It isn't always the case. You might skip up ten flights of stairs without too much effort, Alice, but I'd be a stretcher case!" He chuckled contentedly.

Hugo provided a potted history of the building as they waited for the lift and made their way up to the tenth floor. Ironically, it had been constructed in the 60s to replace slum housing but Divis Flats did not prove to be an ideal solution in Catholic West Belfast. Within a stone's throw of the city centre and housing the parishioners of nearby St Peter's Pro Cathedral, the Divis complex was part of a much more extensive planned development that ran out of money. Twelve eight-storey blocks of flats and one twenty-storey tower were erected between the mid-1960s and early 70s. Poorly designed and badly constructed, the flats provided a notoriously dire living environment that was named in a European Union report in 1982 as "the worst of its kind in Europe". Between dysfunctional buildings and frequent clashes between the army, the residents and local IRA units, it was reported that at one stage something like sixty-eight percent of residents were on tranquillisers. After years of campaigning, the flats were finally demolished in the late eighties and only the tower block remained. The Housing Executive invested in refurbishment and, despite ongoing issues with the heating system and damp, it became a more acceptable place to live. During the Troubles, the army had an observation post on the top of "The Tower" and for some years they also occupied the top two floors with an array of surveillance equipment. As peace took hold, the military inhabitants finally withdrew in 2005 and the whole building became a community residential facility again.

Outside 10B Hugo and Alice rang the doorbell and waited. At the sound of movement inside, Hugo raised his eyebrows hopefully at Alice and prepared to greet whoever opened the door.

Jed was looking pale and more than a little surprised to see them. He was tall and slender and had a shock of long, dark wavy hair that fell across his forehead. Often, unselfconsciously, he swept the hair out of his eyes in a manner that emphasised his fine cheekbones and his serious expression.

Hugo had learnt that Jed worried about getting things right and essentially avoiding any displeasure landing in his mother's lap.

Now, Jed turned around and left them to follow him inside.

"We were wondering how you are, Jed. It's not like you to be out of touch?" Hugo somehow made this sound like a question.

"Would you like tea or something?"

Jed was an awkward host and they declined his offer. Instinctively Alice and Hugo opted for silence and left it to Jed to do the talking.

"Me mam is at one of her meetings but she's not usually too late back."

He motioned towards a leatherette sofa and they both sat down across from the armchair where he had obviously been sitting. On a small table in front of him were arranged a few books including an exercise book and a biro.

"I was doing my writing," he said when he saw that they were looking at his books. "Gary comes to work with me tomorrow and I like to show him I've been making an effort. He gives me his time so I don't want to take him for granted."

"Good for you," Alice said. "You are right to do a bit of practice when you can."

Jed smiled at her approval and relaxed a bit.

"You have a really amazing view from here," Alice continued, waving toward the window that showed a constellation of city lights spread out in all directions. "I guess you don't need curtains this high up," she joked.

The tension in the room eased.

"It's great as long as the lift's working," Jed said good-humouredly and then turned to face Hugo. "I know I should have let you know I wasn't coming," he blurted out. "I had something on my mind and I wasn't ready to talk about it yet. I did plan to call you tomorrow."

He looked so apologetic Alice thought he might cry but he held it together and kept eye contact with Hugo. Hugo had made really solid relationships with these kids, Alice noted.

"Well, we just thought we would call by in case you needed something," Hugo said. "Would you like to talk to us now?" He waited. "No pressure at all, Jed. It's up to you, mate."

Jed looked from Hugo to Alice and back and seemed to come to a decision. "OK. As my gran says, 'No time like the present'." He nodded as if to affirm the wisdom of his grandmother. "Let me see where I can start."

9

After the meeting Brenda did not slip away without speaking to anyone as she usually did. Since starting to attend the meetings, somehow she had found it possible to look at the other people here and see that she wasn't the misfit interloper she often felt herself to be. She had soon recognised that it was lives like hers under discussion at these meetings. Now, by finding her voice she had crossed what remained of some self-imposed boundary that had kept her feeling like an outsider even when it wasn't the case. Her outburst had ended all that. She felt like a better fit in her own skin, never mind a better fit with those around her.

"You spoke for lots of us here, Brenda, when you said how angry and powerless you feel sometimes. I feel like that too, a lot of the time."

Her neighbour was a quietly spoken man who was

just a bit older than her. "I'm Johnny Power," he said and held out his hand to shake hers.

The hand was cool and a little rough and she thought he must do some kind of manual work.

"I don't know what came over me," she said with a laugh. "I'm usually struck dumb in situations like this. I feel like everybody else can say things so much better than me but I suppose that's all part of how abuse keeps us silent."

He nodded sadly and she could see that his story was full of the kind of pain she knew only too well.

"I'm sorry if I upset you," she said but he was quick to reply.

"My upset happened a long time ago, Brenda. You touched a nerve with me right enough, but it was more to do with the ones who abused us and then banded together to cover it all up. You hit the nail on the head with that."

He looked at her with such sincerity that she knew his response came from the heart.

She took his arm and steered him across the room. "Let's get a cuppa and some of those chocolate biscuits they have. I can't stay long as my boy is at home and expecting me."

"I can give you a lift if you like," Johnny offered eagerly. "I go across town to the Antrim Road."

"Great," she accepted happily. "I live in Divis. The Tower, that is, not the mountain."

She laughed at her own local joke and they made

their way to the table at the side of the room where the refreshments were laid out. Several people smiled at her and a few gave her solidarity nods and thumbs-up signs. She felt proud and elated and pleased to finally have made a more solid connection with others who shared her history.

Johnny turned out to be a carpenter by trade. He told her in the car on the way across town that a love of woodwork was the only good thing he had taken from life in An Cuan.

"It's the most ironic thing ever," he said, meeting her gaze with eyes of deep blue. "In Irish An Cuan means harbour or haven, a place of safety, but, outside of a concentration camp, it was probably one of the most harmful places for a child to be in the twentieth century."

When they parted it felt good to say, "See you next week," and she skipped into the foyer of the Tower with a new sense of contentment.

Coming out of the lift on the tenth floor, she heard voices and was surprised to see her own flat door open and Hugo and some woman leaving. She momentarily worried that her son had had an accident but the voices were cheerful and then she could see Jed smiling at the door.

Hugo turned towards her and the woman waved in greeting.

"Hello, Mrs Clinton." Hugo extended his hand to her and she shook it warmly. "This is Alice Fox who works with me and the group in EXIT." As Brenda shook Alice's hand he continued, "We just wanted to check in on Jed because we missed him in the group."

"Hiya, Mam!" Jed called in welcome and she headed to join him at the door. They watched as the departing visitors got into the lift.

Brenda's phone buzzed and she glanced at the screen as she closed the door and followed Jed into the flat.

Fancy a cuppa before your work tomorrow? I got your number too from the sign-in sheet :)

Johnny Power was a man of action, Brenda thought, and smiled to herself at the idea that she had attracted his attention with her outburst.

City Hall at 12? she responded and received an immediate thumbs-up in reply.

10

They were planning to burn the midnight oil in the Murder Squad HQ in the Grosvenor Road police station on the western edge of Belfast city centre. They knew from experience that the ground covered while the murder trail still retained some heat was crucial to any new inquiry. The investigative trio were used to rising to the challenge of a new case.

Paton, Burrows and McVeigh were a lean team that worked smoothly and tightly together. They requisitioned additional leg power and specific expertise as was needed but preferred, in the main, to keep the advantages gained from being a streamlined operation. That way there were no leaks to the press, no loose talk with colleagues and all their energy was harnessed to the immediate task. Nothing got out of control and nothing was wasted. Tonight they were all feeling sharp and looking forward to pooling their findings and first impressions.

"So what have we got so far?" launched Caroline as they gathered around the central table in their discreet office area and helped themselves to the coffee and filled rolls that would suffice as their evening meal.

Burrows had noted that there was less chocolate in the DI's proffered snack options at the moment and wondered if she was on some kind of health kick. He was in danger of becoming a secret chocoholic the way things were going.

Caroline talked and Burrows noted data on the electronic whiteboard that served as their central evidence-gathering tool. They also had a shared drive where they stored and managed documents, reports and images and each kept their own written notes and files for reference and back up. They had grown to trust their diverse perceptions of things and these had made for productive comparisons in the past.

As was often the case, McVeigh began the review.

"An emergency call to St Oliver's Roman Catholic Chapel on Ormeau Road was received at twelve thirty-eight today. The local plods who responded found a woman there who, while arranging flowers on the altar, had noticed a light that should not have been on. When she went to extinguish it, inside the confession box, she discovered the body of a man in priestly garb. He was not from the parish and was not recognised by Mrs O'Brien or by Canon Murphy, the parish priest who later in the day viewed the body before it was removed to Pathology. Initial observations showed the man had been the victim of a fairly bloody assault. The pathologist at the scene said that he might have been there overnight or at least since very early that morning but the autopsy will hopefully reveal more about that." He paused. "We should have photographic images through by now and we might look at those in a bit and see what we can learn from them."

Caroline chipped in at this point. "My conversation with Mary O'Brien confirms all that. Mrs O'Brien opened the front doors of the chapel when she arrived to set up the vestments and other things used by the priest in saying Mass."

Caroline was conscious of a whole language that accompanied the rituals in Catholicism and her own sense of alienation from that world. When this cultural conflict arose she tried to remain respectful but in her gut she thought a lot of it was hokum. She was careful to keep that response to herself.

She continued. "Mrs O'Brien had attended ten o'clock Mass and stayed behind afterwards to 'tidy up', as she put it, after the canon who had said the Mass. Apparently there is laundry to be sorted and certain bits of paraphernalia that need to be locked away. Some of the items used in the Mass are made of precious metals and would be of value to thieves who took advantage of the open-door policy in the church. She told me it was getting to the stage where they'd have to lock the doors but they hadn't gone that far yet." Caroline said all this in a matter-of-fact tone that encouraged them to see only the piece of evidence and not the idiosyncrasy of the detail. "Mrs O'Brien thought that it was unlikely that any of the sparse congregation at the morning Mass would have been aware of there being anything amiss with the confessional. They are mostly elderly, some using walking-aids and for access reasons they tend to sit near the central aisle. Nevertheless, it might be worth trying to track a few of them down and inquire if they noticed anything out of the ordinary. There will be no Mass tomorrow as our forensics have a lot of ground to cover but maybe the day after when we have handed back the scene, you could both go along after the ten o'clock service and see if there are any snippets to be gleaned."

Burrows and McVeigh nodded in agreement and made notes in their diaries.

"I've talked to the Super and made him aware of the details," Caroline continued. "We'll put out a vague press announcement tomorrow morning and wait until the evening or Friday to have a full press conference. That will buy us some time but we might use a meeting with the press to prompt some public response if we still have no ID by then." She sipped her coffee thoughtfully. "The fact that the body is not from this parish is interesting. I wonder if our man is a specific target or a token of some kind. Is the perp somebody who has a gripe with religion

58

and anybody will do? And why deposit him here? It's a very precise location and a considered arrangement of the victim. I'm sensing a convoluted story behind this one" She considered the surface of her coffee for a few seconds and then returned to the moment. "Anyway. How did you get on with the canon?"

"To begin with, he was a little frosty at losing control of his domain," said Burrows, "but we reasoned with him. Ian diplomatically explained that it was to relieve him of responsibility for all those people working there with precarious equipment. That seemed to do the trick. When he balanced his loss of power against his lack of liability he became more friendly."

Sergeant Burrows always took the opportunity to praise the work of his young Detective Constable and McVeigh looked modestly appreciative.

"The canon explained that the numbers in the parish have been dwindling for some years and he doesn't expect they have a lengthy future ahead. Some Church land has already gone to the developers and his parishioners are mostly old or foreign nationals that don't affiliate to any particular parish." Burrows checked his notes as he spoke. "What he said made sense. He said that newcomers don't easily find affordable accommodation in the area and attend whatever church is most convenient at any one moment rather than committing to one particular parish." He looked to McVeigh to see if he wanted to add anything.

"We did get the contact details for a caretaker who opens and locks up the church but we haven't been able to track him down as yet," McVeigh said. "The canon's housekeeper made some snooty noises about him and suggested he would most likely be found in the pub down the road. We have left messages on his phone to get in touch ASAP." He looked at Burrows. "Do you want to report our findings about the side access, sarge?"

"OK. When we finished with the canon we did a recce of the area around the church and the various exits."

At this point he pulled down a retractable white screen and projected a plan of the chapel and grounds onto it. He used one of his new gadgets to talk them through the territory. Burrows loved technology and his new laser pointer-pen was given an outing at any opportunity. Now he deployed the fine coloured beam of light to indicate the orientation of the church, the front and two rear exits. One went from the sacristy to the pathway that led to the parochial house. The other was a side door that opened onto a small car park where there was disabled access to the church for those that needed it. The sacristy door was self-locking but the side door needed to be locked by the key-holder and was the responsibility of the caretaker. Motor access to the car park was through a small side road off the Ravenhill Road which ran parallel to the main Ormeau Road. The heavy metal gates were kept open round the clock, probably to avoid additional calls on the caretaker's time.

"The side door into the car park was open this morning so we will have to check with the caretaker if that was his doing or if it was left open by our killer."

He explained that they had closely inspected the area around the side door both inside and out once the forensics people had finished their work there. There were suspicious traces that had been recorded on the ground outside the door and on the internal tiled floor. An accessible toilet for parishioners was located under the stairs next to a storage place where McVeigh's forensics friend Bryson had pointed out that a wheelchair was stored. The stairs led to the balcony used occasionally by the church choir. Forensics had dusted the entire area, including the chair for prints and other residual matter and found traces of what might be blood or some other body fluid on the seat of the wheelchair.

"If there's a match, we will at least know how quite a hefty body was transported from a car to the confessional."

"Great!" said Paton. "Really good job. Any signs of life in the car park? Any camera there or on the access road?"

"We checked that," said McVeigh, "but there was no joy. We are hoping that maybe the house-to-house being done by the local uniforms may turn up a sighting in the area. If we get word of something of interest we will follow up immediately."

"OK, so where do we go from here? Let's have a look at the images sent through from Pathology and start to get a feel for the victim profile. You can use some more technology, Bill!" She smiled mischievously at Burrows who feigned offence and pulled up the file from George in Cynthia Boylan's office and opened it on the large screen.

Burrows took his place at the table again and clicked on the file from the pathologist's department. "There will be other crime-scene pics to come from forensics but this is what we have so far from Dr Boylan's department specifically to do with the victim."

As he spoke the first image came up on screen. The already familiar image of an open and bloodied mouth screamed at them from the opposite wall.

"OK. What can we see?" Caroline said. "White male in or around mid-sixties. Approximately six feet in height and overweight judging by the strain on the clothing. Blue eyes, very well-manicured nails and an expensive wristwatch. We can rule out theft as a motive so ..." She consulted her colleagues with a questioning look.

"I agree with those estimates," said McVeigh. "He is wearing a black suit and dog-collar, suggesting that he is a member of the Catholic clergy, or disguised as such. There are signs of assault in the area of the mouth where something, possibly a body part has been inserted." He moved awkwardly in his seat and worked hard to control a cringing expression as he continued. "Signs of blood or urine in the genital area too. Query, castration?"

Burrows and Caroline both nodded seriously at this suggestion.

"We'll wait for Cynthia to confirm that but I was on that thought-track too," said Caroline. "We will restrain ourselves too, for the moment, from listing all the possible reasons for castrating and killing a priest. Let's edge forward carefully on this one. I don't want to miss anything or leap to assumptions too quickly." She nodded to Burrows who called up the next image that focussed on the man's crossed arms.

"This staging of the body looks to me like a child's pose or possibly the way angels might have been depicted to children in my young day. It suggests innocence maybe." He looked a bit embarrassed to have articulated this and moved on quickly. "Or the way a corpse might be laid out for a wake. Later you'll see that the writing on the page pinned to the chest is revealed more clearly but this posture seems to me to be about powerlessness or self-protection. What do you think?" He waited. "I'm not even sure it's useful to conjecture but as you say, boss, there are messages in the arrangement of the body that we need to try to read."

"I think we may never know the answer to that one unless the killer tells us but no harm in speculating a bit so as to be conscious that there is a message there. Let's see the next one." Caroline sat back and considered each image as it appeared. "If the arms are about control, the legs are about a loss of it. They are the embodiment of exposure, vulnerability and the removal of dominance ... possibly literally." She grimaced as she said this. "I think we'll get some advice from a psychologist and body-language specialist about all this and also when we have a bit more context we may be able to read the signs more clearly."

"OK. Let's look at the paper then." And Burrows clicked on an image of a sheet of A4 paper that had words computer-printed across it portrait style and in capital letters.

BLESSED ARE THE MEEK FOR THEY SHALL INHERIT THE EARTH

"It's biblical, I think," said McVeigh who probably had the most recent experience of religious education. He was googling on his phone and quickly announced, "It's Matthew, Chapter five, Verse five, and is one of a list of something called the 'Beatitudes' that outline exemplary Christian traits."

"We might surmise that it's being used ironically here!" mused Caroline. "A bit more research needed then with someone well versed in religious matters. When I think about it I'm not even sure what 'meek' means. It suggests subservience to me but I could be wrong. Let's get a good look at the nappy pin too. It must be a bit of a relic of times gone by. Not many people use that kind of thing in these days of disposable stuff." She looked more perplexed than usual and it was clear she felt that there were already more than the usual volume of challenges associated with a dead body. "Carry on with the images, Bill. It's all clear as mud so far."

After an hour or so of looking at graphic pictures of the murder victim, they eventually ground to a halt in their deliberations.

Caroline sighed deeply. "As I said earlier, we need to bear in mind that this may be a man against whom someone has a specific gripe or he may just be some unfortunate cleric being used as a symbol or a token of someone's anger against the clergy in general." She looked at her watch and left that point as something to return to when they had more to go on. "Anyway … that's not too bad for a first review. Let's do what we can do at this point and hold all these questions for later."

The others agreed and felt the relief of getting back onto more practical territory.

"Ian, will you attend the autopsy first thing in the morning? Cynthia is not as much a morning person as she likes to imagine so you may have time to do some online research while you're waiting. Bill, you track down the caretaker and see what the house-to-house is coming up with. I'll look after the press and the Super and get someone onto the Missing Persons files. There must be a bishop somewhere who has a list of priests that have recently gone AWOL. I'll see what I can find out about that. Let's get some sleep now and we'll meet up when you get back tomorrow, probably late morning."

They felt the road ahead was even steeper than usual and rest seemed like a good place to start their ascent.

11

Alice heard nothing from Caroline that evening and she knew that the Murder Squad were probably having a late night and trying to cover as much ground as they could at the start of the new case. She checked the local news on the Internet and realised that they had so far managed to keep reports of the murder away from the media. Caro would be pleased about that, she thought, smiling to herself. Caroline liked to be as far ahead of the public newsmongers as possible and to control the flow of information to suit her investigation. Alice had surmised that there would be a brief statement at some stage and then a fuller press conference when it suited the detectives to go public. She had wondered vaguely what the murder story would be this time but she had slept easily and peacefully in the knowledge that she would hear all about it eventually.

At some stage during the night a cartoon gif of a dementedly busy minion came through to Alice's phone and she laughed when she saw it next morning. Part of her envied the opportunity to be absorbed in solving the puzzle of a new case but she reminded herself that she had chosen her line of work for good reason and that she was happy with that decision.

On her morning run along the Lagan towpath towards Lisburn, Alice replayed the conversation she and Hugo had had with Jed the previous evening. He said he had often asked his mam to tell him about her family and she had put him off with delaying tactics – when you're older, now is not the right time, be careful what you wish for and so on. He knew that she had been adopted and in an orphanage on and off a few times and he didn't like to push her to talk about it in case it made her unhappy. Then one evening a few months previously, when the TV news was reporting on the new inquiry into child abuse, she had told him that she had started to go to meetings of people who had abuse in their family history. She told him that both his gran and his gran's mother had been in institutions where they had experienced terrible neglect and ill-treatment. They had been separated from their children and only later on was a service to reunite family members put in place. Jed remembered then that he had first met his gran when he was already about eleven but at the time he had never questioned why that was. His mam had finally told him Martha's story only a few nights before and he had found it both sad and shocking. It explained why she didn't like to think about all that and made him all the more curious about her own early life. He told Alice and Hugo that he was stuck in his head, thinking about those questions, but he knew he needed to wait until she was ready to tell him.

Jed's great-granny had been in a Mother and Baby home in Belfast when his gran, Martha, was born. At the time, there had been no question of her keeping Martha and so she was sent immediately to an orphanage run by nuns, in a small country town. Martha found out that her mother had a second child in this way and maybe she was considered unfit and that is why the babies were taken from her quickly. When she was in her fifties, Martha also discovered that her mother had some family living in Dublin and so it was possible that they arranged for her to return to her family after she had given birth and the babies were taken into care. But there was no happy ending for Martha in the subsequent revelations about her family. Both her mother and her sister had finished their days in a grim institution for those with mental illness and both had died before she was able to locate them.

Baby Martha hadn't received much in the way of attention and when she was younger people thought she was "a bit slow" because she had limited speech and habitually rocked in her seat for comfort. In fact, she had never really been spoken to by the older orphans charged with the care of large numbers of babies and her formal schooling was sparse. These older girls had their own preoccupations and were not resourced to care for young children. Mostly Martha remembered being cold, alone and sad. One of her jobs was feeding the hens every day and she admitted to helping herself to some of their food when she was hungry.

Jed had retold this tale to Alice and Hugo in detail and with great care and it had obviously made a deep impression on him.

His mam had told him that as a young teenager Martha was sent into service as a maid with a rich family in the Dublin suburbs. It struck him as very unfair that she was expected to look after the small children of that family with no experience of care in her own young life. There would have been toys and other stuff that she would never have dreamt of in her own childhood. While taking her charges to the playground she struck up a friendship with a girl in a similar situation to herself and began to go to Saturday-night dances with her. After one of these excursions, when more than a few drinks had been taken, she met a fellow who made her feel that she was pretty and interesting. Their relationship was short-lived and when the woman of the house found Martha was several months pregnant she was instantly dispatched to the Mother and Baby home on the Cabra Road in Dublin. There, less than two decades further on, her own beginnings in the world were replicated in how her daughter entered the world. When she was born, Brenda was taken from Martha immediately and eventually adopted by a young couple in the North. As part of her efforts to locate her family, Martha learned that the couple's marriage broke up during the Troubles and Brenda was returned to the care of the State in Northern Ireland. Meanwhile, Martha's work as a hospital cleaner in Dublin gave her a weekly wage and days off when she pursued her love of Show Bands and subsequently had two more babies, both of which were also sent for adoption. Jed had been surprised by the additional pregnancies but Brenda had said, "You have to understand, Jed, that she was really not well prepared by her upbringing for the ways of the world and she was easily exploited by men who showed her any bit of kindness. She had never lived in a family until, as a teenager, she became a servant in one and what small kindness she was shown there could not reverse this absence of love in her life. How could she show care when she had never any lived experience of it?"

Only in later years, when there was a lot of talk about institutional abuse in the south of Ireland, did Martha become more knowledgeable about her own history. In the Phoenix Centre for survivors she discovered a whole group of people who had a history like hers. She learned that the Irish State had apologised for treating them so badly and taken the blame for their poor education. She attended some education and craft classes in that Centre and learned to read and write a little through her love of Show Band singer Joe Dolan. She knew the words of all his songs and her tutor wrote them down as Martha sang. Then they both sang them repeatedly with gusto and Martha learned to follow and recognise the words as she sang. She practised in the evenings in her little flat and realised that she wasn't as stupid as she had been led to believe. "I am like her in that way, I suppose," Jed had reflected.

It was in the centre that she also discovered she could try to locate her family through Barnardo's family-tracing service, her search for her mother leading to the discovery she had died in an institution for the insane.

Martha regretted not having even a photo of her. She would say hopefully to Brenda, "Do you think she would have looked like me?"

And Brenda would say, "Well, Mam, we look like each other so I suppose it's fair to say you got your good looks from her," and they would laugh mischievously to fill the chasm of sadness.

Of the three requests Martha had placed in relation to her children only Brenda, her eldest, took up her offer to meet and they were reconciled when Brenda was twenty-eight and Jed a young fellow of eleven. At the time, Martha said she felt lucky that even one of her children was prepared to have her in her life and she consoled herself that the other two must have found happiness that they didn't want to disrupt. Without any further searching she let any hope of meeting them go and then unleashed her entire store of love and good spirits on Brenda and Jed. Jed thought his gran was a hero to have survived her loveless early life and to be such a positive and affectionate character. He spoke of her with great fondness and Alice marvelled at how those who are given so little could manage to make so much of it.

In his retelling of his gran's story, Jed explained that he wasn't able to let the detail rest. It was playing over and over in his head and he didn't have room to come and join in the EXIT group activities until he could make sense of it all. The missing information about his mam's life and by association his own beginnings were niggling at him constantly but he knew he mustn't push too hard at her. He knew she had always done everything in his best interest and he trusted she would tell him when the time was right.

Hugo and Alice had made sure Jed knew they were there for him if he wanted to talk and he said he would be back to EXIT next day for the weekly review session. He seemed much happier when they left and pleased to see his mother home from her meeting. Alice wondered if there had been any further discussion about the Clinton family history the previous night after she and Hugo had left the Tower and headed for their respective homes. There would be many more episodes of this story to come, she surmised.

12

Historic scandals involving the State, religious groups and often indigenous peoples were not unknown to Alice in the US context but she was ignorant of Ireland's past experience of all that. After the visit to Jed's the previous evening, she had done some online research and the findings had made shocking reading. She'd learned that there had been more than a dozen Mother and Baby homes operating in the North of Ireland between 1922 and 1990. Over 14,000 women and girls had been resident in these homes, some just for the duration of their pregnancy, others for their whole lives as what amounted to unpaid workers. Those bereft of family and any independent means worked in religious houses and businesses in exchange for a meagre level of sustenance and protection from the elements.

In similar homes in the south of Ireland, girls were sometimes kept on as maids and kitchen workers and others were dispatched to hospitals and other facilities run by the same religious orders. There they exchanged one form of institutionalisation for another. Many of the women and girls were victims of rape or incest or of having been taken advantage of by men who realised they could exploit their ignorance of reproductive matters. The women had mostly been poor, often destitute, and shamed and stigmatised in those days by their unmarried pregnancy. Alice learned that not all the residents of these places were pregnant. Families opportunely placed women and teenage girls described as having behavioural problems, addictions or learning difficulties in these institutions. Once there, they were treated as penitents who needed to atone for their alleged misdemeanours. They were sometimes made to eat standing up, confess their sins publically and their names were taken and replaced by a new name or a number.

Alice read about the inquiry into abuses in Irish Industrial Schools that had taken place in the South over a number of years between 2000 and 2008. The findings were contained in the Ryan Report published in 2009. She found that the detail in the final report was a gruesome indictment of religious orders and authoritarian attitudes to the care of children. There were entire pages filled with the different instruments fashioned by staff to physically punish children, often

74

without any reason being given. One man had testified that a Christian Brother who had been his teacher had given him the task of boiling his leather straps to make them tougher and more effective implements for beating the boys in his charge. Somehow the deployment of a child to prepare the instruments of his own abuse added another whole layer to the horrors that the Ryan Report contained. Gratuitous beatings, sexual and emotional abuses were widely reported by adult survivors of these places who spoke to the inquiry and the evidence of lasting harm done to them was staggering.

Reasons for taking children into the care of the State were varied. Aside from those, like Martha, sent directly at birth from Mother and Baby homes, there were those accused of petty crimes like stealing food or playing truant from school. In some families when the mother died, the father was deemed unfit to care for the children, especially girls, and they were taken into the care of the authorities. Children of colour, Irish Traveller children, those from poor families and many more were taken into the care of those who saw their task as ensuring that the perceived sins of the parents would not be repeated by the next generation.

All things considered, Alice could understand why Jed was distressed by his gran's story. She felt a little better informed now in terms of supporting him with that legacy and resolved to read some of survivor's published testimonies about what that institutionalised life had been really like. As an experiment in the domestication of some elements of society, seen as undesirable, it was clear to Alice that this was a misguided, harmful and highly unsuccessful project.

13

Alice had planned an in-college day in DePRec on Thursday and, after she had showered and eaten breakfast, she headed towards Belfast's *Titanic* Quarter on her bike. As she made her way down Donegall Pass, the bunting remnants of the celebration of Chinese New Year the previous month fluttered in the gentle spring breeze. A few moments later it was the bedraggled Union Jack flag outside a loyalist bar that caught the eye. A feast of Belfast's visual culture, she thought to herself, smiling and realising that she was growing very fond of this place and all its vagaries. As she crossed the bridge over the Lagan and the salt air from the Lough caught her nostrils she became aware of cycling in time to the soundtrack playing in her head. Her father had loved the music of Simon and Garfunkel and she had grown up to it playing in the background of her life.

Even now, decades later, certain moods generated a particular track in her head. This morning her inner jukebox was playing "Song for the Asking" and her eyes filled with tears as she acknowledged her sense of having been filled with opportunities in her life by this man who was no longer there. He had been so pleased when she had graduated from Police College and joined Lowell PD but he had never put pressure on her to be anything but herself. She hoped he would like the choices she was making now … in work … and in love. She thought he would approve and hummed on as she saw Belfast City College ahead, set against the iconic industrial harbour backdrop.

Junior academics in the US were lucky to find a brush cupboard to work in but back in August, on arrival in Belfast City College, Alice had been given a fine office with a spectacular view. On that first morning she had reported to Professor Jackson Bell who was Head of the DePRec and her host for the year. He was a slim, balding man in his forties who exuded an old-fashioned formality that some might find alienating. That first morning Alice had reserved judgement until she knew him a little better and followed behind him as he led her to her workspace for the incoming year. The departmental admin office door was open and, behind it, regally installed in a purple high-backed office chair, sat Mairéad Walsh.

"I bring you Doctor Fox," announced Bell grandly,

"and place her in your most reliable hands, Mrs Walsh." He then turned to Alice and with a small flourish introduced her to Mairéad Walsh, DePRec Operations Manager.

Bell left with a kind of backwards sweep as if leaving the presence of a potentate whose territorial supremacy he fully endorsed.

Back then, Mrs Walsh surprised Alice by rising and enfolding her in a gentle embrace, as if she were made of fragile stuff at risk of shattering. "*Céad míle fáilte!*" she exclaimed. "Anyone from Massachusetts is welcome here. My son has been there for nearly ten years now so you and I are practically related."

Alice found this woman reminded her instantly of an effusive older sister of her father's that she had always liked.

"Between you and me – I'm Mairéad and you are Alice and we don't need to bother with the formalities. There's more than enough hoity-toity stuff around here to boil your head."

The older woman exuded a heady perfume that Alice couldn't quite place but which she associated with childhood experiences of family gatherings.

"Your room is through here so I can vet your visitors if you like," Mairéad whispered conspiratorially.

Alice couldn't imagine there would be that much traffic through her door but nonetheless she received Mairéad's offer of protection positively.

The older woman shepherded Alice through to the adjoining room and waited cautiously at the door. It was a spacious enough office, comfortably furnished with a desk and a bright-green office chair. There were fitted shelves on the internal walls and a solid glass plate, framed in steel, faced the door and formed the external wall of the room. The view of the harbour estate and Belfast Lough was breath-taking. This was lavish accommodation indeed.

As if reading her thoughts, Mairéad said, "I can't stand heights at all." She gestured dramatically towards the spectacular view from the fifth floor with one hand on her forehead. "They make my knees go weak, so I arranged that they divide this office in two and allow me to stay safely on the inside. A room without a view, so to speak," and she winked mischievously.

Since then, in the intervening months, the two women had grown to like each other and Alice was comfortable in the older woman's company. Mairéad had learned that Alice liked to be left in peace and managed her messages and ensured that uninvited visitors didn't disturb her.

This morning she greeted Alice with her usual warmth and then launched into a commentary on the morning news. "I see our friends in the Murder Squad have a new case on their hands. A body found somewhere up the Ormeau Road they said on the local morning news. No details released until the family is notified." Her familiarity with all things investigative dated back to early

January when they had their own murder inquiry in the department. Her close friend and now senior lecturer, Ralph Wilson, had been a suspect for a short period of time and she had entered into the proceedings like a true acolyte of Miss Marple.

Alice received this news with only a passing interest and the knowledge that as soon as Caroline could afford the time she would be brought up to speed on what was happening. For now she planned to make a start on writing a book proposal that would allow her to give an account of her research comparing practices in youth restorative justice in Belfast and Lowell, MA. She had an idea for how, using photography with the young people, she might make this project a little out of the normal run of academic texts and she was keen to commit her proposed approach to paper. As she sat down at her desk she switched her phone to silent so that she wouldn't be disturbed.

14

McVeigh had braced himself for the morning's autopsy, not just because he was a little squeamish by nature but also because, if it were as they suspected, the detail of the castration would be fairly gruesome. The very idea of it had disturbed his sleep that night.

Sally had been less than sympathetic. "Try actually pushing an entire human being out though a small aperture in your body and you'll really have something to be hypersensitive about!"

Their first child had been born not that long ago and the whole process had been life-changing for them both, in different ways. The baby and his routine governed their days and nights and sleep was no longer something assured, even when you went to bed shattered after a long day pursuing vicious killers. Sally carried the bulk of the care demands but he didn't want to be a disconnected father and liked to do his bit, when work allowed. She often reminded him that he was lucky to have that choice and he knew that she was right.

He had gauged accurately that this autopsy was going to be a messy one. He replayed the ordeal in his head now as he climbed the two flights of stairs from Dr Cynthia Boylan's Pathology Department in the basement, back to the Murder Squad base on the first floor. She had been on time, which was unusual in itself and so he hadn't had his planned half-hour meditation while he waited. He had taken to mindfulness when Sally was pregnant and she also had listened to recordings on her phone to keep herself calm and centred. He found it had helped him too when he needed to switch off from some detail of his work. Anyway, there had been no time for that this morning and Cynthia had launched in straight away with her usual cheerful nonchalance.

Back at base now, he could see that DI Paton was in her office with the door closed and Burrows wasn't back yet from his hunt for the caretaker. Hopefully that meant he had tracked him down and got some straight answers. Ian wouldn't be surprised if the church was occasionally left open all night while the caretaker, Peadar O'Sullivan, swilled pints in the pub down the road. He pulled up his recording of the morning's proceedings on his phone, inserted his earphones and got ready to make notes of the significant findings. The pathology report would be sent through later in the day but there had been a few useful elements in relation to the man's identity that they could get to work on straight away.

There had been no identifying papers in the murdered man's clothing. No wallet or credit cards, no driving licence or papers with a name or address and this suggested that they had been removed to delay identifying the victim. No distinguishing marks had been located on the flabby body that had lain chilled on the pathologist's table, unaware of the imminent ordeal it faced.

To begin with, a penis had been removed from the man's mouth, matched to its place of origin and then laid in a kidney-shaped chrome dish. Ian had momentarily wondered about the implications if there hadn't been a match at this stage but that was not the case. The slight sucking sound as the member was extracted from the rigid lips and throat had made him gag but he hoped he had managed to turn it into a cough before Cynthia or her assistant George had noticed. The lingering sour smell of alcohol had intensified as the mouth was left vacant and gaping.

"Although strictly speaking the term castration refers to the removal of the testicles ..."

Ian braced himself for a potentially difficult learning moment.

"In the case of our victim, it is the actual penis that has been severed. However, the absence of a commonly known term to describe this process means that, should the MO become known, it is likely to be discussed using the better-known but inaccurate term 'castration'."

Ian could see that his contribution to this evening's briefing might raise a few eyebrows.

The pathologist noted that the victim's trousers and underpants suggested the removal of his penis had taken place while the body was clothed. Markings on the body showed that a small, serrated blade had been used to do the cutting and there were a number of small cuts to the surrounding underclothing. Examination of the mutilated area under a microscopic lens clearly showed the pattern of the blade and identifying the type of knife would be straightforward enough. George had taken a range of photos that would be available online for their evening review. The conclusion was that it was more than likely a common kitchen knife, possibly like those designed for peeling grapefruit, and unless the killer was very careless they would have to be lucky to find the exact weapon.

Cynthia's explanation of potential causes of genital mutilation had been a mini forensics' lecture that Ian could have done without first thing in the morning and after a poor night's sleep. She had thrown up three possible motivations that had both interested and shocked him. Firstly, removal or cutting of a sexual organ as in female genital mutilation could be culturally determined – a rite of passage or a mark of reaching puberty for example. Secondly it could be the result of self-harm.

Thirdly it might be the deliberate disfigurement of a body, including after a homicide.

In this case, the lack of haemorrhage indicated that the cutting had been done post mortem.

In response to Ian's question about cause of death, the pathologist had been cautious. "An educated guess, which I'll confirm when I can get around to dissecting the neck, is that this was a homicidal suffocation, probably by a chokehold." She had explained that, as there were no visible red spotting marks on the exterior of the neck or around the eyes, a particular form of neck-hold was indicated. It was possible that the assailant had some experience in self-defence or some form of combat training to allow the skilled use of this particular type of neck compression. Ian mused that what at first appearances had seemed like a chaotic and impetuous killing was now emerging as something entirely different.

Dissection revealed bleeding on internal muscle at the back of the neck as well as at the root of the tongue and the front of the larynx. This confirmed Cynthia's hunch about killing by suffocation. Exacerbating factors to the use of a chokehold, she explained, were intoxication, cardiovascular weakness and hypertension. Close examination of the bodily organs showed that a number of stents had been fitted in the valves to the heart as a result of significant cardio-vascular disease and hypertension. The unknown victim turned out therefore to be the ideal candidate for this mode of killing.

Subsequently, the man's liver had shown that he was overly fond of a drink and his stomach contents revealed excessive quantities of whiskey and very little food. Cynthia had sent samples off to toxicology to determine if the body showed signs of any drugs having been administered. It seemed logical that if they were thinking of this as the work of one killer then it would have made the victim more manageable if he had been drugged prior to being killed and then mutilated. The motive then had been more about leaving a message with the treatment of body than torturing the victim and that was a telling fact about the killer.

The deceased's few belongings had been subjected to forensic scrutiny and were then placed in an evidence box and sent directly through the internal mail to the Murder Squad offices. They would be available for examination that afternoon and by the time of the evening review they might have a few interesting findings. Ian had gleaned some useful detail in the course of the autopsy. The expensive watch spotted by Caroline was indeed a Rolex and Ian thought that he had read somewhere that each watch had an individual identification number. He would check what information that might give. The labels on the man's clothing suggested they came from a clerical outfitter's shop in Dublin. Perhaps all priests were fitted out there irrespective of whether their parish was North or South but again this was something he could follow up on immediately. The company might even recognise a photo of their deceased client if other sources of ID didn't prove fruitful. Finally the paper and the nappy pin that had been attached to the man's clothing were bagged separately and sent to forensic specialists for any information they could glean from them. The pin looked old and might be a relic of bygone days.

Ian compiled a list for what he might get done that afternoon and was just thinking about lunch when Burrows arrived back.

The older man had a healthy appetite and derived great pleasure from food. "I'm ready for today's lunch special," he announced enthusiastically as he hung his coat on a hook inside the door. "Any takers?"

Ian was already on his feet when the DI's office door swung open.

"Did I hear talk of lunch?" she said happily. "Let's build our stamina for the day ahead with some gourmet delights from the staff canteen."

And the threesome headed off in good humour, ready for the worst the staff eatery could throw at them.

Johnny Power was leaning against the perimeter railings of the Belfast City Hall when Brenda arrived. He looked relaxed and smiled broadly as she approached. Brenda noted the flecks of grey in his hair and the spots of amber in his blue eyes. He was wearing a navy donkey jacket, a blue checked fleece shirt and faded jeans.

Brenda liked how he looked and marvelled at how, after years of solitude while she raised her son, she suddenly found herself meeting a quite presentable man for coffee or lunch or whatever.

"Hiya, Johnny!" She found she was laughing as she spoke. "I'm suddenly really hungry. Do you mind if we have a sandwich with our cuppa?"

He took her arm easily and directed her to the crossing in front of them and down a narrow road where there was a small café. The smells of coffee and homemade food were good and they were lucky to be ahead of the lunchtime rush and to find a table for two in a corner by the steamy window.

"I start work at one," Brenda told him, "but the good news is it's just across the road so we don't have to hurry too much." Then she realised she was gabbling like a schoolgirl and stopped herself.

"Let's order our food and then we can chat."

Johnny spoke quietly and with an accent that wasn't just Belfast. She could hear strains of the west of Ireland lilt that she was used to now in her mother's partner, Brian. Funny, she thought, that they both might end up with men from the west and then laughed inwardly at how hasty she was in her prediction. She determined to stop dreaming and listen to the man beside her and see what he was actually like before jumping to conclusions. For all she knew he might turn out to be a serial killer.

15

At the end of a satisfactory day's writing in DePRec, Alice Fox got on her bike and headed for the EXIT youth project. It was a gradual uphill climb but the wind was in her favour and she would get there in less than half an hour. There would be time for a chat with Hugo before the group arrived at seven o'clock.

Dusk was creeping in and the Falls Road was a mishmash of brightly lit shops and buildings, shadowy side streets and noisy traffic that moved in fits and starts. It was Thursday and late-night opening in city-centre shops so there were plenty of people about and a collective air of cheerfulness that the working week was nearly over.

This part of the city was identified as almost entirely Catholic although that reflected past housing policy more than current religious belief. People held on to old habits and some still blessed themselves, making the

Sign of the Cross passing by any chapels on the road. When the Angelus bells rang at noon and six o'clock, you could see an occasional older person stop in their tracks, muttering under their breaths and beating their breasts with a clenched fist. This was the Falls Road call to prayer, Alice thought cheerfully.

At the top of the Donegall Road she stopped to buy an evening paper from a grubby young fellow who was promoting his product with bursts of inarticulate shouting. None of what he said was intelligible to Alice but that was the way of paper-sellers the world over.

A small piece on the front page announced a suspicious death at an undisclosed location on the Ormeau Road. There was nothing to expand on the morning news delivered by Mairéad Walsh and Alice deduced that progress in identifying the body and informing the family was moving slowly. She wondered when Caroline would take a break and call round to see her but knew from recent experience that she might be in touch very little until the case was beginning to make some progress. With a faint sense of regret, she climbed back on her bike and powered up the final stretch to the EXIT base off the Glen Road.

It was just coming up to six-thirty as she stowed her bicycle and sat down facing Hugo in his office, to prepare for their evening. The weekly review didn't involve any facilitated input from them so it was really about listening and taking direction from the young people about what was needed. They were both good at that so the evening would go smoothly.

At about ten minutes to seven they heard the front door open and moments later someone tapped on Hugo's door and Jed came in. The more established group members had a code that allowed them to come and go on the premises when they needed to and this was a prized right that was never abused.

"How are things, Jed?" Hugo asked casually. "It's good to see you back."

"Thanks, Hugo. And thanks to you both for making things so easy for me last night."

He was a bit flustered making this announcement and Alice stood up beside him and rested her hand lightly on his shoulder. She waited quietly for him to regain his momentum.

"Me mam and me had a good talk last night," he continued, "and I'm feeling better about things. My gran and her fella are coming up for the long weekend and Mam wondered if you would both like to come and meet them for a drink after the session tonight." His expression was earnest as if he was determined to deliver his mother's message accurately. "She says that she wants to thank you herself and also to let you know about the group that she's going to. She wants you to know my background so that you'll understand me better."

There was no inkling that Jed found any of this proposed closeness in any way awkward and he showed that he fully trusted his mam's strategy.

He looked hopefully at Hugo and then at Alice who had both already nodded imperceptibly at each other.

"Well, we don't really need to be thanked for looking out for you, Jed," Hugo said, "but we will happily come by and meet your folks. Where are you heading?"

"The Felons," Jed announced, pleased at his success in arranging the outing.

Outside, the raised level of chatter signalled the arrival of some of the others in the group and Hugo stood up and began to move towards the door.

"We'll see you over there, Jed," Hugo said. "Alice and I will need a little while to wrap things up here after the session and we'll come across to you and your folks then."

Alice looked questioningly at Hugo as Jed left. "Need a little while to do what?"

"Nothing! It's just that I don't want to make it an obvious social occasion. We don't want the whole group joining us at the club!"

He laughed at the prospect and Alice understood that he was managing the group dynamics as carefully as ever. For all his relaxed approach, he was always vigilant and watchful about the entire group's wellbeing.

"The Felons is an interesting name for a club," Alice said. "How does one become a member?" She smiled wryly at Hugo who laughed heartily.

"Well, as an ex-detective you might not be top of the

member's list but, don't worry, guests are allowed and my dad is on the committee. It's an interesting local spot and they may even have some live music tonight."

And, laughing teasingly, he moved out into the meeting space and joined in the banter that was a regular feature when the EXIT group was gathering.

16

Under DI Paton's direction the Murder Squad met at some point every evening during a case to review progress and agree their next investigative steps. This Thursday was no different and the three met after seven and spent just under two hours pooling and mulling over their discoveries and agreeing next steps.

The second day of what Burrows had dubbed the "Confession Box Case" had seen some surprising discoveries and some that had been well anticipated. Burrows' meeting with Peadar O'Sullivan had confirmed that he had been on a bit of a drinking spree and had left the side door of the chapel open all night on Tuesday. The interesting snippet had been that on that same morning he had received a card and a very generous donation, thanking him for all his support in a recent bereavement. That in itself was not unusual but the sum was much greater than he was accustomed to and "Sure it just called out to be celebrated," he had told Burrows earnestly. O'Sullivan had spent all Tuesday evening and most of Wednesday in a local club and only heard about the murder in St Oliver's on Thursday morning when his wife was berating him at the same time as she prepared his cooked breakfast. Burrows said the caretaker still wasn't in great shape on Thursday morning when he found him leaning on a brush at the back of the church. The interview had been torturous and O'Sullivan had said that he felt sick at the prospect of cleaning the confession box when all the fuss had died down.

"That suggests some local knowledge on the killer's part if it was known that the caretaker could be got offside so easily," McVeigh said.

"It could do," responded Paton. "Or some careful preparation at any rate by someone intent on finding a suitable location to place their victim. I don't think any of this happened by accident. We need to find out the possible significance of this parish, the confession box, the treatment of the body and the message pinned to the corpse. There is a definite narrative being constructed there and we need to get to the bottom of all the elements." She tapped her pen rhythmically on the desk as if to reinforce each step in the process. "Let's stay focussed on what we have found and then we can speculate when we have that core work done." She was adept at keeping the inquiry grounded in facts and they knew from experience that her instincts were very good.

Burrows continued with his report on the house-to-house calls made by the local officers. No one had seen anything out of the ordinary but one elderly woman who didn't sleep too well had talked about hearing a car with "a rickety engine". She couldn't say what time this was because she was not fully awake but it was possible that she heard it more than once. The uniformed officer thought that might be relevant in terms of delivering the remains and leaving some time afterwards. She said that it was definitely during the hours of darkness and when the area was quiet so that narrowed it down slightly.

"It might be worth revisiting that one when we have a bit more context?" he added and made a note for himself.

Caroline turned her attention to McVeigh. "What have you got from the autopsy? I see that Cynthia's report won't be through until the morning now as she has a few more unexpected customers to deal with."

McVeigh summarised his notes from the morning's session in the basement, focussing on the information that would help the inquiry. They would all read the rest when the report came through. "OK! We have a man in his 60s, overweight and with a heart condition. He had a number of stents fitted and signs of liver damage from excessive alcohol. There was little food and a lot of whiskey in his system."

"I think we got that from the aroma in the confession box," quipped Paton.

"The damage inside the neck showed he was killed by a chokehold applied with sufficient skill to avoid the tell-tale red marks on the face and neck." McVeigh hesitated at this point, unsure whether to deliver the information about terminology for removal of male body parts. He decided they would get the information from the report and he didn't need to pre-empt that. "The victim was castrated post mortem with a serrated blade, probably a common kitchen knife. The tox report will tell whether he was initially drugged or whether his level of alcohol alone made him more compliant to his attacker."

"What about time of death?" asked Burrows.

McVeigh nodded. "Cynthia said that, based on the level of rigor and lack of decomposition, we are looking at more than twelve hours before the time of discovery and less than thirty-six hours. She says that he was killed elsewhere and transported to the church, probably in a seated position. That fits with the wheelchair theory and the fact that he was seated when found. The broad parameters for time of death are between early on Tuesday morning and late Tuesday evening."

"OK," said Burrows. "So we have a priest, or someone dressed as a priest, in his sixties, possibly drugged, fed a load of whiskey, strangled with a chokehold, castrated and then transported we don't know how far and placed in a confession box in Belfast."

"Right," said McVeigh. "There were no documents or credit cards or any other material that would have identified the victim. Sergeant Burrows and I have spent the afternoon following up on the deceased's belongings that were sent through from Forensics. We have made some progress with identification but are just short of absolute confirmation."

He paused and looked at Burrows who signalled to him to continue, happy to allow him to have the glory.

"Well, ma'am, I thought I had read somewhere that each Rolex watch had an individual identification number and so I followed up on that hunch and got onto Rolex HQ in Geneva."

Caroline and Burrows both smiled and nodded enthusiastically in their appreciation of the constable's ingenuity and he flushed with pride.

"Well, Sergeant Burrows had a lot of work to do on proving our bona fides and bypassing the security but eventually the number on the watch belonging to the deceased was matched to a jeweller in Dublin. They, in turn, after the same security wrangles, confirmed they had sold the watch some years ago. The buyer was named as Nicholas Quinn whom we now know to be a producer of religious memorabilia who supplies anyone wanting a holy picture, medal or glow-in-the-dark statue."

Burrows chipped in at this point. "We have phoned Quinn and left messages for him to contact us. His secretary told us he was travelling for business and would collect messages when he reached his hotel in the evening. He is doing a tour of sites of religious pilgrimage in France. Apparently it's an annual trip to maintain friendly relations with very lucrative customers. He is due home first thing on Saturday morning."

"Hopefully he will contact us this evening. Keep trying him anyway." Caroline was energised by this progress. "It would be good to be able to announce tomorrow morning that we know who the victim is. Shows we're not hanging about."

McVeigh signalled that he had more to report. "The Sergeant and I did some Google searches and came up with images of Nicholas Quinn at various meetings and dinners in high places. There were also some family shots, one of which was a photo of him playing in a charity golf game with his brother: Father Michael Quinn. Michael Quinn, the priest, bears a very close resemblance to our victim. Bill has been trying to plumb the depths of the Catholic system of governance so that we can track down Father Quinn's place of residence and see if he is by any chance missing."

Burrows was nodding in agreement with all this. "I am fairly certain we have an ID for our victim, ma'am, and that opens up the options for moving forward."

Caroline visibly relaxed and they set to work on plotting their next moves and what they hoped to achieve by the same time the following day.

*   *   *

After the review, Caroline sat alone in her office refining the detail of the next morning's meeting with the press. She paused in that process and considered why this case was causing her such an underlying sense of anxiety. It was clear from the outset that this was a complicated one but that didn't explain her consternation. In fact, usually the more complicated the detail of a killing the more she rose to the challenge. She had slept badly the previous night and had been slightly ill at ease all day. The feeling was not one she often experienced but she had a serious case at the moment. It was as if she was about to undergo a test under public scrutiny, for which she knew she was ill prepared. She recognised this as the stuff of nightmares and scanned her inner consciousness to try to locate the source of her disquiet. It was certainly not to do with the mechanics of the investigation. She was an experienced professional with an unparalleled record in bringing killers to justice. With Burrows and McVeigh she had developed a methodology that allowed them to apply their diverse strengths to the challenge each killing presented to them and follow the evidence threads through to conclusion. They were already making good progress with the current case in that regard. Better than she had initially hoped for, thanks to McVeigh's sharp thinking.

When had she begun to feel rattled? Carefully she scanned through the previous two days to see if she could remember the root of this creeping dread. All had been well yesterday when she had left Alice's flat to head to the new murder scene. She shook her head at the very idea that Alice was any part of her agitation. The visiting scholar had broken through Caroline's protective shield with one winning sideways smile. All her sturdy defences erected over decades had crumbled … joyfully, as she remembered. She smiled now, two months later, at the memory of that visceral, undeniable jolt to her system. A *coup de foudre*, the French called it … a bolt of lightning … love at first sight. Caroline had thought she was much too sensible to buy into such notions but she had definitely fallen for Alice Fox – hook, line and sinker. She had a compelling urge to go back to Botanic right now and be wrapped up in that unfaltering confidence of hers, but there was a press conference to prepare for and a briefing paper to send to the Super. Better not get distracted. She would get to the bottom of this nameless angst when she had more time to spare. In the meantime she would, as always, cope with it.

17

Nicholas Quinn phoned DS Burrows that night from his hotel in Lourdes. Burrows could hear an apocalyptic thunderstorm in the background and Quinn explained it happened regularly in Lourdes because of the proximity to the Pyrenees. Burrows wasn't in the mood for a meteorological lecture but he guessed that Quinn had consumed a fair amount of wine with his dinner and he realised he was going to have to manage this conversation carefully.

"I'm sorry to intrude on your trip, Mr Quinn," Burrows began, "but I need to ask you some questions about your brother Michael. We have had an incident here in a church in Belfast and we have reason to believe that your brother may have been involved. Can you tell me when you last spoke to him?"

It transpired that Nicholas hadn't spoken to his

brother for over a week and had no idea of his movements. He gave Burrows the name of the parish in north Dublin where Father Mick was a resident and promised to get in touch with the PSNI when he landed in Dublin on Saturday morning. He evidently was either very drunk or had no worries about his brother's wellbeing as he made no inquiry about him whatsoever.

Burrows then phoned the Dublin parish and asked to speak to Father Quinn. The housekeeper said he had been away for a few days and was due back the following evening. She explained that he had some business to do in the North where he was previously a curate. Burrows googled the Dublin parish and consulted the gallery of photos of parish outings and events. Father Mick was clearly a gregarious character as he featured in the majority of the images, frequently holding a glass. Burrows noted that he often had a scarf thrown round his neck in a cavalier fashion that also concealed his dog collar and he wondered when this habit of hiding his priestly identity had developed.

The light was still on in the boss's office and he tapped quietly on the door and went in.

She looked up from her laptop and smiled tiredly. "Bill. You're still here. We should all be heading home soon, I think."

He brought her up to date with the recent details about the murder victim and his brother. It was likely that Nicholas Quinn would be asked to come to Belfast to identify his brother's remains and until that happened the identity would not be made public. Tonight's discoveries would not change their position for the press conference but required setting up a collaborative understanding with colleagues in the South. They agreed that Paton would immediately set in train the cross-border protocol that would allow them to retain primacy in the investigation, as the location of the crime, but give them access to valuable support from the Garda Síochána south of the border. Tentatively they agreed that Burrows and McVeigh would, as planned, attend the ten o'clock Mass the following morning to speak to those attending. After Mass and the press gathering they would all meet up and plan for a trip to Dublin that afternoon and the ID of the remains on Saturday. Nicholas Quinn would have an unexpected detour to make before he finally headed for home.

18

Alice and Hugo locked up the EXIT premises and made their way the few hundred yards along the main road to the Felons Club. It was pitch dark where they stopped and there were no lights outside the dark shell of a building or any sound to indicate there was some life within. It was enclosed at a distance of a few metres by a metal cage that reached from roof to ground level. Alice recognised the architectural feature she had noted on police stations in the north and it was clear that nobody would be launching any unwelcome devices at the façade of this fortress.

Hugo pushed a buzzer in the front gate and it swung open. When they were safely inside the protective perimeter and the outer gate had clicked closed, a door opened in the dark and they were assailed by loud music, cheerful voices and the smell of hot bodies coming from the brightly lit interior. The contrast between inside and out struck Alice as massive.

"How's our Hugo then?" said the heavy man sitting at a small desk inside the door. He was a hulk of a man who looked as if he could pack a punch yet he was smiling kindly at Hugo and Alice as if he was the most gentle of beings.

"Grand, thanks, Matt, and yourself?" Hugo responded amicably. He was clearly not a stranger in these parts.

"I'll just ask your guest to sign the visitors' book and you're free to join the throngs! It's really packed in there tonight. Thursday is definitely the new Friday in West Belfast. Everybody is getting into practice for Paddy's Day next Monday."

As Alice added her name to the impressive tome on the desk, she heard Hugo enquire if the Clintons were there and Matt directed him to where they were settled at a corner table. He evidently already knew or had vetted and tracked everyone who entered the premises.

"The band's about to go on a break so you might get half an hour of conversation before they start up again." Matt turned his gaze to the monitor on a shelf to the right of his seat where another hopeful couple were signalling their desire to gain entry. He pushed a buzzer that allowed them through the first line of defence.

Inside the doors, Jed was waving from the corner to attract their attention and they weaved their way around the crowded tables until they were beside the three generations of the Clinton family. Alice recognised Jed and his mother Brenda, and a woman in her early sixties who had to be the granny, Martha. There was a strong family resemblance between Martha and Brenda and Alice thought that at their first meeting all those years beforehand that striking family likeness must have been particularly poignant. The fourth person at the table was a spritely-looking man in his sixties who had the weather-beaten complexion of someone who likes the outdoor life. Martha's partner was called Brian Mulgrew and he seemed like an affable man whose careful attentions demonstrated that he was quietly protective of her.

After a round of introductions, Hugo and Alice took their seats which had been preciously guarded for them by Jed.

As promised by doorman Matt the group playing lively Irish music went for a break and they were better able to hear what the others at the table were saying. Jed was dispatched to the crowded bar for beers for Alice and Hugo and another round for the others. Alice was sitting between Brenda and Brian and looking around. She was amazed by the number of people and the seeming intensity of their concentration on having a good time. There was a buzz of energy in the room and a sense of good-humoured camaraderie that Alice hadn't encountered before in any social venue. She wondered if there was a parallel meeting place in a

Loyalist community and how it would compare with this one. She would have to ask Caroline.

"Where do you live, Alice?" Brenda enquired.

When she said she had rented a place in the Botanic Area it was arranged that Brian and Martha would give her a lift home as they were staying in a B&B near the university.

"You don't want to be cycling over there too late," said Brenda.

She had planned to get a taxi and collect her bike the following evening but this was another option, provided they didn't plan on a late night.

"I don't like to be too late," said Alice and Brian had looked relieved.

Now that she had the chance she could see signs of pallor and fatigue behind the healthy skin-tone. He must be tired after the drive up from Dublin, she speculated. She thought it a bit strange that he was wearing a tweed cap indoors but perhaps he felt the cold and wanted to retain his body heat.

"Don't worry, love," he said. "Martha and I will be happy to go when you're ready. We are here for the whole weekend so we don't have to do all our chatting in the one night. These young ones can stay on as long as they like."

Brian had a strong accent that Alice hadn't encountered before. It was more musical than the Belfast flat vowel pronunciation and she had to strain to attune her ear to what he said.

109

"I'm a Connemara man," he said by way of response to her puzzled expression.

Martha leaned across him to say, "Just tell him to slow up, darlin'. He speaks too quick for me too and I've known him nearly five years!"

Martha and Brian turned their attention to Hugo who was sandwiched between them, smiling contentedly. He was clearly very much at home here and occasionally made a gesture of recognition in response to a greeting from a passer-by.

Brenda took hold of Alice's arm and spoke confidentially to her. She thanked her for the support she and Hugo were giving to Jed. She explained that she was very much caught up in the detail of her family origins at the moment and that Jed had been feeling some pressure because of that.

"He's a very sensitive wee lad," she asserted. "There were only the two of us for all those years before I met up with my mam and suddenly we started to have a bit more of a family life. Before that we only had each other and that meant we were very close. What annoyed him annoyed me and vice versa. It's still quite a lot like that."

Alice could imagine that intense relationship had both advantages and drawbacks. In her own experience, the presence of siblings and another parent could dilute family tensions and bring a range of perspectives. She could quite easily understand that Jed and Brenda must live in a very close-knit and maybe sometimes oppressive unit.

"Jed mentioned that you are part of a new group," Alice said, giving Brenda an opening to give the explanation that had prompted this get-together.

Brenda explained the purpose of the survivors' group and how they met in the offices of Amnesty International. The background detail wasn't entirely new to Alice who had read about the survivors' movement in the research she'd done after the chat with Jed. What she hadn't understood was the limitations of the Northern inquiry that had started recently and the groups that were omitted from its reach.

While the others at the table chatted and distributed the second round of drinks, Brenda told Alice about her adoption, the unhappy circumstances of that family break-up and her subsequent return to State care.

Before she reached the point in her life where she became pregnant with Jed, the band started up again and serious conversation became impossible.

"We'll do this another time," Brenda said into Alice's ear. "I'd really like to talk it all through with someone who would understand and who would be able to help Jed if he struggles with knowing the details about his own start in life." She looked enquiringly at Alice as if keen to get her agreement to this future conversation there and then.

"Just let me know when suits you," said Alice, "and

I'll be sure to be there. Do you like to be outdoors? Maybe we could walk and talk?"

"Sounds lovely. I'll get back to you soon about the when and where." Brenda was visibly pleased to have an understanding with her new confidante.

Alice put her name and number in the contacts on Brenda's mobile phone and then they both turned their attention back to the group chat. Those around the table who were hoping for conversation were now vying for survival with music that seemed to have gone up several notches in volume. Alice relaxed into doing what she liked best – observing the behaviour of those around her.

She could see that Jed was delighted to have brought his family together with Hugo and her. His fine features were lit by a constant smile that was a hopeful outcome given his recent angst. Brenda too looked contented as if she had a pleasant secret that was giving her cause to smile a lot. Martha was enjoying a pint of lager and singing along heartily to the music when she knew the words. At the same time she kept a close eye on Brian and blew him copious kisses. This didn't in the slightest seem to disturb Hugo who was sitting in between the couple. Hugo and Brian were attempting to chat but it was a lost cause with the volume of the music and, increasingly, the added accompaniment of the audience.

Brian was struggling, Alice thought, to refrain from yawning and to prevent a rather strained expression from taking hold of his features. It seemed he really would be glad to get away early.

It was after ten thirty when Martha, Brian and Alice stood to leave. It looked as if the others were there for the duration.

The drive home in Brian's smooth hybrid car was straightforward at this time when traffic was minimal.

Once inside Alice had locked up and was thinking about going to bed when the front door buzzed. She went to the window to check who was there.

19

Caroline came through the front door of the first-floor flat and fell into Alice's waiting arms.

"My tired woman," Alice murmured into her partner's hair. "And I've been off drinking beer in the Felons Club. What colourful lives we lead!" She chuckled playfully.

The detective broke free from the embrace with a look of disbelief on her pale face. "Really? You've been reaching dubious depths of community immersion there?" She laughed a little scathingly at Alice's most recent adventure.

There was a conversation to begin about their different ideological positions on the North's identity issues but Alice could see that now was certainly not the moment. However, she couldn't let it pass without some response.

"Well, Caro," she said, approaching the core issue

head on, "for me that is just a place where I could meet the family of a young person I'm working with. I guess I'm lucky not to have all the sectarian baggage that others here have accumulated. I hope that you can you see that?"

Her message hit home.

"I'm probably not in the most open frame of mind, Alice. My spirit is fragile and I needed an extended hug to calm my demons."

The senior detective was demonstrably less than her usual capable self and Alice set aside their differences and became more alert to what was happening.

"I won't stay long," Caroline said, "because I have a press conference first thing in the morning and then a trip to Dublin for a few hours in afternoon. Things are getting a little convoluted with the new case."

Alice knew better than to open up that subject when their time was limited and she put on the kettle to make some herb tea for them both. She knew the DI's propensity was probably for chocolate but she didn't have any and plumped for the nearest healthy option. "Have you eaten, Caro? I could make some toast and honey to go with a relaxing tea."

"That sounds almost enticing," Caroline said, laughing, and then stopped herself short of becoming offensive. "Thank you, I would love that ... and then I would also like that extended hug."

"Deal!" said Alice, aware that this was an unusually

needy Caroline who had now dumped her shoes where she stood and flopped onto Alice's comfy sofa. She let the silence calm the atmosphere, aware that this was terrain where banter could go badly wrong.

After she put the tray on the coffee table in front of them, she took her place beside her lover and opened her arms. "Hugs in abundance ready and waiting."

"Thank you."

Alice felt the tension ease as she held her partner close.

When Caroline surfaced, she reached for some toast.

"Do you want to offload some troubles, Caro? Or would you rather just recharge your batteries and leave the soul-searching for when we have more time?"

"I don't want to talk about the case just yet, but I do need to broach something it has dredged up for me from the very distant past."

Alice saw that this was more than a minor irritation and held unwavering and attentive contact with Caroline's troubled green eyes. She felt the other woman falter and watched her wrestle with how to continue.

Finally and characteristically, Caroline opted for a question as the way forward. "Do you think that it's possible to bury something so deeply in your subconscious that you become completely unaware of the fact that it happened?"

"Yes, I do," Alice said without hesitation. "There's a lot written about that in the literature about surviving childhood trauma. Sometimes the body remembers what the mind has buried and silenced and things can resurface in response to an unanticipated stimulus." She kissed Caroline's hand gently and waited for her response.

Minutes slipped by and some boisterous students passed by in the street outside, singing at top volume. Neither woman reacted. Eventually Caroline took a deep breath and began speaking quietly.

"When we were kids my mother had a brother who was studying to become a minister in the church. I suppose I was just about four or five at the time. He was in our house a lot at mealtimes and he used to bring puzzles for me and help me to get them started. He didn't bother too much with my older brothers and they were often out playing in the street. I guess I got used to him being alone with me."

Alice could see where this was going and felt a surge of compassion and fierce protectiveness for her new lover. She held her hands more firmly and waited quietly for her to continue.

"One evening when he was there I remember getting upset about something … although I can't recall any detail of why that happened. That's all a blank – just a sliver of a memory." She paused and appeared to grapple with how to proceed. "I do remember there was a scene when my very quiet, eldest brother gave the would-be minister a bloody nose. There was quite the row that evening and after that my uncle didn't come to visit any more."

She looked at Alice as if hoping that she could see into the past and fill in the gaps for her. Alice slowly stroked Caroline's hands and remained silent.

"Well, now, since this case has begun, something is stirred up in me that makes me feel vulnerable and insecure. I have to work harder to be across my game which usually comes very easily to me." Her frustration with the impediment this new recollection had generated was palpable as she struggled to make sense where no hard evidence could be found. "Of course I can see there was an abusive event happened in my past and I am able to see from my lack of comfort sexually around guys that there is a root to all that. I told myself I was a career cop and hadn't time for relationships and I didn't think about the possibility of being close to women in those days … or ever really until you hit me with your particular charm." She smiled feebly and then looked as if she might cry but held it together. "I need to get my equilibrium back, Alice, or I won't be able to do my work." She sat back and allowed herself to breathe slowly for the first time since she'd arrived.

"You poor love," Alice said and waited before adding, "Is there something else you want to say or is it OK for me to chip in here?"

Caroline nodded for her to continue and reached for another piece of toast to nibble on.

"The first thing is thank you for bringing this to me. I'm glad that you know you are not on your own with this now. Something has awakened this memory in you. It may be the current case, and I also don't think we should talk about that now ... or it may be that at the moment every news bulletin has something about the Historic Institutional Abuse Inquiry on it. We are dealing with this stuff in EXIT at the moment too so I think that for some people a lot of forgotten histories are being disturbed right now."

She watched as Caroline nodded in agreement.

"That's all possible," she said quietly.

"As well as not being on your own, you are also a grown-up now. Your feelings are those of a small child who didn't understand what was happening ... and who may never remember what that was. But now you are a strong, capable woman who is well regarded for her work and well loved for the good person that you are ... This is in the past and it can stay there... or you can take it out and look at it, deal with any remnants and lay them to rest. That's work to do with a good counsellor who we can find and who will help you deal with this stuff without disturbing the balance of the rest of your life. You don't need to decide what to do now ... just realise that this doesn't need to control you. You are not that small Caroline any more."

"I feel a bit better just for letting it all out," Caroline said with some relief. "I'm sorry ..."

Alice raised a hand. "No apologies, Caro. Wait till I start revealing some of my dusty secrets!" She smiled her sideways smile that made everything seem a lot better. "I think we'd better plan a holiday in the sun before the lid comes off that one." She gently kissed Caroline's cheek. "Now I'm going to get really bossy. I suggest that you get into bed right now and sleep until six. Then you can get up and go home and do what you have to do to prepare for the day but you'll have had some sleep. I'll be beside you to deal with any demons and we can let this all settle until there is time to take it on in whatever way you decide is best for you. Is that a plan? No self-interest at all in my suggestion ..." And she jumped up and gently pulled Caroline from the sofa and steered her towards the bedroom.

By the time the light was switched off they were both smiling peacefully.

20

Alice and Brenda had arranged their get-together by text on Friday morning and agreed to meet at the front gates of the Botanic Gardens around half past eleven. It was bright and blustery and carried the promise of warmer days to come. Buds were beginning to appear on trees and bushes and there was that hopefulness that accompanies regrowth and the end of winter. Alice was still wearing her many winter layers but was aware that a number of those passing her to go into the park were anticipating warmer weather than she expected. Caroline had warned her that at the first sign of better weather young men moved directly into shorts and T-shirts. Many never actually got to the stage of wearing a coat even in the depths of winter. She thought it must be an element of young Irish masculinity that required you to be impervious to the cold ... or at least appear to be. She loved getting to know all these signs that were particular to a place. It was like learning a language only the locals could hear and allowed you to feel less of an outsider.

At twenty to twelve Brenda came into view, moving rapidly and appearing flustered, even at a distance. Alice was always on time, often early in fact, but she really didn't mind others being late as she enjoyed the slices of unexpected time it gave her for people-watching. She welcomed Jed's mum with a wide smile and they headed into the park.

Brenda was quite out of breath and so when they found an empty bench in the sun outside the Palm House, they sat down and Brenda had a drink from the water bottle she was carrying. She met Alice's eyes decisively, took a deep breath and began to talk.

"I'm so glad that you agreed to meet me, Alice. I really need to talk to someone who will understand my story and will also know what is best for my Jed."

Her facial expression was both determined and anxious and Alice understood something about this woman's struggle to be a good mother whilst shedding the burden of her family history. Brenda had dealt with the part that involved her biological mother and now her own abusive past needed to be reckoned with.

"I am happy to listen, Brenda," Alice said sincerely. "Jed is a fine young man and anything I can do that will help you or him is okay with me. I enjoyed the meet-up last night too. Thank you for organising us all." She could see that Brenda was encouraged by this acknowledgement and settled more comfortably into the seat.

"It's not a complicated story I have to tell, Alice. It is the experience of many women and girls … especially poor uneducated women and girls who have been brought up to see the clergy as totally trustworthy. As you know from Jed, I was adopted as a baby and I lived with those parents until I was a young teenager. There was a lot of stuff going on for my mam and dad and their relationship was getting more and more violent. My social worker saw that it wasn't a good place for me to be and they were not up to being parents at the time. She got me into an aftercare place where I had my own room and there was a resident care worker. That person changed often and they didn't really know us all that well. If you wanted to, you could easily fool them into thinking you were an angel even if you weren't. It was a job for them and it stopped when they went off duty." She smiled sadly at the memory of those times.

Alice listened quietly and attentively. Stories of the weaknesses in social-care systems and how vulnerable kids fell through the cracks were familiar to her.

"Anyway …" Brenda was impatient to get on with her account. "I wasn't a bad kid really and if someone was kind to me I was ready to lap it up. Now as an adult I can see what I really needed was to be well loved but that wasn't on the menu. When I was fifteen, me and some other girls from the after-care unit went for the summer to a camp run by the Catholic Church. I was there to help look after small kids from poor families caught up in the Troubles and give them some sort of a holiday. Each group was only there for a week so we didn't really get to know them and anyway we were really more concerned with our own needs than theirs." She hesitated slightly as she came to the crux of the issue. "There was a priest there who ran a youth club in the evenings for older kids and he gave me a lot of attention. I was needy and flattered and I trusted him. I'd been told all my life that priests were good and holy and I wasn't very worldly wise. He groomed me well and truly. He gave me drink I could never afford for myself and told me I was special. He said he would never hurt me … but he did … and by the time the summer was over I was pregnant and my options were limited."

Brenda's face showed the abject desolation she must have felt back then and Alice was reminded of Caroline's sadness the previous evening. Abuse was definitely a long-term issue as well as a cause of immediate harm.

"I remember he got his sister-in-law to come and talk to me and try to coax me into his way of seeing things but she wasn't really convinced by his position any more than I was. He wanted me to have the baby in a place he knew run by nuns and have it adopted. Just like I was myself. I wasn't ever going to do that so I told him to leave me alone and I'd cope with it myself.

He sent me money for a while but I knew he wanted nothing to do with me and my baby and he very soon disappeared without trace from my life. I let people call me Mrs Clinton because it sounds kind of respectable but there never was a Mister anybody. There's always just been me." She looked earnestly at Alice and continued quietly. "So you see, Alice, Jed's dad is a Catholic priest who wanted nothing to do with him. How do I tell him that without causing him harm? Is it better to lie and let him think he was the result of a drunken fling or do I tell the truth and hope he can cope with it? What do you think?"

"Well, that's a difficult one, Brenda. It makes me so angry that the Church has caused such havoc in people's lives. There have been similar revelations in the States so I'm not shocked by what you're telling me but I'm furious that this happened to you when you were young and you're still dealing with it all these years later. And now you have to figure out how to make this part of Jed's life too." She paused, conscious of the weight of Brenda's question. Her gut said that the truth was always the best route but sometimes hearing the truth all at once was a bit brutal. It needed to be heard in episodes, one piece at a time.

"You know Jed better than anyone, Brenda. I don't think any decision you make will take away his certainty of your love for him or the fact that you want the best for him."

They talked until they were too cold to sit outside

any longer and went into the museum to get a warm drink and talk some more. Alice knew from experience that people often wanted to meet an absent parent so that they could identify something of themselves in that person. Sometimes that led to disappointment and more damage when the enthusiasm about that discovery wasn't reciprocated.

She asked if Martha and Brian knew about her quandary.

"He doesn't need a scumbag like that in his life," had been Brian's reported comment and Martha had not argued against that view.

Brenda was more conflicted about what was for the best. She talked about the survivors' meetings and the importance of knowing the truth about your identity that was often expressed there. She didn't want to deprive Jed of the right to know who his father had been. Alice could see that her dilemma was torturous and she felt her anger rise against this man who had abused a vulnerable teenager and then left her to deal with the lifelong consequences of his self-indulgence.

Alice said she thought that the place to begin, irrespective of Brenda's decision, was to put supports in place for both her and Jed so that she felt less alone. She assured her that Hugo and herself would be there for them and suggested that Barnardo's would also be a good source of help. They dealt with complicated family issues all the time and would be sure to have experienced people and practical supports in place.

They decided to pause the discussion and let it rest for a while. Alice would talk to Hugo and Brenda would see what Barnardo's had to offer when she was there for her meeting the following week.

"I've met someone I like at the meetings and I saw him for a chat yesterday," said Brenda. "He's a survivor of An Cuan so he understands about neglect and lack of family life."

The source of Brenda's smiles became suddenly clear.

"Somehow, even though I hardly know Johnny, I feel less alone. I realise that I have more of my own life left to live as well as being the best mother I can be to Jed."

Life could get very damned complicated, Alice thought as she smiled in admiration at this woman, who despite having had a fraught childhood and turbulent adulthood, had nonetheless learned about the essence of good parenting.

Brenda looked at her watch, jumped to her feet and thanked Alice for listening. "I need to get to work. I can really do without getting sacked right now." And she grimaced helplessly at that prospect in her already difficult life.

The sky outside had darkened and it looked like it might rain soon. Brenda went off to clean offices in the city centre and Alice walked home through the park, wishing she had a fire she could light to warm the chill that she had in her bones.

21

Hands wrapped around a mug of hot chocolate, Alice Fox sat in her comfy armchair and mulled over the number of times some form of abuse had edged up very close to her this week. None of it was entirely new to her but the layers of intensity of damage wrought in one small family were shocking. There was the story of Jed's granny Martha – second generation born into the stark, loveless care of the State, where the whole purpose was to produce docile, obedient servants of authority. The image of the baby left to the care of young orphan girls, who were themselves deprived of any family experience, made Alice sad and angry for all those children. There could be no flourishing in that environment where everything worked to a military-type schedule. From her reading she knew that bells or whistles were sounded to waken children, to tell them when they could eat and when they must stop eating, to permit speaking and to bring conversation to an end, to signal time for learning and work and even sleep at the end of a regimented day until the cycle of control began all over again with the loveless signal for rising next morning.

Baby Martha would have been lucky to have even her most basic bodily needs catered for, yet the reports that Alice had read suggested that even these spartan requirements for cleanliness, comfort and nourishment had rarely been satisfied. In the same vein, young Martha's responsibility for feeding the orphanage's hens, when she herself was often hungry, was indicative of a regime full of contradictions. The state took children from parents viewed as unfit to raise their young and then failed to give those children even a minimal taste of affection. It had taken a long time too for them to admit any culpability and from the testimonies Alice had read that delay had caused irreparable damage in some cases.

The in-depth inquiry into institutional abuses in the Irish Republic had recognised 'loss of opportunity' as an abuse of children in State care. Education in the State care facilities was authoritarian and brutal and adults who had lived in fear of lavish amounts of corporal punishment reported that terror blocked their capacity to learn even the basics of literacy and numeracy. Some were not even given the fundamental building blocks of language development. There was no one with the time or the skill to be a model for little ones to emulate in learning language. Often children were expected to remain silent for long periods of time and those without any residual experience of family life had no example of rich vocabulary and family chat to draw upon. There was no adult or older sibling to marvel at the small child's production of a new sound or word, no one to repeat the correct pronunciation or encourage communication. There were no nursery rhymes, songs or bedtime stories, just harsh commands and rebukes and endless fearful isolation. In this loveless scenario the language code of many remained restricted and, although most expanded their vocabulary in adult life, some who remained alone had little opportunity to do so.

In the cases where children in care homes were sent out to a local school, the story wasn't any better. They reported being singled out for ridicule and exclusion on the grounds that they had no one to defend their rights or speak in their defence. In the Redress part of the national inquiry, a points system determined monetary compensation. Lost opportunity was seen as a lesser form of harm than sexual and physical abuses. Not being given the basics of language development seemed like a pretty big form of damage to Alice's mind and she wondered how the immediate and long-term impact of such things could begin to be fairly measured. She was sure that there could be no adequate compensation for lives filled with such childhood atrocities.

Now, as well as Martha's story, there was the subsequent Clinton generation of Brenda who had some experience of family life but lost even that when she was a young teenager. Without any stable, supportive adults to watch out for her, she was preyed upon by a cleric who left her pregnant at sixteen to cope alone with bringing up her son. A lone parent, living in social housing and cleaning offices for a living did not earn much respect and admiration but Alice recognised and admired the courageous spirit and survival skills of these women. They were way above and beyond the plaudits easily heaped on the achievements of the privileged, herself included. She tried to quash her fury at the ways of the world and think of the small amounts of potential progress in Jed's life, the third generation Clinton who had benefitted most from family care. His mother had kept him and loved him fiercely. Although he was going to have to accept some harsh realities about his parentage, his mother was involved in fighting back against historic abuses and he would hopefully get strength and some sense of justice from that. She smiled when she thought that now Jed was in the care of Hugo and the EXIT group and the power of that was not to be underestimated. At least there was some light in this grim tunnel.

And then there was Caroline and her early brush with some forgotten episode of childhood abuse. Small Caroline had stored that experience away in a dark corner but it had been disturbed and was now demanding attention. In the time she had left in Ireland they would deal with that and begin to lay it to rest. She would be beside her ... wouldn't she? Alice was unexpectedly wrong-footed by the extent of the dilemma that the future posed. In only five months there would be the outcome of complicated decisions coming down the track about the way forward ... But for now she would finish her book proposal and see if she could find at least one element of certainty on her increasingly hazy horizon.

22

By coffee time on Friday morning DI Paton had successfully conducted the Press Conference with her superior and was back in her office. Thanks to Alice and her steady head, she had regained her composure and what had seemed like an intractable issue now seemed totally manageable. She was resolved to approach her childhood ghosts as she did a murder investigation: gather the evidence, examine it forensically and resolve matters in whatever way was most appropriate. She would track down an experienced counsellor that she could feel comfortable with and make time to do the work needed to lay this demon to rest. With Alice Fox at her back, she felt able for that.

While waiting for Burrows and McVeigh to return from speaking to Mass-goers at St Oliver's, Caroline followed up on the documents that needed to be sent ahead to the Garda in relation to the current case. She and McVeigh would drive to Dublin as soon as the three of them had a quick confab and Burrows would hold the fort in Belfast. She wanted him to take care of the diplomatic contact with the Catholic hierarchy in such a way as to allay any tendency in that quarter to obscure detail that might be relevant to the case. If this cleric had done something that had incited someone to murder in the particularly graphic manner that they had found, then she wanted no opportunities for a cover-up. It was no secret that this was often the Church's approach to impending scandal. The Murder Squad would delay releasing the ID of the victim until the family had been officially informed and that would be Saturday at the earliest. She was sure that Canon Murphy had already spoken to his superiors so some courtesy gesture was called for from the police towards the Church authorities. At the same time, the cross-border facet of the case complicated and delayed it somewhat. Burrows would be conciliatory and gain them some time. Her plan that afternoon was that she and McVeigh could get to examine Michael Quinn's rooms and belongings before any clean-up had taken place.

It was one o'clock before they finally set off, taking sandwiches and coffee with them in the car. There was an easy silence between them. McVeigh drove and Caroline relaxed and mulled over what she wanted to achieve from this outing. They would drive to the

Garda Metropolitan Region Headquarters in Harcourt Street in Dublin and meet up with the officer who had been appointed to accompany them on any enquiries they would make south of the border.

The guy she had talked to the previous evening when she had launched the North/South Protocol had been warm and friendly and clearly relieved that the crime had happened in the North. That being the case, the bulk of the inquiry would be the responsibility of the PSNI. An Garda Síochána (which meant the "Guardians of the Peace" in Irish) would share intelligence information and facilitate visits from their northern counterparts as and when required. Since the Good Friday Agreement had formalised the process of peace-building, relationships between the two forces had been cautious at first but there was easy cooperation in both directions now on most matters.

"I'll have a suitable buddy sorted for you by the time you get here tomorrow, DI Paton," he had said in a gentle, lilting accent.

As they got nearer to the border there were increasing signs of the forthcoming St Patrick's Day holiday and Caroline wondered how that would impact on the investigation.

Crossing the border, she remarked that the weather often changed quite dramatically at that point and wondered if that climactic detail had been taken into account when the border was originally drawn. More likely the Cooley Mountains were the determining factor. The area was often referred to as "bandit territory" and down the years had been known for smuggling of goods that were less expensive or plentiful on one side or the other of the line between the two jurisdictions. There were stories of lucrative trafficking of butter and bacon, cheese and jam from South to North during the Second World War and for as long as food rationing continued. More recently diesel was the profitable commodity and there were frequently queues of cross-border traffic at whatever petrol station had the best bargain at any given time. For the most of the thirty years of the Troubles, it was guns and explosives, the chattels of war, that were the reason for cross-border scrutiny. Then the border had been the site of British Army bases, 'listening stations' that were heavily fortified and the location of numerous bomb attacks and exchanges of gunfire. Civilians crossing from one side to the other had their vehicles, and sometimes their bodies searched and the process was both nerve-racking and time-consuming. Probably just about everyone had breathed a sigh of relief when the posts were finally demilitarised and the frontier was returned to its slightly shabby, sparsely inhabited landscape.

Caroline noticed that McVeigh too relaxed a little when they crossed the border and understood the complexity of meaning behind that response for someone brought up as Catholic.

They drove into Harcourt Street not long after three o'clock and were met by Detective Inspector Orla Hegarty of the Garda Criminal Investigation Department. It was customary to match the ranks of cooperating officers in cross-border investigations and in Caroline's experience this approach worked smoothly.

They all shook hands and headed for DI Hegarty's office where they would talk over coffee and cake. A very good place to start, Caroline thought to herself.

23

It was after seven that evening when Caroline and McVeigh drove back through the heavy security gates at the Grosvenor Road police barracks. It was hard not to compare the relatively relaxed nature of policing in the South with the harsher realities in the North. History had left its different mark on each culture and to Caroline's mind the northern lot, on the surface at least, seemed darker and more joyless. She could see from his slightly more sombre expression that McVeigh might be on a similar page in his thinking.

"Let's raid the chocolate store," she said roguishly to her young colleague.

"I'd say Sergeant Burrows will be with you on that one," McVeigh said with a laugh and they headed up the stairs to their base and the review meeting that would bring their long day's work to a close. They had significant findings to bring to the table and by the smile on Burrows' face he had not been idle either.

"You look pleased to see us, Bill," said Caroline and lifted the nearest phone to put a call through to the canteen. "Hi there, Eileen. It's Caroline Paton here. What gourmet delights have you got there for three Hungry Horaces?" She listened attentively as she looked at the whiteboard on which Burrows had begun to sketch in some detail. "Sounds good, Eileen. Thanks. Oh, and by the way, the chocolate embargo is off. Back to business as usual." And she laughed out loud at the look of relief on Burrows' face. "Just give me five minutes, gents. I want to make a call before we start."

Their meeting was light on detail but what new information they had edged them forward in a significant way. Burrows and McVeigh had found two parishioners of immediate interest to the inquiry. One who had noted the light over the confessional and wondered if confessions were being heard. She had been on her way over to investigate when she had been waylaid by a friend and instead gone for coffee and a chat with her in a café down the road. "A lucky escape for her," quipped Caroline.

The second person of interest was a Filipino nun who had used the parishioners' toilet after Mass and noted that it was not as clean as usual. There was dirt on the floor and she had got oil on her jacket when she brushed against the wall or the door. Burrows had taken her contact details and asked her to call at the local station to give prints and a DNA sample so that forensics could eliminate her from their inquiry. She agreed also to bring in her jacket although she said she had tried, not very successfully, to remove the greasy mark. Burrows said that he and McVeigh had distributed flyers giving the contact of the local station, in case any others were prompted to pass on information.

"That's all progress," said Caroline. "It helps us narrow down the relevant trace evidence and our estimates of when the body may have been put in place. How did you get on with the church authorities?"

Burrows reported on his conversation with the bishop's private secretary who had indeed been informed by the canon of the findings in St Oliver's. He said that they had no knowledge of any member of the clergy who had gone missing and suggested that this might be some attempt to implicate the clergy in a secular matter. Anybody could replicate the appearance of a priest, he had suggested.

"The fact that he adopted that position made it easier for me to avoid getting into too much detail and yet to satisfy our wish to appear cooperative. He did also agree to circulate the enquiry to his colleagues and let us know if any missing person report surfaced elsewhere."

"I think from my research into the Catholic system of governance that those communications will be all-island," said Caroline. "That suits us very well now as we hold off on naming our victim until we have a solid ID. Afterwards, when we need to be able to address those south of the border who may be of interest, those good relations with the Catholic hierarchy may be helpful." She signalled to Burrows to continue his report.

Burrows said he had checked in with the local station on the Ormeau Road and there hadn't been anything further forthcoming from the house-to-house. They were ready to help in any way they could. He confirmed that the toxicology and the autopsy report were both available now on the shared drive. Toxicology showed that the victim's system had contained enough whiskey and Diazepam to ensure that he would have been comatose for a considerable period of time. The autopsy report confirmed McVeigh's initial account and additional graphic photographic images from pathology had also been uploaded.

Caroline nodded to McVeigh to deliver the feedback from their trip to Dublin. She had driven on the return journey and Ian had been busy on his iPad, making a record of their findings. Aside from anything else, Caroline would have been sick if she had needed to focus on writing whilst in a moving car. She had suffered from carsickness ever since childhood unless the road was fairly straight and she could just focus on the horizon.

McVeigh explained that DI Orla Hegarty had been appointed as their liaison officer for the duration of the investigation. He handed Burrows a card with her contact details. After they had briefed her, she had driven them to the Church of the Redeemer on Dublin's north side. The parochial house was a large, double-fronted detached residence with well-maintained gardens. It was in sharp contrast to the modest social housing in the nearby area where there were all the signs of poverty and hardship. Outside the church railings was a row of dingy shops and every free piece of wall space was well graffitied with illegible names and some fairly explicit messages. On a grassy patch in the middle of an expanse of housing, there were a number of ponies grazing, and as they passed by a young lad had jumped on the back of one horse and begun to ride it bareback across the grass. The overall impact was hard to put into words but was in the general vicinity of anarchy and a rejection of a more conservative value system that offered little real hope to those who lived thereabouts.

Their visit to the priest's residence had been unannounced and the housekeeper was put out by their request to be shown to Father Quinn's rooms. DI Hegarty had smoothed the way and they had been taken upstairs to a spacious bedroom with a bay window looking out to the front of the house. The room was tastefully decorated and had an en-suite bathroom. As well as a double bed, it had a large leather-topped desk and office chair and beside an open fireplace there was a reclining leather armchair. The two alcoves on either side of the chimneybreast were lined with books. There was a political thriller, a glasses' case and a half-full bottle of Bushmills whiskey on a small table beside the armchair. The room was not untidy but neither had it been cleaned in anticipation of their visit. Paton and McVeigh were relieved that there had been no attempt to tidy away papers. A large diary and a laptop were open on the desk.

When the housekeeper had left, they had donned their gloves and gathered the diary, the computer and other items of interest into evidence bags which McVeigh had produced from his briefcase.

"We noted as much detail as we could," said McVeigh, "and then DI Hegarty instructed the housekeeper to lock the room and admit no-one until she gave permission for her to do so. The gardaí will organise a full forensic search of the premises as soon as the official ID has taken place. While the evidence that we removed was bagged and recorded back in Harcourt Street, DI Paton and I had a few moments to look at the papers, diary and other notebooks we found. In his appointments for Wednesday he had planned to visit someone in the Divis Tower so bringing that person in for interview will be top of the agenda tomorrow as well as getting Nicholas Quinn here to identify the remains."

Caroline placed an evidence box on the table. "I'd like us to get started on sifting through all this stuff now, so that we can get clarification from the brother tomorrow, if need be."

As they all gloved up and settled down to examine the paper trail left by Father Mick Quinn, Burrows sighed contentedly and reached for a chocolate bar.

When Caroline phoned around seven, Alice had just finished a long phone chat with Hugo where she had brought him up to date on her conversation with Brenda that morning. The evening review was about to take place in the Murder Squad HQ and Caroline wanted Alice to know that she was in a much better frame of mind. The following day would be busy so she wouldn't be about before that, but if things became a little calmer by the evening she might not be too late finishing.

"I really think I need to take the work-life balance of the team more seriously," she said roguishly.

"Sounds good to me," Alice said with laugh. "I'll make us something to eat that can survive a shifting time plan." She had delighted in the fact that even the thought of time with Caroline still produced those delicious, involuntary sensations in her body. She was quite sure it was life-extending.

By the time she had finished her Saturday-morning run, Alice had a plan to go to the weekend St George's Market in the city centre and get some large fresh prawns from one of the excellent fish-sellers there. They would only take a few minutes to cook with garlic, parsley and butter and she would have a green salad ready to go with them and bottle of chilled white wine. No need to make things complicated.

On her short cycle to the covered market her phone buzzed in her pocket and she stopped and checked the origin of the call. It was Hugo and she answered immediately. He wouldn't idly disturb her on a Saturday.

"I've just had Jed on the phone in a bit of a state. Two uniformed PSNI officers arrived at their door at nine this morning and asked his mam to go with them to Grosvenor Road barracks. She wasn't arrested but asked to 'help them with their enquiries'. Jed wanted to go with her but Brenda refused that offer and told him to phone me and ask if I would get you to meet her there."

Hugo paused but Alice had nothing to say at this point. She was trying to think of the possible reasons why Brenda could be of interest to the police.

"Jed thinks she wants somebody with her in case there is reading and writing involved and she feels that she can trust you. Are you free and willing to go, Alice? You're a better prospect with the forces of law and order than I am. My family history gives me bad press in a way that yours demands respect."

She could hear that he was teasing her slightly but also making a valid point.

"Remember that if she needs a lawyer my cousin will be happy to go in and meet you there."

Hugo's cousin, Shane Ramsey, was a solicitor who had been called in during the murder investigation in

DePRec when a young colleague Hugo knew had found himself to be a suspect in that crime. No doubt Shane would similarly be available to help Brenda if this became necessary.

Alice felt she was becoming part of that local community network and the idea pleased her.

"I'm actually on my bike and not too far from Grosvenor Road at the moment. I can go there directly. I'll call you when I find out what is happening. It's good that you're available for Jed in case he needs you."

And with that the plans for dinner were waylaid and Alice Fox found herself yet again drawn unexpectedly into Northern Ireland police matters. She was plainly aware that unlike the last time, her invitation did not come from the lead detective in the Murder Squad but someone who was on the other side of the table. For now Alice's priority was responding to a request for help and how or if that impacted on her relationship with DI Caroline Paton would no doubt become apparent all too soon.

24

Nicholas Quinn's bag of French liquors was clinking loudly as he made the long walk from the arrival's gate to baggage reclaim in Dublin Airport's impressive Terminal 2. It was only eight o'clock in the morning and he was not fully awake and just a little hungover. The brandy in his coffee on the plane had not helped matters.

Behind the passport-checking desks, a uniformed garda was waiting with a copy of the photograph page of Nick Quinn's passport. DI Hegarty had briefed him earlier that morning. He was to meet the early flight from Toulouse and ensure that Nicholas Quinn made his way directly to Belfast either by air coach or in his own car if it was in an airport car park. He was to give Mr Quinn an envelope that contained all the details of the PSNI officers he was to meet and the location of the police station. As it turned out, Quinn was not unfamiliar with Belfast as he supplied a number of outlets there with religious merchandise and had visited the city a number of times. He had found them to be a rather serious crowd who were not usually interested in his offers of hospitality but business was business and he knew his way about the city.

He phoned his wife and told her he was delayed and would be home whenever he could be. They were no longer close and he doubted she would be too disappointed if he were a day or two later than expected. And anyway – he laughed to himself now – he had been quite pickled for most of the past few weeks. He might book in somewhere in Belfast and see what entertainment he might find for himself.

It was only as he approached Belfast on the motorway that it struck home that he was going to have to confront the remains of someone who might be his brother Mick. He had not allowed himself to consider that fact before this. He had always had a knack of avoiding responsibility if at all possible. Even when he had started his business it was a bit of a joke really and then he had seen that there was a fund of gullible money out there that he could be accessing.

What might Mick have got himself into now? His brother was younger than him by only a little over a year. They were what was known as Irish twins and had always been partners in crime. Nick and Mick had been an infamous pair throughout school and into early adulthood where they had done their share of carousing and womanising together and not all before they had both settled down into their adult lives. There had been a few moments much more recently than that and he chortled as he remembered. It had been a bit of a shock when Mick had opted for the priesthood but then he had made his own money from religious trinketry so he couldn't criticise. It was an easy business – the faithful, as he liked to refer to his clientele, could find hope in the most tasteless of items and he had been catering to their bad taste for decades now.

It was just after ten o'clock as he pulled his Lexus into the entrance of the police station that was conveniently situated just near the end of the M1 motorway. He hoped that this wouldn't take too long and he would head around to the Europa Hotel afterwards, check in for a few nights and see what mischief he could get up to.

The heavily fortified entrance to the Grosvenor Road Police Station was not unfamiliar to Alice Fox. Burrows and McVeigh of the Murder Squad had taken her there in January to give a statement about her close encounter with a murder suspect. Her reception in the station that night had made it clear that word of her skill in martial arts had preceded her. As someone who disliked to be noticed, this had made her a little uncomfortable but also in a way she had been quietly pleased.

Today she was more concerned that her arrival would be awkward in terms of Caroline and the unresolved matter of how public their relationship should be. She had decided not to phone ahead and cause additional anxiety and trusted that they would both manage the situation with discretion. Alice was there at the invitation of someone helping the police with their inquiries and most particularly because of the woman's worry about any literacy demands that might be made on her. In her work in the US Alice was often called as a supporter for vulnerable or intimidated witnesses. In addition to her skills and experience gained in LPD, since she moved into academia Alice had done rigorous training for the 'supporter' role and was often called on to help in awkward interviews. She had no idea why Brenda had been brought in and whether or not it coincided with Caroline's work or some other police department's business. In any case, Alice had no information whatsoever about the nature of the current case that the Murder Squad were dealing with and could say in all honesty that there was nothing compromising about her presence.

In the reception area she presented herself at the desk and explained that Brenda Clinton, who was already there for interview, expected her. The uniformed Desk Sergeant asked her to take a seat in the waiting area and phoned through to announce her arrival. In a short space of time the swing doors to the right opened and

Alice recognised DC Ian McVeigh. So now she knew Brenda's request for assistance had in fact come from the Murder Squad. The dapper young detective smiled and shook her hand and they exchanged pleasantries. Her previous dealings with Burrows and McVeigh had been very amicable. In fact McVeigh had dropped her home earlier in the year after she had made her statement in relation to the DePRec killing and they had chatted a bit about her work in restorative justice. He had seemed interested, she recalled.

"Mrs Clinton has asked for you to be present to support her. She explained that she doesn't want legal representation but has concerns about her understanding of written materials and would be more relaxed with you here. It's all been cleared with the DI. We are just about to begin questioning so I'll sign you in and we can get started." He hesitated for a moment and then asked, "How do you know Mrs Clinton, Dr Fox?"

"Actually, I've just met her recently – in fact, earlier this week." Alice was surprised, given how much she knew of the woman's life, at how little time had passed since she had first met Brenda. It seemed they had known each other longer. "Brenda's son, Jed, is a member of the EXIT group that I work with as part of my research here in Northern Ireland. It's a restorative justice programme and I work there several times a week."

"I see," said McVeigh. "I remember that we spoke a little about that back in January." And he smiled meaningfully at her, not least because his memory of her impressive actions that night back then was still clear in his mind but also because her Boston drawl was somewhat incongruous in this place and very pleasing on the ear.

"I'm not informed in any way about why Brenda's here but I guess I'll catch up as you explain."

Alice followed McVeigh downstairs to the interview rooms in the basement and was relieved to see Burrows sitting across the desk from Jed's mam. Caroline had evidently been forewarned and taken herself out of the picture.

Brenda looked cowed but managed a fragile smile for Alice as she came in and took the free seat beside her.

Burrows smiled at Alice and nodded at the tape machine, which was already running. "DC McVeigh has returned with Dr Alice Fox who will be here to accompany Mrs Clinton while she is helping us with our inquiries." He smiled encouragingly at Brenda who looked close to tears.

Alice placed her hand on Brenda's arm and squeezed gently. Brenda turned and made eye contact with her and Alice gave her a look of reassurance. Then she nodded to Burrows that they were ready to begin.

"I realise, Mrs Clinton," said Burrows, "that you don't know yet why we've asked you to come to the station and so I'm going to explain that now. I know that it's upsetting to be brought to the police station first thing on a Saturday morning and we'll make this all as easy as possible. Just answer our questions as fully as you can."

McVeigh took over at this stage and Burrows made notes on the iPad in front of him. "Earlier this week, Mrs Clinton, we began a murder inquiry. We have not as yet officially identified the remains but are fairly certain that we know who it is and we hope that a family member will confirm that later this morning. A search of this person's papers showed that on Wednesday of this week your name and address was recorded in a diary, suggesting that the person in question had a plan to meet you."

Alice noted that McVeigh had not alluded to the gender of the victim, where they lived or any details of the proposed meeting with Brenda. He was making a familiar play, hoping to lead the interviewee into disclosing any prior knowledge they had of the deceased.

Brenda looked blankly at the two men opposite as if frozen in time and was clearly confused, perhaps just by the formality of the language.

Alice gently touched her arm again and spoke quietly. "Maybe if you just think back to Wednesday, Brenda, and tell them what you did that day. I think that would be helpful. Just tell them what you remember about your day."

Brenda looked uncertain but began to speak hesitantly, working the palms of her hands against each other as if trying to remove some stubborn stain. "I do my messages on a Wednesday morning and that takes a while as I get the bus up the road to the big shopping centre. Our Jed usually comes with me to help carry the bags. He's been in a funny mood this past while and so I went on my own this week." She looked at the detectives as if seeking affirmation that she had answered correctly.

McVeigh nodded and Brenda continued a little more confidently.

"When I got back he helped me put away the messages and we had a bite of lunch. I was going to my meeting straight from work that night so I made a pot of stew so that he could have something to eat at teatime. Then, at about a quarter to three, I left for my cleaning job in the city centre. I do four hours' office cleaning on Monday, Wednesday, Thursday and Friday. It's usually one o'clock till four but on Wednesdays it's three to seven and I leave a bit early to get the bus up the Ormeau Road to Barnardo's for my meeting at seven o'clock." She was speaking quickly now as if she wanted to get her account of the day over and done with all in one go. "I don't usually stay for the tea after the meeting but this week I did. I texted Jed to say I'd be a bit late … so that he wouldn't worry about me. There's just the two of us, you know, so we look out for each other …" She looked at Alice now as if she had come across the perfect alibi. "Sure you and Hugo were there when I got home. Weren't you?"

"We certainly were, Brenda. It was about nine-thirty or so, I think, when you came back as Hugo and I were just leaving."

McVeigh was nodding and looking not unkindly at Brenda. "Can you tell me, Mrs Clinton, if you had made any arrangement, out of your ordinary routine maybe, to meet anyone on that Wednesday?"

"Definitely not," she replied without hesitation.

"Would you know if someone had made an arrangement to call at your home when you were out on Wednesday?"

"Of course I would," she said. "My Jed doesn't have many callers. There's a chap from the EXIT group who comes around a few times a week to help him with his lessons but it's a Tuesday and a Thursday when he comes."

"OK, thank you, Mrs Clinton. That's all very clear. Can I ask you now what the meeting is that you referred to? You said that after work on a Wednesday you go to your meeting. What exactly is that meeting?"

Brenda's face darkened and she looked at Alice for guidance. She clearly was not sure about telling her story to these detectives.

Alice turned to McVeigh. "I think if Brenda knew that what she says here is in confidence within the parameters of your investigation, she would be happier about answering that question, detective." She looked meaningfully at McVeigh.

"I can assure you, Mrs Clinton, that what you tell us

155

will not go beyond those concerned with our inquiries."

McVeigh's wording was cautious but sounded sufficiently comforting to put Brenda at her ease. She took a deep breath and faced the detectives bravely.

"Every Wednesday I go to a meeting in Barnardo's on the Ormeau Road. It is for people who are survivors of abuse in their childhood. Some were in children's homes or orphanages but others were in clubs or other types of groups where someone was harming children. Everyone who is at those meetings is on the side of the children. I suppose you know that there is an inquiry going on at the moment about historic abuses in Northern Ireland. It just started at the beginning of this year and we are trying to make sure that no-one is left out." She paused and was clearly wondering about where to go next with this. "You might have heard of Kincora ..." She watched as both McVeigh and Burrows nodded seriously and sympathetically.

These were kind men, Alice thought, and had quickly understood that they were moving into territory where their interviewee was fragile and needed to be treated as such.

"I go to those meetings because my grandmother, my mother and me have all been treated badly as children and as adults too. I want the abuse to stop before any more young people or women get harmed." She spoke bravely and proudly and there was silence in the room when she finished.

Alice smiled at Brenda and nodded to affirm that she had made her point well. McVeigh's facial expression made it clear that he understood and sympathised.

"Did anything unusual happen at the meeting this week?" he asked gently.

"Well, it was the first time I spoke at the meeting and I was proud of myself for that, so I stayed for tea for the first time. That was all unusual." The honesty with which Brenda spoke made it clear that she was concealing nothing. "A man called Johnny gave me a lift back into town and that never happened before ... but apart from that everything was the way it always is."

Alice had noted the slight softness in Brenda's voice when she referred to Johnny and she hoped that he was worthy of this good woman's affection.

"Can you tell us anything at all about this man who gave you the lift, Mrs Clinton?" McVeigh asked respectfully.

Brenda replied immediately. "I didn't know much then but I do now, because actually I met him again on Thursday for lunch before I went into work at one. I know that his second name is Power and he works as a carpenter. He makes furniture and he's a skilled tradesman. He learned the woodwork in the Industrial School in An Cuan and he says it was the only good thing that he got from being there." She looked at the men to see if what she had said sufficiently answered their question.

McVeigh probed a little further. "So let me be clear.

Wednesday evening was the first time you spoke to this man. Before that you didn't know him?"

"I hadn't spoken to him but I had noticed him at the meetings. We are both very shy in groups so Wednesday was the first time either of us had spoken to each other, or to anybody else in fact."

"Thanks, Mrs Clinton. That is very clear."

McVeigh and Burrows exchanged a look and Burrows switched off the recording machine. McVeigh said they would take a short break and asked if the two women would like tea. Brenda asked for tea and Alice for some mineral water and the men stood and left the room.

"Was that alright?" Brenda looked to Alice for reassurance.

"You were perfect," said Alice and smiled with genuine admiration. "You were brave and you made your point clearly and honestly."

Brenda relaxed and they both sat back and wondered what was going to happen next.

25

Caroline Paton thought she had enough excitement for one day already when her phone rang and DI Orla Hegarty asked if she was free to talk. It was clear that the conversation was going to happen whether she was free or not, so Caroline greeted her southern counterpart and prepared to listen.

"I assume that Nicholas Quinn arrived as planned?" Orla asked. "My officer reported that he appeared unconcerned about the need to go directly to Belfast. He had a large consignment of alcoholic airport purchases so perhaps he wasn't thinking too clearly."

"He arrived just after ten and confirmed that our murder victim was indeed his brother, Father Michael Quinn. In the heel of the hunt, he was more shocked than I expected given the lead-up to this ID. But then, by his own account, he is an inveterate pleasure-seeker and identification of family members in the mortuary doesn't really fall under that umbrella."

"Interesting," said Orla in a slightly detached way that gave Caroline the distinct impression there was something else coming down the line.

"I've asked him to come back and give us a better insight into his brother once he's settled into a local hotel. There'll be arrangements to be made for later on in the week when we're ready to release the body. Thanks for all your help so far, Orla. The cooperation is much appreciated."

Caroline waited now to see what would emerge as the real purpose of DI Hegaty's call.

"Well, it looks like we're going to have a lot more opportunities for collaboration."

Caroline wondered what she meant and listened hard.

"The fact is, we have a new body here, just discovered this morning but it may have been in situ for four or five days. So we're talking about some proximity in the timing of the two killings. It also sounds very like your MO in that our pathologist thinks that it may be a case of suffocation prior to the removal of a body part and significant posing of the corpse. And there are other features that coincide with your confession-box find, like the attachment of a piece of religious text to the victim's chest with a nappy pin."

Caroline Paton's mind was racing in a number of

directions at the same time. "It must be our perpetrator. And it sounds as if he has a carefully composed signature. Have you an ID in your case?"

"Yes, we do. The victim is an elderly man who lived alone in an isolated place in the Dublin Mountains. A carer called every Saturday to bring some groceries and do a bit of cleaning. She discovered him this morning. Apparently he was an ex Christian Brother, known as Brother Francis Twomey. He formerly taught in a notoriously harsh Industrial school called An Cuan, which is in the west of Ireland. When the teaching element of the Brothers fell apart in Ireland, he moved back to Dublin and settled in this remote place where no one knew him. He did not mix much and the carer who kept a distant eye on him was organised through some sort of religious support group."

Caroline had begun to make notes as she listened while at the same time casting around wondering what this would mean for their own case.

Orla explained that given the similarities in the cases and her appointment as liaison with the team in the North, she was now heading up the investigation of this latest killing in the South. They agreed that they needed to change the protocol to reflect the more equally shared nature of the investigation. The Belfast Murder Squad no longer had primacy. They now had a joint inquiry into two murders with a seemingly religious element, that were almost certainly linked.

They agreed that they would open up all possible digital channels for sharing documents and images. The two DIs would have joint progress reviews by conference call twice daily and staff would meet in person whenever necessary. These meetings would be in either of their respective bases so as to make the sharing of evidence as secure as possible. In the meantime they would both continue with their full-on inquiries and try to cover as much ground as possible. They arranged an introductory conference call with core team members for later in the day when they could share intelligence on the cases and see how best they might proceed.

When the call finished Caroline sat and considered the position she now found herself in. She didn't like to be pushed into corners but the fact that Alice was yet again appearing in one of her investigations meant she needed to act positively in order to keep her team above reproach. Decisively, she phoned the Detective Superintendent's mobile and asked his PA for a meeting to discuss some urgent matters of relevance to the case. There was the issue of the expanded investigation and then there was the professional propriety around the involvement of an intimate partner in an ongoing inquiry.

Almost immediately the Super's PA returned her call and suggested that Detective Superintendent McCluskey would be available in half an hour in HQ on the Knock Road.

Caroline left a message for Burrows and McVeigh

that she would be back soon and had significant developments to discuss with them. That was one way of putting it, she thought to herself, and headed out to her car with slightly less than her usual composure.

26

Burrows and McVeigh returned to Brenda and Alice in the interview room after about fifteen minutes. McVeigh carried a metal tray on which rattled three thick white delft cups with a green stripe around the top, a stainless-steel teapot, milk, sugar and a plate of digestive biscuits. Burrows was holding a bottle of mineral water and a warm glass which he offered to Alice. She opted to drink from the bottle.

Brenda had relaxed a little and the tea seemed to make her feel even more at ease.

The two men had decided that they needed to be very cautious in their questioning of Brenda Clinton. She was clearly fragile and three generations of women in her family had experienced abuse at the hands of the Church, the State care system or possibly both. In the first instance they needed to try to find out what possible explanation there could be for the murdered priest to have Brenda's name and address in his diary. Father Quinn had never kept that appointment but it may well have been his primary reason for travelling north and could potentially be connected to the motive behind his killing. They could see that Brenda Clinton was not capable of committing this murder on her own but that didn't mean that she was not implicated in some way. They had permission to name the victim now that Nicholas Quinn had confirmed the ID. Nonetheless they wanted to proceed with caution.

Burrows stated the starting time of this segment of the proceedings for the recording machine.

"Mrs Clinton, I'd like to ask you what you meant earlier when you said that you, your mother and grandmother all had experience of being treated badly."

Brenda looked at him in disbelief.

"How long have you got, mister?" she asked, not insincerely. "You're asking me for the story of our lives so that would take us a fair wee while. In the first place that information is confidential and also it's not for me to tell you my mother's business. She can do that herself as she did to the inquiry in the South." She thought for a moment. "I think she's got it all written down somewhere when she was preparing to go before the Inquiry Board."

Alice thought Brenda was dealing well with what appeared to a very vague line of questioning and perhaps this judgement showed in her facial expression.

She understood that these men were kindly and trying to cover difficult ground without causing any upset but in the business of child abuse that wasn't really an option. Burrows seemed to have come to the same conclusion.

"The person who is the subject of our murder inquiry, Mrs Clinton, is a Catholic clergyman from a parish in Dublin. We are trying to find out why he may have had your name and address in his diary. I don't want to cause you any upset but I need to ask you if the name Father Michael Quinn means anything to you."

All eyes were on Brenda who, in response to the victim's name had inhaled deeply. Her face had become deathly pale. She had moved her hand instinctively to her chest where it magnified the increase in pace of her breathing as she showed all the signs of shock.

"Good God Almighty," she said directly to Alice, "that's him that I told you about just yesterday. That's the one that groomed me and got me pregnant with our Jed. You and me talked about putting supports in place for Jed and me." It was as if she needed to replay all the detail to assure herself that her experience was real. "I thought about telling him about his father last night but then I thought he looked so happy watching the telly that I decided it would keep for another bit. I know he thinks he wants to know all that but it's a case of be careful what you wish for." She shifted her gaze to the two detectives. "And Mick's dead? Is that what you're saying? He's actually been killed by someone?"

"We're sorry to give you this shocking news, Mrs Clinton. I'd like to show you a recent family photo of Father Quinn to make sure that we're talking about the same person." McVeigh took a photocopied picture from his file and turned it towards Brenda. "Does this look like the same Michael Quinn that you knew, Mrs Clinton?"

"That's him all right. That's the same bastard that took advantage of a poor kid who had nobody to look out for her. Imagine if he'd turned up at my door unannounced!"

Alice thought it was better that Brenda felt angry rather than distressed and she nodded gently to show the other woman her approval.

Brenda suddenly looked horrified.

"Jaysus Christ! Ye don't think I killed him, do ye?"

"We are just trying to find out what we can about Father Quinn's recent movements. Our job is to discover what led to his death and your information is a piece in that puzzle." Burrows was trying to allay Brenda's anxiety without being untruthful.

Alice could see that this woman's list of problems was not getting any shorter.

"When did you last see Michael Quinn, Mrs Clinton?"

"That's easy to answer. My Jed is twenty-three and a bit so you could say over twenty-three years and you wouldn't be too far out. When I turned down his offer to dump my baby and come and be his live-in housekeeper, he stopped having any interest in me." She was losing her bluster and beginning to look exhausted.

Alice raised a hand slightly to indicate to the detectives that it was time to stop and they responded immediately.

"Thank you for giving your time this morning, Mrs Clinton. You have helped us understand a little more about our victim. It appears that he planned to make contact with you but was stopped before he got to do that. We just need to find out who stopped him."

When the recorder was switched off there were a few more niceties exchanged and Burrows said they would probably need to talk to Brenda again if they found out why he was going to visit her after all this time.

Alice and Brenda headed for the door and Brenda went into the women's toilet in the reception area. Alice left a message for Hugo to meet her at the Clintons' flat and was mentally preparing for the surprise coming in Jed's direction when the doors were thrust open and DI Caroline Paton strode in, looking preoccupied.

Both raised their eyebrows slightly in unison and Alice spoke quickly with one eye on the door of the women's toilet. "We need to talk but not now. Let's make time this evening when you get finished up."

"Agreed. I'll get there as soon as I can but we can relax a bit. I've just had a chat with the Super so we can stop with the secrecy about us. I don't mean we should shout it from the rooftops but we don't need to worry now." And she squeezed Alice's arm affectionately and headed for the stairs, making a big effort not to grin too widely.

168

27

Brenda emerged from the toilets and told Alice she had called Johnny Power because it seemed likely the police might follow up with him and she didn't want him to be taken unawares. Alice thought that they would probably want to talk to all the Clintons but thought it best to leave that be for the time being. This was going to be a process of small, careful steps so that everybody could be kept as safe as possible.

She collected her bike outside and the two women set off on foot for Divis Tower, huddled into their coats against the bitter east wind.

By the time they arrived at the tower block Hugo was attaching his bike to the railings outside. Alice locked hers alongside. He looked at her with concern and she tried to communicate wordlessly that things were bad but it would all be okay. He seemed to understand and gave Brenda a hug that she did not resist.

As they headed into the lift, Brenda looked at Alice and voiced her immediate panic. "How can I tell our Jed that not only is his father a Catholic priest but also that he has just been murdered?"

Alice responded without hesitation. "We're here to help, Brenda. You're not alone. Jed is well loved and he'll be all right. Yes, it'll be a blow but he'll cope and we'll all be there as best we can to help him, and you, through this storm."

Hugo reinforced the message. "Jed has you and his gran and he has all of the EXIT group who care about him and will know how to help him get through this. They've all had incredibly hard knocks to deal with and they'll know what to do to make this easier for Jed."

As the lift doors opened and they approached the door of Flat 10B, there was the incongruous sound of laughter from within. Martha and Brian had come straight over when Jed had called them and they had convinced him with their reassurance that his mam would never have done anything against the law.

Jed was only a little surprised to see Hugo and Alice arrive with his mother. "Well, Mam, what was that all about? Have you been robbing banks in secret?" Jed's relief to see his mother home after not too long was soon replaced with anxiety as he read the tension on her face. "What is it, Mam?"

He moved towards her and she put her arms around him.

"I'm all right, son. I only had to answer some questions and Alice was beside me all the time. But now I have something I need to tell you and I think we'd better all sit down before I start."

"I've just made a pot of tea," said Brian. "I'll get a few extra mugs and a plate of biscuits."

Martha went with him to help carry things to the small table in front of the sofa. Jed moved towards the window and faced his mother expectantly.

When the tea had been poured and they were all settled, Brenda took a deep breath and began.

"You know I've been going to my meetings every Wednesday, Jed?"

He nodded cautiously.

"And you understand about your great-gran and your gran both having been abused in Mother and Baby Homes?"

Martha lowered her head and rocked almost imperceptibly. Brian edged a little closer to her.

Jed nodded again, waiting for the new piece of information that was obviously coming.

"Well, there is another thing that I haven't told you yet, mainly because I wasn't sure how best to do it without upsetting you too much."

Now Jed was looking at Brenda with rapt attention. Martha was holding Brian's hand and rubbing it fretfully while Hugo sat very still and fully focussed on Jed and his impending distress. It was as if he was

171

poised to catch a child who might fall if he lost his footing in a balancing act.

"Go on, Mam," Jed said tetchily. "Spill the beans. Enough of the pussyfooting!" He looked long and hard at his mother and frowned. "How bad can it be?"

A gust of wind blew a plastic bag filled with air past the tenth-floor window and Brenda was momentarily distracted. Then she met her son's intent gaze. She could see he was wound up very tightly and she persisted in trying to frame her bombshell of a message as clearly as possible.

"OK, son. There'll never be a good time so here goes. Remember everybody in this room cares about you and is on your side."

Jed bared his teeth and placed his hands on his head as if to hold some explosive material inside.

She took a deep breath and continued. "The police called me to ask me questions about a priest that was found murdered in St Oliver's Chapel on the Ormeau Road." She paused.

"Why? Did you know him?" Jed looked bewildered.

"They found my name and address in his diary. It seemed as if he planned to visit here on Wednesday but got killed before he got here."

Again she hesitated and silence filled the room.

Then she looked at Jed, willing him to understand her next words. His face was frozen in an expression of utter frustration and she forged ahead with a sinking heart.

"The fact is that the priest who planned to come and see me was the same priest that got me pregnant twenty-three years ago." She looked at her son's devastated expression. "Michael Quinn was your father, Jed."

"*What?*" He gasped and his face flushed with anger. "He was my *father!*" He choked on the last word as his frustration turned to rage and he screamed, "*What are you saying? My father was a priest and now he's dead?*"

Brenda spoke quietly now, desperate to complete her story but uncertain if Jed was hearing her now.

"I was a sixteen-year-old living in a care home and helping out with poor kids on a summer holiday. He was the one in charge of the youth club in the parish and he took advantage of me. Now that's the whole sad story for you." Tears ran slowly down her cheeks and she rustled in her sleeve to find a paper hankie.

Jed had turned his back and was banging his fists on the windowsill as if fiercely intent on working out a new drum rhythm. The others sat silently, each unclear about what to say or do and opting for inaction. Eventually he turned, wringing his hands and looking from one person in the room to the other as if expecting someone to contradict this new reality and bring him back to safe ground.

For a while no one spoke and then Martha piped up in a small voice. "Sounds as if he was maybe coming looking for you both," she said, innocently looking for something positive in the story.

173

"Maybe so," said Brenda kindly to her mother, "but we have some rights in that too, Mam. He couldn't just land in here after all these years without so much as a by-your-leave. Who knows how many kids he fathered around the country? I'm sure I wasn't the only one he picked on." She fought to curb her tears that were flowing freely now.

Alice and Hugo had both been watching Jed carefully and had seen his facial expression change from shock and disbelief to anger and then finally concern for his mother. He looked at Hugo for direction.

"I don't know what to feel," he said quietly.

"Of course you don't, Jed," Hugo said gently. "That's a lot of information to get unexpectedly. But you heard your mother say she was trying to find a way to tell you that wouldn't be too hurtful for you. She has always had your best interests at heart and that won't change because this has all come out in a way that she would never have chosen for you. You still have to look after each other and we will all help you in whatever way we can. You can be sure of that, Jed."

Jed met his mother's searching look and opened his arms for her. "Come here, Mam," he whispered tenderly. "Sure what will be any different … except that now I know the answer to the question that was torturing me. There's still just you and me but that's not too bad, is it?"

Then Brenda really gave way to sobbing that sounded as if it came from the depths of her being.

"You're the best wee son a mother could have," she said through her tears. "That's some really enormous good that came out of all that awful stuff."

Alice and Hugo stood up together. "We'll go now and leave you in peace and quiet," she said. "You both know where to find us when you want us. Any time is fine with us both, I think." She looked at Hugo.

"Agreed. For sure," said Hugo, nodding wholeheartedly. "Phone when you need to or call by the Centre for a chat when you know I'm there."

Brian and Martha got up to go as well.

"We'll call after and see what you feel like doing about tea," said Brian. "Maybe we can get pizzas or maybe you two will feel like a quiet night and Martha and me can eat somewhere near the B&B. We'll take it as it comes."

They hugged Brenda and Jed and the four left.

"I hope they'll be okay," Martha said as if talking to herself, as they went down in the lift together.

Brian put his arm more tightly around her. Alice thought that he looked suddenly exhausted by the weight of care. He answered quietly and as if he had moved some distance away.

"They'll be fine when things settle down. And in the meantime we will keep a close eye on them. Don't you worry, my darlin'."

By the time the one o'clock radio news came on, Jed and Brenda were listening on their own, immersed in the dark clouds that had descended on the Divis Tower. It was shocking to hear the death of someone, who was a complicated part of their history, discussed in the dispassionate language of a radio announcement. It was even more shocking to hear that he was no longer the only victim in this case.

The Saturday lunchtime news on Radio Ulster had a new headline story. A carefully timed press release from PSNI headquarters made its way to the top of the news without leaving time for a deluge of calls to PSNI HQ. The bank holiday for St Patrick's Day on Monday would dilute the attention to the news and allow the two murder squads to forge ahead without the full distraction of the media being on them.

PSNI Murder Squad detectives are investigating the discovery of the body of a Catholic priest in St Oliver's Chapel on Belfast's Ormeau Road. The remains were found around midday on Wednesday but formal identification has only taken place today. News of the discovery was delayed until family members could be notified. The deceased was resident in the south of the country and close cooperation with An Garda Síochána has already been established. Members of the police force in both jurisdictions believe that a second body found this morning in the Wicklow Mountains is linked to the Ormeau Road discovery. A full joint murder inquiry will now begin led by DI Caroline Paton of the

PSNI Murder Squad and DI Orla Hegarty of An Garda Síochána Criminal Investigation Department. No further details of the killings will be released at this time for operational reasons.

Press conferences will be held simultaneously in both Dublin and Belfast at seven o'clock this evening when there will be an update on the progress of the joint investigation.

Details of confidential phone lines were included for anyone who wished to provide information in relation to the murders.

Listening to the news in the Grosvenor Road Barracks canteen, the three members of the Murder Squad felt the surge of adrenalin that was the result of the discovery of a second body.

When Caroline related the details of her conversation with DI Hegarty, Burrows and McVeigh recognised the link to Johnny Power that had emerged from their interview with Brenda Clinton that morning. The man who had been in An Cuan as a boy and was now friends with Mrs Clinton suddenly became a person of much interest to the inquiry. A uniformed officer was immediately given the task of tracking down Power's whereabouts and bringing him into the station for questioning.

"Ian, can you keep an eye on Mr Power until Bill and I are done with Nicholas Quinn? Offer him witness support and if he accepts then you'll need to get Dr Fox back in again. We need to make sure we treat all these vulnerable witnesses appropriately."

The three approached the rest of their lunch with increased enthusiasm when they realised that the afternoon was filling up and they had their first meeting with the southern team later that evening. It would make Caroline Paton very happy indeed if she was able to introduce a possible murder suspect so early on in the proceedings. Johnny Power might well be a very interesting person indeed.

28

The image of Brother Francis' corpse that was uploaded to the joint investigation digital drive was both horrifying and intriguing. McVeigh looked at it for a long time without allowing any definite thought to settle. It was as if his eyes were thinking wordlessly, scanning all the elements of the photo but not making any connection to the verbal part of his brain. Only after he was lost in this soundless place for a matter of minutes did the ideas start to rush forward in a way that made him sit back sharply in his seat as if to cushion the brunt of the impact.

Here was an angelic, smooth-skinned face framed in pure white hair and wearing an expression very like a smile. McVeigh was reminded of Clarence, the wingless angel from the old Christmas movie *It's a Wonderful Life*. He had a gentle, strangely ageless complexion that had somehow defied the ravages of time. He and Sally watched the old black-and-white film in December each year and it always did the trick of getting them into the holiday spirit.

The man's hands rested on his portly stomach, one on top of the other with thumbs intertwined. Only in following the view of the hands as they disappeared into the woollen jumper sleeves did it become apparent that the right hand was actually holding the upper left hand in place. It had been severed below the wrist bone, leaving the impression of a strange, clotted bracelet just visible below the sleeve line. Something that looked like a piece of bread hung from the mouth as if mischievous children who had eaten their fill had formed a pipe from their unwanted crusts. A flash of memory flicked through Ian's mind – of constructing smooth pyramids out of mashed potato and being mildly rebuked for playing with his food. His mouth began to form a smile until he realised that it was inappropriate, given the image before him. He instinctively checked to make sure no one was watching.

Brother Francis was seated on a wooden chair with a high curved back and armrests. He was dressed in a dark-green, fine-wool sweater and black trousers and his feet that were crossed at the ankles and nestling in a pair of tartan slippers. His chin was slumped forward so that it rested on his chest just above the page that was fixed with a large nappy pin. The message was printed in capital letters and read:

BLESSED ARE THOSE THAT HUNGER AND THIRST AFTER RIGHTEOUSNESS FOR THEY SHALL BE FILLED

An incongruous smiley face was drawn in green pen below the typed message.

Around the man's neck and adding a fine, almost beautiful finishing touch were two strands of daisy chains. They were faded and dried now as if they had been made in a summer long past and stored carefully until the moment they were intended for had arrived.

Ian retrieved the image of Michael Quinn from his digital files and placed the pictures side by side before him on a split screen. The two men were decades apart in age and bore no physical resemblance one to the other. Quinn's face was stuck in a shocked and horrified expression whereas the older man was almost smiling. The similarities arose in the arrangement of their bodies, the religious phrase attached to their chests with identical nappy pins and the unique cutting of a body part. He understood clearly why these repeated behaviours over and above the MO were known as a signature. Rather like an actual way of signing a name, they were unique to the perp and could be read to reveal psychological traits behind the murderer's actions. The images here, although not identical, were strikingly similar and he could almost sense the satisfaction of whoever had posed these bodies and in so doing had finally released their deep and abiding anger, resentment and their need for others to understand the basis of that anger. He wondered if the killer's wrath had been assuaged or if there were still more of these messages to come.

That afternoon while DC Ian McVeigh waited for Alice Fox to make her way back to the station, he loaded the relevant files to make them accessible to the members of the joint investigation team. At the same time Paton and Burrows were in an interview room, seated across from Nicholas Quinn. The older Quinn brother appeared to have finally begun to absorb the fact that his sibling was dead. He had called his wife and asked her to join him and she was catching an afternoon Enterprise train to Belfast. They were booked into the Europa Hotel for as long as was needed to have the remains released and plan a funeral. His wife would take care of those details. What he had intended to be an extension of his boozy French trip had become a much more subdued affair and with that realisation he had lost all his previous swagger.

Caroline reflected that these must have been two handsome brothers who would have cut quite a dash in the city nightspots in their day. Now the ravages of drink had taken their toll on those fine features and, Caroline could see that Nicholas was essentially an unpleasant type and that was the dominant message etched into his every expression. She dismissed her bias and turned her mind to work.

Burrows started up the recording machine and announced the time and the names of those present. Then he asked Quinn to tell them about his brother. He explained that, in a murder inquiry, the more they understood the victim the easier it was to piece together what might have happened to them.

"This is not the time to give the sanitised account of your brother," he explained. "We want to know what kind of a man he was and if there might be those who would be angry enough with him to end his life. And of course I will remind you that what you tell us remains confidential to the investigation. We are on the same side here."

Caroline watched carefully as Nicholas nodded slowly and pressed his lips closely together as if to stop the words from escaping. Then, as was often the way with interviewees, he seemed to decide to put his trust in Burrows.

"Well, I suppose I should begin by saying that Mick was never an angel. He had a wild side to him that he made little effort to control and that also made him great fun to be with." He got lost for a few moments in some reminiscence that made him smile and then returned sombrely to the moment. "I mean we were both tearaways as lads and no one was more surprised than I was that Mick decided on the priesthood." He shook his head slightly as if reaffirming the incongruity of his brother's career choice. "You know, he never showed any signs of being devout but our mother had an uncle in the States who was a cardinal and I concluded that he liked the idea of the power and pomp that he saw in him. He liked all the fancy vestments and the ceremony and the way the priest was looked up to ... literally. He was made for the pulpit and everyone hanging on his every word." Quinn made some affirming sounds and smiled at the strange contradictions raised by his recollections.

Burrows waited to see if he would continue unprompted but then followed up with another question.

"When you say your brother was wild, Mr Quinn, what exactly do you mean?"

"He was wild about women and drink in equal measure, I'd say. That was both before and after he joined the priesthood, to be honest. He got himself into some close scrapes with young girls that he'd crossed the line with but always managed to tidy up after himself, if you know what I mean."

Both Burrows and Paton looked questioningly at him and he rose to the bait.

"What I mean is that before he learned to choose more judiciously, he became over-friendly with young women who might have had reason to cause him trouble ... with the hierarchy. I needed to help him out financially on occasions when young ones needed to take the boat to England at short notice. You know?" Quinn paused and checked to ensure they were following his meaning.

"Did you ever meet any of these women, Mr Quinn?" Caroline mostly succeeded in keeping any harsh judgement out of her voice although Burrows knew her long enough to identify the irritation in her voice and demeanour.

"Well, yes. Sometimes he would bring a young one from the north to Dublin for the night and I'd have a meal with them and book him into an appropriate hotel. It was always in my name of course, for reasons of discretion. He didn't have that kind of money and it was the least I could do for my kid brother." Nicholas Quinn seemed to expect that his behaviour merited some kind of praise but there was none forthcoming. "Look. Mick used his connections to put a lot of business my way and this was a small way I could repay him."

Caroline pursued the line of questioning. "Did you know if any of these women were under age, Mr Quinn?"

"Sometimes, especially when he was younger, he blurred the lines of what was legal and what wasn't but I didn't see it as my role to judge him." Nicholas Quinn appeared to become conscious that others might not view his brother's habits as benevolently as he did. He wiped his hand across his brow and took a different tack with his argument. "Celibacy is a mad rule for the church to try and uphold. The truth is it is widely ignored all over the world. A housekeeper's role is often more extensive than appears on the surface, I believe."

He had warmed to this subject now and cast around for substantiating evidence. "You know, before contraceptives were freely available in Ireland, Mick got his supplies from a cardinal in New York who understood his needs." He was satisfied that he had made a fair case and then added a final point. "Surely none of that would be a cause for murder. I'm talking about harmless fun, mostly between consenting adults."

Paton and Burrows remained expressionless in response to Quinn's words although each recognised a growing sense of exasperation in the other's responses – the quality of the silence, the barely perceptible sound of air being drawn through clenched teeth and the hand movements that were replete with suppressed annoyance. Nonetheless, they forged forward to find out about his brother's more recent past. His move to Dublin ten years previously was possibly, his brother admitted, because of a complaint in his previous diocese about excessive drinking and inappropriate behaviour. Burrows could see another difficult conversation looming with a reticent member of the Catholic hierarchy. The Church was known for moving problems from one parish to another rather than dealing with the core issue and it looked as if this was another example of that approach.

When asked if he knew why his brother might have planned to head north the previous week, Quinn denied any knowledge of the trip. Finally Burrows asked him if Father Michael ever talked about any past relationships in particular. Nicholas hesitated and looked loath to continue.

Caroline wasted no time in coldly interjecting, "Might I remind you, Mr Quinn, that your brother has been brutally murdered in a manner that suggests there is a connection to his sexual past? Whatever you know is important to us to get to the motive for that killing and maybe preventing the death of others. Now, please tell us what you know and stop delaying our process."

Burrows sensed his colleague was near the point of losing her temper.

Nick appeared somewhat contrite and spoke hesitantly. "He got involved with a young girl over twenty years ago and he always maintained that she meant more to him than all the others. He asked her to stay with him then but she was pregnant and wouldn't give up the child." He made it sound as if the young woman was being unnecessarily awkward in the circumstances. "A young housekeeper he might have got away with, but not one with a child that resembled him. That would have been a step too far and he wasn't prepared to leave the Church under any circumstances."

Caroline noted how Nicholas had a way of presenting his brother's behaviour as perfectly acceptable but she was careful to restrict her response to the detail of this case.

Quinn was continuing his sympathetic account of

his brother's life. "At the time he let it go but recently, as he's got older and reached retirement, he had become obsessed with finding them. There were others afterwards but none that chose to continue with the pregnancy. I suppose he became conscious that he had a child and that was a game changer in later life. I told him that in over twenty years people make new lives and that he might be walking into a situation that could lead him into trouble or maybe even danger. This is Belfast, after all." He looked between his questioners for affirmation of the obvious. "I thought I had convinced him but apparently not, if as you say he was headed up here to find her."

"What was that woman's name, Mr Quinn?" Caroline asked curtly.

"I only remember the surname as it has been in the news a lot down the years. She was called Clinton but the first name is gone. Sorry, but the old memory is not what it was." And he laughed, slightly nervously. "There was at least another one who got pregnant after the Clinton girl before the bishop stepped in and moved him to look after the oldies in Dublin. But, to be honest, you'd get more information from my wife about that. Nancy would have been the one who did the admin for all that."

Burrows moved on in the hope that he could deflect the DI's suppressed anger.

"Did anyone else know about your brother's past,

apart from the young women with whom he had these … relationships?"

"Well, he was close to the cardinal in New York. They used to meet up in Lourdes every year when he went with the youth group. I guess he may have confided in others but I honestly don't know who they might be."

"Have you spoken about your brother's affairs with anyone? For example, have you told your wife or other family members that Michael Quinn had a number of sexual relationships while being a member of the clergy?"

"I'm not sure my wife listens very attentively to me any more, Detective Inspector, and even if she does I'm certain she does not retain that information long enough to repeat it to anyone."

Caroline's patience with Quinn was again showing signs of fatigue. "Nonetheless, I would be grateful if you asked your wife to contact me when she arrives in Belfast," she said, "and I will arrange to question her for myself." She could see that the potential list for those who might have a grievance with Father Michael Quinn was extensive but she followed her gut to ensure nothing was left unscrutinised and knew that it rarely let her down. She was not surprised that Mrs Quinn tuned her husband out whenever possible but that didn't prevent her from being the custodian of information that might help this inquiry.

At a nod from Caroline, Burrows stopped the machine.

He escorted Quinn to the exit, made sure that he had a card with the Murder Squad contact details and reminded him that his wife should call as soon as she arrived.

As he left, Nicholas felt an unaccustomed loneliness descend on him. He had a sudden insight into the reality that he had lost one of the few people who loved him without question and he realised that brotherly bond would never be replicated.

29

The lunchtime news that Jed and Brenda had heard in the Divis Tower had been interesting on a number of counts. Those present in the tenth-floor apartment had been better informed than the newscaster and most listeners – in that they had known the identity of the Belfast victim to be Father Michael Quinn.

For Brenda, as well as the instant trauma of a teenage pregnancy, without any family support, there was the deeper long-term hurt that Quinn had caused and that would involve a lifetime of recovery.

For Jed, the headline referred to the man he had just discovered was his biological father and who by all accounts had intended to come and visit him and his mother. The newscaster was publicly announcing that this same individual was now dead, killed and left in a Catholic chapel in Belfast and the subject of a murder inquiry.

And all of this was before Jed and Brenda took on board that there was now another victim and began to wonder what this second person might possibly have to do with the Clinton family and its past. Jed was struck by how just a small number of words contained a message of huge significance.

As she read the news online in her rooms back in the Botanic area, Alice carefully considered this turn of events. On top of the Belfast murder was the revelation that a second, probably related, killing had taken place in the tranquil Wicklow Mountains where she had spent the Christmas holidays. It seemed that her life in Northern Ireland was fated to include a succession of unplanned involvements in mysterious murders. Ironically, this seemed to have nothing directly to do with the fact that the head of the Murder Squad was now her lover, although that had certainly complicated things somewhat. On a more mundane level, she smiled with satisfaction that she had managed to get the last of the large prawns from the stall of the Ardglass fisherman where she frequently bought a weekend treat. If dinner happened, she was ready to shine with the minimum effort. If not, they would be fine for a few months in the freezer.

Thinking about Wicklow brought Tara Donnelly into Alice's head and she dialled her friend's number on the off-chance that she might be free for a chat. The founder of DePRec, where Alice was now the visiting scholar, Tara had moved to the South after some disturbing intimidating behaviour had threatened her and her family. For over a decade since then, she had worked in the South Dublin University (SDU) where she specialised in studying community-based evidence of State Harm. She and Alice had linked up at the annual conference on Harm that had taken place in SDU the previous December. They had found that they had much in common in their academic interests and a love of hillwalking, which they had found some time for over the break. Thanks to Alice, Tara had played a part in solving the DePRec murder some months earlier and the two had kept in touch. Now, Alice wanted to know what Tara made of these recent killings that crossed the border and targeted members of religious communities. It was clear to Alice that Brenda Clinton was not a suspect in the murder of her former abuser but it seemed likely that clerical or institutional abuse was a common factor that would bring the survivor community under the investigation's scrutiny. As a result of her reading, Alice was drawn to pursue that possibility for herself and she had a hunch that Tara might have some survivor groups amongst the many communities with which she carried out her research.

"I've just heard the announcement on the *News at One*," Tara said in response to Alice's initial inquiry if she had heard about the murders. "The word here is that the southern victim was a Christian Brother associated with one of the infamous industrial schools in the west of the country. It sounds as if someone might be executing their own form of justice against these historic harms that went unregulated by the State. I'm actually quite surprised it hasn't happened before and on a grander scale."

Tara told Alice that she worked closely with one of the main survivor groups that operated in Dublin as a social, educational and cultural centre.

"Monday's a bank holiday here so nothing very much will be happening. However, I'm actually due to go there on Tuesday to conduct a focus group. Do you want to be my beautiful assistant?"

Alice laughed. "I'd like nothing better, Tara."

They arranged that Tara would meet Alice off the early train from Belfast. They would go somewhere for coffee and Tara would bring her up to speed on the plan for the session. Afterwards, there would be time to hang out a bit in the Centre and gauge opinion about any further developments in the news.

As they said their farewells Alice's phone buzzed to alert her to a new text message. **Hope to get away around ten. Cx**

Alice thought she would take some time to inform herself a little better about the survivor groups north and south and particularly if there was any overlap or cooperation between them. They needed to find a person who was linked either in the past or the present to both murder victims. She settled down at her desk and fired up her laptop for an afternoon of online detection.

Only a short time later, as she had begun to read the chapter in the Ryan Report that dealt with An Cuan, her phone rang and Ian McVeigh began by apologising for disturbing her a second time that day.

"You probably won't be surprised if you've heard the news, Dr Fox, but we have Johnny Power, who was mentioned earlier by Mrs Clinton, coming in for questioning later this afternoon. His link to An Cuan makes him interesting for our inquiry. Some uniforms are trying to track him down at the moment. The DI wants him to have the services open to a vulnerable witness and asked for you to be called in. Are you free?"

"I can be there at three," Alice said, allowing herself a little reading time before heading out again. "I'll see you then." And she picked up her reading of the report on An Cuan where she had left off.

Back in the Divis Tower, Jed and Brenda had talked intensively for over an hour and then decided they needed to get out for a breath of air. They called Brian and Martha and suggested a drive to the coast, a walk along Helen's Bay and maybe an ice cream, before it got dark.

When they were suitably wrapped up for a spring walk, they waited across the road to be collected from the tower block so that they could get on the road as soon as possible. They didn't have long to wait.

"I'm so glad you called." Martha twisted round in her seat and patted Brenda's leg. "I was worried about you both but not sure what I could do. Brian said you needed time on your own."

Martha usually managed to make her point even though, as she said herself, she wasn't the best talker. So many aspects of her development had been neglected that her positive attitude and sense of empathy for others was a wonder to those who got to know her well enough to learn about her past. Despite having no education to speak of and no evident example of affection in her life, she had worked hard and managed her modest earnings well. She was well advised by a kindly trade union rep in the hospital where she had been a cleaner and had opened a Credit Union account. She lived in sheltered accommodation owned by a religious order in an area in southwest Dublin known as The Ranch. Aside from a modest rent, her outgoings were slight and she saved most of what she earned. Once a year she went with other residents on an organised pilgrimage to Lourdes or Medjugorje. She didn't really care that much about the religious parts of these trips but she enjoyed the company of the others in the group and having a few beers and a singsong in the evenings in the small hotels where they stayed. Most of all, while some of the group were afraid of flying, Martha loved the thrill as the aircraft accelerated and lifted off the ground. While others prayed, she whooped happily with the exhilaration of take-off.

When she went to the Redress Board that was established as part of the measures to deal with the legacy of abuses in the south, she had received an unexpectedly large payment. Initially, in her case, the psychologist's report had said she merited little compensation. After a barrage of tests that had left Martha baffled, it was asserted that she had severe learning difficulties that would have limited her achievements in life whether she was in care or not. Because of this, Martha, like Irish Traveller children and those from communities with a likelihood of low educational attainment, was not deemed to merit any compensation since, even if left with their family of origin, they would never have achieved anything.

In Martha's case, this was contradicted by a second report from a literacy expert who had worked with her in the survivors' centre and was able to show that the issue was not so simple. Martha's oral language development was that of a very young child and therefore, in order to begin to understand most of what happened around her, she firstly needed a basic knowledge of spoken language. Without some very basic vocabulary, she could not have understood the instructions for completing the psychologist's tests, never mind the content of the tests themselves. The second report showed she was actually an intelligent person deprived of the primary tool of language.

As her linguistic capabilities developed, so the signs that had been misinterpreted as intellectual limitations had diminished and she began very slowly to regain some lost ground. Her spoken language and confidence increased considerably but time was against her. The few hours a week available to her for basic language and literacy classes made very slow impact on the mountain of lost educational ground she had to cover. Possibly her enthusiasm for having a good time also slowed her learning progress but in any case she seemed happy with her life and realistic in her ambitions.

"I'd love to be able to sit by the fire with a book or a magazine and read it," she had once told Brenda when they were talking about how their lives had turned out. "But I know it would take a lot of hard work and I'm not sure I have it in me any more. Brian likes me the way I am, so that's good enough for me."

Now, as they drove towards Helen's Bay in his very smooth car, Brenda thought about how Martha had been transformed by meeting Brian. It was like a fairytale outcome for someone with the challenges that Martha had faced, to find herself with a devoted partner and to be financially very well off. Of course, Martha's lack of understanding of monetary matters meant that she had little or no understanding of her financial situation. She had already been saving consistently from her occupational and state pension and the award from the Redress Board had added a substantial five-figure sum to those savings. Brenda had worried that Martha was vulnerable to being exploited and Brian had been suspect in her mind until he had shown himself to be above reproach. More than that, Brenda had seen that he was Martha's devoted protector and, without smothering her independence, he watched out for her and shielded her from harm.

Brian and Martha lived in single flats in the same sheltered-housing complex in a sprawling social-housing estate in a suburb of southwest Dublin. The supported-living residence was owned by a religious order and run in an institutional manner that made Brenda irate at times. However, Martha felt safe there and there would be no point in Brenda disturbing that security. When Martha and Brian had been together for a few years, they had asked to be transferred to a double apartment but the request had been refused on the grounds that they were not married. Brenda had been incandescent when they told her that news but, instead of making a fuss, they had quietly acquired a mobile home on a plot of land along the coast north of Dublin. They escaped there as often as they wished and so maintained their single lifestyle in the flats complex and their freedom to be together in the coastal resort.

By Brenda's side in the back of Brian's car, Jed was doodling in the window condensation and lost in thought. He was dealing with so much these days, Brenda thought, but he was able for it and he had great support from the EXIT group. Hugo and Alice were full of concern for him and Alice was turning out to be a solid companion to her in these turbulent times. Despite everything, she felt fortunate with the number of people she had who cared about her and were ready to help when she needed them. She leaned forward and kissed her mother's wrinkled cheek. She smelt of soap and cigarette smoke. Martha smiled at her in the manner of an innocent child who realised that she had gained the favour of those that she most loved.

"Here we are, Clintons!" announced Brian cheerfully. "I give you the delightful resort of Helen's Bay. Let's get the wind in our hair."

Martha snorted loudly. "Oh, Brian," she said with all sincerity, "you are so funny. Sure you're bald. You don't have any hair now for the wind to blow through!"

30

While the Clintons had a blustery walk through the forest park and along the coastal path at Helen's Bay, Burrows and McVeigh took their seats in the interview room, with Johnny Power and Alice Fox, and began their questioning.

Johnny Power was a good-looking, well-built man in his early fifties, Alice estimated, and she could see that Brenda had accurately judged him to be shy and a little fragile. From the perception of the police, Alice could see that this was a man with the strength and the motive to kill. On the surface, he appeared calm but Alice could see that this was a way of being in the world, learned by someone self-schooled in remaining unnoticed. His eyes showed that he was agitated about being questioned by the police and he was relieved when Alice was introduced as someone there to support him.

Burrows asked the questions this time and McVeigh was the note-taker.

"So, Mr Power, we understand that you have recently become friendly with Brenda Clinton, is that correct?"

"Yes, that's right." Power was open and direct in his response. "I go to weekly meetings in Amnesty International and I met Brenda there. This week's meeting was the first time we actually spoke to each other. I offered her a lift home and we met on Thursday for coffee and a bite of lunch."

"Was there a particular reason why you spoke to her this week?" Burrows said gently.

Power seemed a little uncertain about the question and answered a little hesitantly.

"Well … I had noticed Brenda before in the meetings but we are both very quiet by nature and I had no opportunity to talk to her. She always rushed away after the meeting and I never stayed for tea before either."

"What was different this week?" Burrows pursued his line of questioning.

"It just happened that I was sitting beside her and when she spoke up about all the cover-ups by the religious orders and others I really admired her courage." Power paused and then seemed to gather his thoughts. "If you haven't been through what we have, it's not easy to understand." He looked from Burrows to McVeigh and they waited for him to continue. "When you are not very educated a lot of what people say goes over your head but she just got it right ... in what she said. People even clapped for her. I just had to say to her that she had done a good job ... that was how it started."

"And then you offered her a lift home and met her again the next day. Is that correct?" Burrows spoke quietly and without the level of accusation Alice was familiar with in US interview rooms. "Did you know anything about Brenda Clinton before that evening?"

Power's answer was immediate. "No. I didn't even know her name until I read it on the attendance sheet."

"Thank you, Mr Power. That is very clear."

Burrows was admirably careful in his approach to this man, Alice thought.

"I'd like to ask you a little bit now about the reasons why you attend these meetings. I don't want to upset you in any way and if you are uncomfortable at any point we can take a break. You have only to ask."

Alice nodded in agreement with this boundary. She touched the arm of the man beside her.

"Johnny, you are here so you can help the police with a current murder inquiry," she said. "There are no trick questions. You can stop any time you like. Just take your time."

Alice's voice rather than what she said had a calming effect. She was on his side of the table and looking after his interests and Brenda had told him she was sound. He smiled at her and nodded.

"I don't mind telling you." He addressed himself to Burrows. "As a boy I was brought up on the outskirts of Galway. I lived with my mam and dad and my younger sister. When I was seven and she was three, our mam died. She was giving birth to our new baby sister but they both died." He paused and took a slow breath as if to delay the next part of his story. "My dad went to pieces a bit afterwards. He started drinking and me and my sister were made Wards of Court. I was sent to An Cuan and my sister went to the nuns. I lost touch with her and, although I've tried, I haven't been able to find her. She may have been adopted and no record kept or she may have been taken to the States. That was common enough in those days."

He halted his story at this stage and those listening remained silent.

He continued, "I was lost in An Cuan but most boys were. If you had any spirit it was beaten out of you. If you were quiet then you were likely to become of interest to one of the brothers who was an abuser. That was my case."

He stopped at that point and Burrows left the silence uninterrupted. Then Power continued with a little more energy.

"Some of them were beaters – they enjoyed giving you a good hammering ..." and he rubbed his hands together as if to ease the sting of a blow. "Others abused us sexually – both day and night. They would take any opportunity they could. It was impossible to escape. Many tried and were brought back by the gardaí or the Brothers and then it was even worse for them."

Burrows appeared genuinely moved by the account. "Did your father visit you there?" he asked.

"He might have come once but visitors weren't encouraged and he disappeared for good from my life when I was still very young. By the time An Cuan closed in 1974, I was fourteen. I had been in the woodwork section for most of my time there and I'd been lucky to learn a useful skill. I did a lot of carpentry work all over the place and eventually moved north because in those days the chances of work were better there. I liked it here and I've stayed and made a life for myself. I teach young lads in the Youth Training Programme in North Belfast."

He fell silent, seeming exhausted by his recollections, and sat very still, waiting for what would come next.

"Would you like a break?" Burrows asked but Power shook his head.

"Let's just keep going," he said. "I'd rather get finished and get home."

"Do you live alone?" Burrows asked almost conversationally.

"I do, sir," Power said, assuming a position of greater deference.

This led Alice to decide they were nearly done here. She would ask for the interview to be stopped as old patterns were reemerging and she didn't want him damaged by the experience.

But Johnny was continuing. "An Cuan didn't prepare us very well for future relationships. I've been in counselling for a long time and am just beginning to feel like some company in my life wouldn't be a bad thing." His faint smile at this progress in his life was touching.

Alice found it hard to see this man as the killing type but that wasn't her job and she sat quietly, alert to his needs.

"I just have a few more questions, Mr Power," said Burrows. "Thank you for your cooperation. I know we are asking you to revisit old wounds here and it's not easy." He turned his pen a few times in his hand and then continued. "I was wondering if you knew a Brother called Twomey from your time in An Cuan?"

Power nodded, drew his eyebrows together in a frown and made a slight sucking sound through his teeth as if he had tasted something bitter. "We called him the Smiler," he said. "Even when he was beating you severely he seemed to be smiling. I was lucky to be with the woodwork guy who was gentle by An Cuan terms. I didn't have many direct dealings with Twomey except occasionally at mealtimes. I did hear a lot of awful tales about him but he wasn't one of my demons. They were another breed altogether."

"And your sister, Mr Power? I'd like to confirm that you never heard anything about what became of her?"

"No ... her name was Mary ... but Barnardos weren't able to track her down at all."

Burrows nodded to Alice that they were finished for the moment.

"Thank you very much for your time, Mr Power," he said. "Your answers have been very useful to us. We may need to get back in touch with you again but hopefully that won't be necessary."

He switched off the recording device, gathered his papers and stood to see Alice and Johnny out.

In the foyer Johnny offered Alice a lift but she had her bike and needed the air to lift the cloud of gloom that this history of mass abuse to Irish children had brought down on her spirits. She realised that she was lucky to be able to shed it so easily, unlike those for whom it was ever-present. She gave Johnny her DePRec card with her phone number on it and told him to call her any time he needed a chat.

He nodded and smiled. "I've promised to let Brenda know how I got on so that will be my comfort for the time being."

"You have excellent taste, Johnny," Alice said and headed for the bicycle rack and home to continue her reading.

At ten minutes to five that evening the Belfast Murder Squad took their places in the digital suite equipped for secure conference calls between individuals and teams in different jurisdictions. McVeigh had spent every moment he could that afternoon with someone from DI Hegarty's Garda team, dealing with setting up systems for the sharing of documents and reports. Because of the confidential nature of much of the work done in this facility there were super-strong firewalls and tight controls on the nature of evidence that could be shared in this way. In reality, after this initial introductory session, the two teams would work more or less autonomously, sharing information online daily or more often as was deemed useful. McVeigh and his southern counterpart would manage this exchange and where physical evidence was involved and the chain of evidence custody was paramount, this would require frequent trips between Dublin and Belfast. Most importantly they would be able to benefit from each other's different approach to the investigation and the wider pool of evidence this would inevitably produce. Full staff conference calls like this one were not seen to serve a very useful purpose and would only take place when a full review of progress was deemed appropriate. Otherwise it was agreed that doing the actual detailed and time-consuming work of detection was the best way for each investigation team to deploy their resources.

Caroline liked to stay very much on top of the detail of a case and the communication delay that was inevitable in these collaborations was frustrating for her to contemplate. Luckily her counterpart Orla

Hegarty was of a similar mindset and they had agreed to stay in regular contact and minimise loss of time.

This initial conference call set the tone of the joint investigation. It was business-like and collegial and they were all agreed that the perpetrator's MO and signature was almost identical.

The initial verbal pathology report on the southern victim suggested the actual cause of death was also homicidal suffocation with the removal of Twomey's hand being done post mortem.

"As is thought to be the case for Michael Quinn," the young Dublin Detective Constable Molloy making the report said, "death was probably inflicted through the application of a particular chokehold used in martial arts, combat sports or sometimes controversially in law enforcement." He seemed to be particularly knowledgeable and added that the hold was also used in professional wrestling to put pressure on an opponent to submit. "The chokehold is seen as a particularly skillful and dangerous move in that an adversary is likely to pass out in as little as ten seconds and it is possible to inflict permanent brain damage in a very short amount of time."

Someone on the southern side asked what difference a chokehold and strangulation would indicate.

Molloy answered without hesitation. "Well, in terms of giving us an insight into our perp, it lets us know that we are dealing with someone who has been trained to use lethal force. Also, it doesn't mean that we are necessarily looking for a big muscular type. This chokehold is seen to be a superior move to manual strangulation in that it takes know-how rather than physical strength. The small guy can conceivably take on the big guy with fatal consequences."

An estimated time of death in the same verbal report was set at less than twenty-four hours before the killing of Michael Quinn. This meant that although Brother Francis was discovered afterwards, the pathologists were testing the hypothesis that he was in fact the first victim, followed in a relatively short period of time by the body that subsequently ended up in St Oliver's. The discovery of the Belfast body gave a certain precedence to Paton's Murder Squad in the matter of litigation and prosecution but to all intents and purposes this was a joint investigation.

The signature posing of the body in the first instance in the victim's home was then adapted in the case of Michael Quinn who was transported after his killing and purposefully located in St Oliver's. It was agreed to look into the possible significance of this location and what connection it might have either specifically or symbolically for the victim. The question was: why go to the bother of moving the corpse and if, as might be the case, Quinn was killed in the South, why move him to the North?

Burrows reported on the interview with Brenda

Clinton and the entry in Quinn's diary signalling his intended visit to her on the Wednesday. He voiced the view that Brenda Clinton was a victim of Michael Quinn rather than a potential murder suspect but this was all speculative for the moment until further evidence was gathered. She had an alibi provided by her son and her workplace for the Tuesday and had no means of transport that would have allowed her to deliver on the MO that they knew to have been used in the two homicides.

Burrows then described the follow-up interview with Johnny Power who had links both to Brenda Clinton and to An Cuan where he had been as a boy. Furthermore, Power had a younger sister (now forty-seven) who had also been in care and with whom he alleged that he had no contact for the past four decades. The sister was older than Michael Quinn's usual targets but it was another element that required checking. Power had provided a work alibi for Tuesday and Wednesday, which they would check out after the bank holiday, and only then could they eliminate him from their inquiry.

"Perhaps we are looking at more than one killer?" speculated one of the team in Dublin. "But I agree that your Mrs Clinton doesn't seem a likely culprit."

Caroline intervened at this point and they agreed to take the inquiry steadily, remain open to possibilities but take care that these were grounded in solid evidence.

The indicative schedule of murders was focused around the Tuesday of that week with the killing of the Christian Brother in his remote Wicklow home at some stage on Tuesday morning. Later that same day the killer or killers proceeded to meet and murder Michael Quinn in an unknown location and subsequently transport his body to the church in Belfast. Finding where the second murder had taken place and how the body had been moved to its confessional on the Ormeau Road was a priority. Both teams would look again at identifying CCTV footage in the relevant areas and see if there were any obvious overlaps between the two locations.

Orla Hegarty agreed to get a forensic team into Father Michael Quinn's residence and to determine if he had a vehicle and, if so, attempt to establish its current location. That might bring them a little closer to identifying where he was killed and possibly allow them to find out something about his activities on the Tuesday when he died. It was agreed that a thorough profile of the two victims would be updated as new information was received. The southern team would interview the parish priest in Michael Quinn's parish and establish what he could about the deceased's lifestyle of late. Those who knew Quinn from his time in the North would be located and interviewed and Brenda Clinton would be asked about recollections of the younger man who had been intent on catching up with his past. Burrows would speak to the members of the Church hierarchy who had dealt with Quinn's indiscretions and he and Mc Veigh would follow up on the information they could glean from Nicholas Quinn and his wife about those who had become the victim of Father Quinn's charms.

As the call ended, in the Belfast Murder Squad HQ the weight of their task seemed to have multiplied. Caroline read the mood and took the situation in hand.

"I prescribe a snack in the canteen before we speak to Mrs Nicholas Quinn and the fine representatives of the Northern Ireland press. Can I get an 'Amen' on that?"

And in the space of a few seconds energy filled the room.

31

Nancy Quinn had many years previously learned that she was alone in her marriage and developed the capability to get along quite happily without her husband. Nicholas provided materially for her needs but, other than having been a most attractive partner when he was younger, he was no longer a source of any satisfaction. She frequently upbraided herself for having been so heavily influenced in her attraction to him by something as vacuous as physical appearance. He had in fact turned out to be a very ugly man in every way other than that.

As a lover he had always been clumsy and self-centred. She was not even sure if he was always aware of the identity of the person beneath him in these soulless couplings. When they had sex he had usually consumed a fair amount of alcohol and was increasingly unable to deliver on his objective. Surprisingly, he showed no regret about this growing inadequacy and was quickly unconscious beside her, snoring like a pig. Nancy was an avid reader and always had a good book on the go to distract her from these momentary intrusions on her person.

During the day, when he was at his office in the factory, she took care of her very comfortable home in South County Dublin and socialised with a group of women who had similarly chosen to make a relatively independent life for themselves. One was widowed at an early age and the others, like Nancy, were called on only infrequently to cater for business clients or be the decorative, well-preserved appendage to their husband at a social function. They managed these unpalatable aspects of their lives and found each other to be diverting company the rest of the time. They had a book club, visited gallery exhibitions and attended theatre performances; they were members of an up-market sports centre and were stalwart players on the women's team at the local golf course. They knew when, in order to maintain their lifestyle, it was necessary to fulfill their wifely duty and were supportive and sympathetic to each other when these demands interrupted their otherwise very rewarding routine.

When Nicholas had phoned her from the airport with the news that he had to go to Belfast before coming home she had been unperturbed and planned to have a friend over for a peaceful evening meal. His second call had delivered the bombshell that Mick had been brutally killed and she had deduced immediately that he was unable to cope with the fallout from that on his own. She had agreed to get the afternoon train to the North and do whatever was needed to cope with this crisis.

Sitting in this grubby police-station waiting area she tried to maintain her sense of decorum as she waited to be interviewed by the Murder Squad. She was not alone in the room. A young man in a grey track suit was sitting along from her picking at his nails and seeming extremely agitated. He had spoken to her when she arrived but it might as well have been in Urdu for all she understood. She hadn't fared much better with the Belfast taxi driver from the train station but the journey had been swift and he had soon realised that she wasn't going to engage in any chat.

At the hotel, Nicholas had told her that she was required to go to the police barracks to be interviewed. She was to answer their questions honestly as there was no point in trying to whitewash Mick's propensities or indeed his colourful past. They were trying to find out why he had been killed and would probably unearth stuff even they didn't know about. He had seemed grateful to her for coming and visibly shocked at his brother's death. The identification process had been more exacting than he had expected and she was surprised that he had called her rather than resorting to drink as he usually did when under stress. It promised to be a long evening and she

216

hoped that he would be exhausted from his travels and have an early night.

She heard her name being spoken aloud and looked up to find a smartly dressed woman with expertly cut chestnut hair and very green eyes.

"I am Detective Inspector Caroline Paton, Head of the Murder Squad. Thank you for coming to speak to us, Mrs Quinn. If you follow me I will show you to the interview room." And she had turned and walked away on the obvious understanding that Nancy would defer obediently to her command. And of course she did.

Burrows and Paton had not minced their words with Mrs Nicholas Quinn. The fact that Mick's penis had been removed suggested that there was a sexual element to his killing. Could she shed any light on that? Her husband had made reference to Michael having been involved with numerous women. What could she tell them about those relationships? Had her husband told her about them? Had Michael ever brought women to her home? Had she ever met any of these women? Had she any information that might be of use to them in understanding how her brother-in-law had become a homicide victim?

She had told them what she knew without making any attempt to hide her contempt for Mick and his reckless behaviour. Mostly, she explained that she had left her husband and Mick to their own devices but in the course of several decades she had occasionally become more embroiled than she would have wished. There was the young one in the North whom Mick had got pregnant and he'd been deluded enough to think he was in love with her. He had hatched the plan that she would have an abortion and then live with him as his housekeeper. The young woman, whose name Nancy remembered was Brenda Clinton, had more wit than him even though she was barely sixteen. Nancy had been drafted in to talk to her "woman to woman", as he had said at the time. Mick was then in his forties and the girl was only a teenager. She couldn't understand how Mick and her husband had thought that it was acceptable behaviour in any way.

"Were you aware that Father Quinn had planned to visit Brenda Clinton and her son the day after he was murdered?" Caroline asked.

"I was not," Nancy responded emphatically. "I haven't seen or heard anything about Brenda in over two decades." She momentarily recalled her meeting with the young woman. "I liked her when I met her. She was brave and smart and more clued in about life and reality than either my husband or my brother-in-law. I told her at the time to get as far away from them as possible and make whatever life she could for herself. I hope she managed to do that."

Caroline did not pursue that line of discussion. If Nancy Quinn had wanted to know what happened to Brenda Clinton she could have found a way to do that at some stage in the intervening twenty-three years.

"Was there another occasion when you met with a young woman who was involved with your brother-in-law?"

Nancy hesitated and then remembered she had been told not to withhold anything so she continued. "Well, yes, Detective Inspector. There is one other encounter that has remained with me down through the years. There was another young woman, some years after Brenda Clinton, who decided to take the boat to England when she became pregnant with Mick's child. She was older but much more timid and malleable than Brenda." Nancy Quinn opened her handbag and removed a small tin of mints. She opened the tin, placed a mint in her mouth and continued. "Nicholas was brought in to fund that procedure and I made the appointments and booked the boat. Her name was Theresa and she was in service in a family in County Down. They were called Ganley, if I remember rightly, but she left their employ before she went off to England. I don't know what became of her. Mick was moved shortly after that episode and I opted out of their affairs from then on. There are limits after all to the expectations that can be had of a wife and a sister-in-law, don't you think?"

Neither Burrows nor Paton offered a view on that question but they realised that there were any number of people who would have reason to find Father Michael Quinn unpleasant enough to murder. It began to look as if they might be spoiled for choice.

32

The evening meetings with the press were crammed full of TV and newspaper journalists and it was clear that this story was going to be the headline in the Sunday papers and on all the Saturday evening news bulletins. Paton and Hegarty had synchronised the quantity and depth of detail that they were going to release as well as the responses they might expect from the viewing and reading public. The names of the two victims were released as well as their religious credentials. The relative police silence until then meant that the joint inquiry was garnering maximum attention now and the detectives wanted to provoke as much reaction from the public as they could. Sometimes the work done by good investigative journalists was of immense help in a police inquiry as was the information that such press announcements stirred up in the general public. They had timed this press launch to generate an optimum amount of public interest, as they reckoned this was where their most crucial responses would be located.

Both jurisdictions had set up free telephone lines to receive calls from those who felt that they had useful information to share. This inevitably included a proportion of pranksters and individuals who just wanted to have their say generally on the issue of historic abuse associated with religious orders. They might have little or no bearing on the murders in question but both Belfast and Dublin were prepared to note every offering and follow up on all leads no matter how absurd they might seem at first.

National survivor helplines had also been alerted and Burrows had spoken to their managers and set up procedures for them to pass on information while respecting the confidentiality of callers. These groups had already anticipated that the volume of calls would increase as it always did when issues of abuse were in the news. They had brought in extra volunteers and had a number of counsellors on call for those whose level of distress was extreme. The history of clerical and institutional abuse across Ireland meant that advocacy and support organisations were skilled at responding to the fallout from any escalation in the amount of attention to the issue. Burrows had been impressed by their professionalism.

When he had a minute, Burrows hoped to design

some means of gathering telephone data that could be shared with colleagues both north and south but as yet he had not managed to make the time. They were all at full stretch answering queries as it was, without contemplating keeping on top of an onslaught of new information that would result from the press briefing.

As they waited for the press conference to begin, Caroline reviewed her earlier conversation with her boss. Detective Superintendent McCluskey had received Caroline's news of her relationship with Dr Alice Fox with his usual reserve. She was breaking no law by being in a same-sex relationship and the fact that her partner had some involvement in a police inquiry was only relevant if ethical lines were not observed. From what he could see both in the DePRec case and the current investigation, Dr Fox contributed positively to solutions and this was what they needed above all else. She was qualified to support vulnerable witnesses and they were about to have an abundance of those by the look of things. If she had the trust of the witnesses and the PSNI then this was a win-win from his point of view. He advised Caroline to stand back from direct involvement in interviews where Dr Fox was present but otherwise to run the case as she would otherwise do. He was supportive of her work, recognised her formidable record in bringing murderers to book and that was all that concerned him.

"I am not attempting to silence you in any way,

Caroline," he added in an almost paternal manner, "but I would counsel discretion until you see where this is all going." And then he had unexpectedly dropped his usual impenetrable sense of formality. "My middle son is gay and although I cannot say that I share his dress sense," he had laughed awkwardly at his own witticism, "I can say that he is a fine human being of whom I am very proud." He sat back and removed a few small pieces of lint from his immaculate uniform jacket and then stood to indicate that the meeting was at an end. "We will face the hordes together at seven o'clock, DI Paton. I will expect your final briefing paper by six."

The statement to the press had been detailed enough to satisfy those present that they had enough text for their first story. A woman from Channel 4 News had asked how they knew the cases were connected and had been told that was information that was being reserved inside the investigation for the time being.

A tabloid journalist asked if it was true they were interested in groups of survivors as a potential source of suspects. McCluskey had floored him with his response and said he hoped that the vulnerability of all concerned in the inquiry would be respected at all times. "We are conscious of our ethical responsibilities in terms of speaking to vulnerable witnesses and hope that the media will behave in a similarly considerate manner. Our business is about ending hurt, not adding to it."

Caroline had been surprised and impressed at

McCluskey's smooth response which had been masterly on many levels.

When asked if the police were considering that these two murders signalled the presence in Ireland of a serial killer intent on punishing members of religious orders for past offences, Caroline had given the stock answer.

"We are in the early stages of an inquiry and are keeping an open mind about everything at this stage. This is a joint inquiry because we have observed similar MOs in the murders. Our goal is to apprehend the killer before any further harm can be done."

The various telephone numbers had been given a high profile and the timing of the event meant that everyone was keen to get away and prepare their copy for the late-night news and the early papers.

Both McCluskey and Paton had declined doing TV interviews and had quickly left the room as soon as the conference had drawn to a close.

"I think that went well, DI Paton. Thank you for your excellent briefing. I hope we will have some good outcomes in the very near future. These high profile cases put us fairly and squarely in the media limelight so we need to play our best game. I will take calls from you whenever you need."

And he had headed back to his office and then no doubt home to collect his wife for their Saturday evening dinner at the golf club. Caroline had learned over the years that very little would disturb that routine.

For her part, she headed back to the Grosvenor Road to confer with her southern counterpart and to agree the way forward with Burrows and McVeigh. She was still hopeful of a late dinner with the new expert support worker for vulnerable witnesses. The spring had returned to her step and she looked forwarded to letting Alice know how much she appreciated her support both professionally and personally. Until then, she would order some pizza for their evening review meeting … as a small snack to keep her going until ten o'clock.

33

Despite the fact that they were now two murder squads working in tandem, for Burrows it meant that they had even more detail to digest, analyse and store. His talent for systematic, orderly organisation of findings was a real mainstay of the Belfast team.

As soon as she got back to base, Caroline could see that he was under enormous pressure. There were not only the interviews and reports from two squads of detectives but now also the information coming in from the confidential telephone teams North and South and the survivor helplines. She acted immediately.

"Bill, I think this would be a good moment for you to start to train an assistant to deal with digital storage and analysis of investigation data. McCluskey has given us the green light to swell our numbers to meet the demands of this very sensitive inquiry so let's not wait till we're snowed under."

Burrows' furrowed brow relaxed right away and Caroline knew she had read the situation accurately.

"Let's second a bright young thing from the IT section," she said, "who will jump at the chance of working weekends and providing solutions to the management of our impending data mountain? What do you think?"

"I think it's an inspired idea." Burrows feigned mopping his brow with a rather crumpled paper handkerchief. He smiled and nodded slowly. "The head of that section has already helped me out a few times so I'll get on to him right away. They work twenty-four-seven as it is, so there may even be someone available now."

He lifted the phone on his desk and in no time at all had enlisted the support of Constable Zara Pradić. She was a thirty-something woman with jade-green hair, a brilliant mind and an appetite for creative digital solutions that couldn't currently be satisfied in her own section. Given that she was at her desk at eight o'clock on Saturday evening, she was able to become involved in the inquiry evening review meeting within the minimal time it took to agree the terms of a secondment. Initially the move was for the duration of the current investigation to be reviewed by all parties whenever the case was concluded. And then they were four.

As they sat down for the evening review Paton, Burrows and McVeigh had a strange sense of having adopted an additional family member. The IT section leader had said, "Think *Girl with the Dragon Tattoo* ten years on, same number of piercings and a lot less attitude. Zara just wants to work all hours and you'll wonder how you ever got anything done without her. She doesn't like to discuss personal stuff and it can be a bit unnerving having this very clever, very quiet person around all the time – but you'll get used to it."

When Burrows passed on this introduction to his colleagues there had been some raised eyebrows but a general sense of relief that they had tracked down another workhorse.

Caroline had welcomed Zara and said they would look on this arrangement as a test drive to see how it worked out for everybody. She explained that their approach was to work hard, communicate clearly and kindly with each other, and solve murder cases as efficiently as possible. The new team member had made no comment but appeared eager to get on with the work and so they had moved directly to the regular progress review.

Constable Pradić listened as McVeigh outlined the case so far, alluding to information sources on the shared drive where relevant. He had shown the images of the two victims side by side and talked through the forensic and autopsy reports. Burrows summarised what they had learned so far and the profile detail of both victims and what they could infer about their perpetrator. It was a useful exercise for them to perform and helped clarify the next steps. They would maintain compilation of thorough victim profiles as a priority. Pradić would immediately establish systems to collate and filter new data forwarded from both jurisdictions. This would be messy to begin with as the calls were already beginning to come in but that could easily be taken into account, Pradić had assured them. The following day, Burrows and McVeigh would interview Quinn's brother and sister-in-law again and Brenda Clinton and her son would be brought in too. It was possible that the son's interest in finding out about his father, which was mentioned by Brenda, might have involved him in a little investigative work of his own. It was worth exploring that possibility.

Paton would revisit the reports from forensics and the local uniforms that had done the house-to-house calls to make sure they hadn't missed something. She would also follow up on the religious and body-posing messages for how these might be interpreted. As the amount of detail about the victims grew some of these messages became easier to read. The bulk of everyone's time would be the scrutiny of the incoming call detail that would be collated by Pradić on an ongoing basis over the next forty-eight hours. This would encompass responses to the television news bulletins North and South as well as the substantial newspaper coverage that the press conference would prompt.

It was after ten by the time Caroline responded to Alice's request that she text when she was leaving.

Pradić had already established a station for herself that involved a number of screens and other equipment that suggested they were about to enter a new era in digital discovery. Caroline suspected that they had found a gem in their new colleague and headed for the exit with a sense that everything was in safe, and possibly even revolutionary hands.

34

A heady odour of wine and garlic greeted Caroline as she arrived at Alice's door. She had gone easy on the pizza and her appetite responded enthusiastically to all the sensory signs of this late dinner. The table was set with candles and enough cutlery to suggest there might be a dessert of some kind. As she ditched her shoes inside the door, Alice met Caroline with a welcome long kiss and a glass of cool white wine. There was gentle jazz music playing in the background and the night held much promise. Caroline gave in to the temptation to go right off duty.

"Everything is ready if madam would like to eat now." Alice laughed at Caroline's dubious expression. "OK. So my butler act needs a bit of work but I'm a good student. Just cut me a bit of slack, Caro. My garlic prawns will hit the spot, I promise."

They were settled at the table and tucking into skewers of grilled prawns when Alice said: "So tell me about your 'chat' with the Super today?"

"You see, he hates to be caught out hearing something he feels he should have known already," Caroline responded. "That's the number one thing to avoid. Any threat to his departmental supremacy causes a severe allergic reaction." She grimaced to illustrate just how disagreeable this could be. "He's a fair man and we work well together but I know the red lines and am careful not to go anywhere near them." She deftly removed the head, tail and body armour of the crustacean with her fingers and popped the rest of it in her mouth. "These are so good, Alice. Thank you for your labours."

"But what did you tell him exactly about us? And why did you?"

"Well, I realised that you were becoming involved in the investigation in a more direct way than the last time and I couldn't risk compromising the evidence in any way. I panicked momentarily and then I thought – there is nothing improper or illegal in the situation but if I behave as if there is a need to be covert then I am asking for trouble down the line. I needed to let him know we were getting into a joint-inquiry situation anyway and I thought I'd clear the air about us at the same time. He appreciated that, I think, and said we were lucky to have an expert witness support in an investigation where that was going to be a vital resource."

Alice nodded slowly and smiled flirtatiously. "And were there any nuggets of advice about how to manage the practicalities of my being about the inquiry?"

Caroline became stern. "Well, he did say there was to be no snogging in the stationery cupboard. I said I would personally make sure that you were properly inducted into acceptable behaviours in the workplace."

"I look forward to those lessons," Alice said with her mouth full and reached across to fill Caroline's glass.

The soft light and the louche mood of the music made serious work talk unappealing but Alice felt there was one thing she should mention.

"I can see that you're really not in the mood to talk about work but I need to tell you just one thing. I talked to Tara today and she works closely in a centre for survivors of institutional and clerical abuse in Dublin. I've arranged to go there on Tuesday and conduct a focus group with her about remedies to state harm, but I think the murder of the Christian Brother will probably be on the agenda there as well. If I'm to be the support person with survivors I'd like to be as well informed as possible. I'll go along to the Amnesty meeting with Brenda as well on Wednesday and see what the mood is there."

"That's a good plan all right. Thanks for keeping me up to date. Burrows and McVeigh and the new staff member, DC Pradić, know now to keep you in the information loop. I'm going to spare you the details from my side and that way we can stay above reproach in terms of bias or partiality. I want to keep both you and the work safe." She looked fondly at her new love and sipped happily at the very good wine. This had been a full and satisfying day and it was her earnest hope that there would be ice cream on the menu to finish things off. "Tell me, Alice Fox. What are your plans for this very enticing small spoon in front of me?"

"Ah now, DI Paton, I may need to request a short interlude before we get around to the chocolate stage of the evening." And she stood up from the table and walked slowly but purposefully towards the bedroom. Caroline learned in that moment that she liked Alice Fox more than ice cream and that was a very significant development indeed.

35

When DI Paton arrived at her desk just after eight-thirty on Sunday morning there was already a bustle of activity. McVeigh and Burrows were seated either side of Zara Pradić who was explaining something on one of her computer screens. She was still dressed in the same brightly coloured top and long black flouncy skirt as the previous day and Caroline wondered if she could possibly have been there all night.

"Morning all," Caroline announced and proceeded briskly to her office and closed the door. She planned to have a close read of all the reports already submitted and to give some serious thought to the issue of body placement and religious symbolism. It was good that the extended team were collaborating and she knew it was best to stand back and allow that to happen without her interference becoming a distraction. There would be time to discover how the collation of incoming data was going later in the morning.

Checking through her emails, she opened an email update from Orla Hegarty, giving her the numbers of calls so far to the police helpline number in the South. The appeal for information and the freephone number in each jurisdiction would be repeated in all news bulletins that day and they expected the lines to continue to be busy. DI Hegarty noted that her staff had found the pro forma for message-taking, provided the previous evening by Constable Pradić, had been enormously helpful. As well as listening carefully and recording the proffered information, responders had prompts in relation to types of physical violence, categories of sexual assault and other experiences the callers had of the victims. The record also probed for respondents who might have known both victims, which was a long shot but worth exploring. They were grateful to have such a sophisticated organisational tool in place at the outset. The first examples of received data were already being digested and followed up on by southern detectives. At the meeting the previous evening the northern team had agreed to keep Johnny Power in their sights but if his work alibi checked out on Tuesday then he would cease to be of interest.

Orla also observed that it was great that survivor helplines were included in the same system so that comparisons and overlapping detail could be identified.

These were great developments for such complex data-collection situations and she was glad to be involved in the implementation of such a ground-breaking tool. Caroline felt she was the recipient of high praise for very little personal effort but was pleased that her intuition about needing another pair of hands had been accurate. The DIs had another person-to-person check-in arranged for later that day and it would be interesting to see what the systems had produced by then.

A bright purple file on her desk caught her eye and she lifted the front cover. There was a blank pro forma for telephone staff to use in gathering information from each call. Then beneath that an example of the processed call reports completed until midnight and sent through to Pradić as agreed. There was already a substantial body of phone evidence from callers who knew either one of the victims. Pradić had created a visually accessible reporting document that contained the caller-contact details, the summarised evidence, any subsequent action to be taken and the outcome. There were audio recordings of all calls and the composite report included embedded links to the actual call that was the source of the data. Finally there was a third report that demonstrated how verified findings contributed to a growing profile document on each victim. Paton could see that this would soon be extended to creating an ongoing digital profile of the perpetrator as more information was accumulated. She had a comforting sense of having a secure repository that would buttress the joint inquiry against the menace of overlooked connections. The inevitable management challenge created by having large numbers of uniformed staff and civilians working on telephone data in two different places seemed much less daunting. She made a note to update the Super on these system innovations. He would appreciate that positive development.

The door knocked and Eileen from the canteen came in with a tray holding coffee and some Danish pastries. Eileen was a wiry local woman in her fifties who had been running the barrack's canteen forever. She made it her business to know everybody and take their eating preferences seriously. She was attuned to staff moods and idiosyncrasies in a way that no one else was.

"I knew from the TV news last night that you'd all be here early so I thought a bit of brekkie wouldn't go amiss." She unloaded the contents of the tray onto Caroline's desk. "I see you've got a new member in your team. Zara is one of my very early birds so I know her likes and dislikes already."

Eileen prided herself on storing away her customers' preferences in her head and Caroline thought that she was a bit of an old-school memory system in her own way.

"You are a great woman, Eileen. You know just how to keep the Murder Squad working at full throttle and I thank you for that."

Eileen smiled and left without any further chat.

Caroline dunked a large Danish into her coffee and ate it with noisy satisfaction. She knew that Alice would be in later on when the Clintons were in for interview. The women had agreed earlier that morning that they would take the day as it came. If their paths overlapped in the course of the normal routine they would behave as if they had no recollection of their time together the previous night. Caroline knew that they would be utterly professional but she still smiled at the certainty of the immense effort that feigned amnesia would require.

36

The previous evening, Nancy and Nicholas Quinn had eaten an unexceptional dinner and drunk two bottles of wine in a subdued corner of the Europa dining room. It was hard to imagine now that the hotel had been one of the most frequently bombed buildings during the Troubles. In fact, after over thirty explosions the hotel was known as the 'most bombed hotel in Europe' and on occasions the 'most bombed hotel in the world'.

"I suppose this place is a little like us," Nancy had said thoughtfully as they finished their meal in relative silence.

"Whatever do you mean by that, Nancy?" Nicholas stared vacantly at her.

"I am often surprised at how resilient our relationship is," she replied.

He watched her closely, waiting for the sting in the

tail of her remark. It did not come and he relaxed a little and gave her his attention as she elaborated.

"Many couples would not have persisted in the face of the number of bombshells we have withstood in our time together but here we are … still carrying on. I'm not saying it's love that keeps us together. There is a limit to my gullibility but something has allowed us to survive and if it's laziness or loyalty or perhaps just that we can accommodate each other's idiosyncrasies, then so be it. We are not unlike the Europa in our stickability."

She looked at him in search of a response but there was none forthcoming. Maybe, she thought, he is just too dense to imagine a life other than the one he's got. And she wondered how he would cope without his brother's ever-ready absolution for all their laddish misdemeanours.

"I think I'll turn in," she said, rising and lifting the access card for their room from the table. "You have your own key?"

"I do," he said and headed to the bar for a brandy as she made her solitary way towards the lift.

Now the Quinns were eating breakfast silently in the Europa's dining room and flicked through the Sunday papers. Nancy found it shocking and a little unreal to see the news of Mick's murder on the front pages. They had unearthed an old photo from a parish magazine that showed him laughing, almost coyly, with a group of elderly women parishioners. He was a handsome man but prone to put on weight from his habits of self-indulgence. The picture could just as easily have been a younger Nick although she knew that the older women certainly wouldn't have held her husband's attention for long.

The headline, '**JUDGEMENT DAY?**' occupied half the front page of one of the tabloids. For the most part there was little personal detail about Mick but a few journalists had done their investigative work thoroughly and had begun to ask some awkward questions. She could see that this whole business could get very nasty if some of Father Michael Quinn's past secrets were dragged out into the public's line of vision. She wondered if Nicholas could escape being tainted by it all but she knew he had a Teflon surface that dirt just slid off, leaving no trace.

'**TIME FOR PENANCE?**' the headline in one broadsheet posed the question and argued that in the context of inquiries into clerical and childhood abuses one had to recognise that some form of retribution wasn't that surprising. The article said that the number of people from Catholic institutions who had old scores to settle with clerics were not few and far between and that must make major headaches for the police.

Nancy read that the victim discovered in the south was an elderly Christian Brother called Twomey who had been in the Industrial School known as An Cuan until it closed in 1974. He had still only been in his forties at that point and had been redeployed to a number of secondary schools around the country when there was need for a replacement teacher. A grainey image of a line of a dozen Brothers identified him as third from the left but this gave little sense of the physique of the younger man. Much of the detail of his life after An Cuan was equally hazy. Nor was it clear how he had come to be living in isolation in Wicklow. The writer suggested that in the wake of the report on abuses against children in the south, a number of those implicated had sought relocation and anonymity for fear of reprisals against them.

Francis Twomey's name had been cited in official reports on a number of occasions in relation to physically abusive behaviour towards boys who were resident in An Cuan. He was reputed to have been a harsh disciplinarian and to have been implicated in the public and violent humiliation of boys who transgressed even the most minor regulation. Someone had interviewed the local woman in Wicklow who cleaned for him and did his weekly shopping. She said he was a quiet old man who wasn't capable of doing any harm to anyone. Nancy wondered how the boys he'd brutalised would feel about that remark and hoped that Mick's actions were not subjected to the same public judgement. He might not fare too well either in that court of public opinion, she thought.

Nick's phone buzzed and he answered swiftly.

"Good morning, Detective Sergeant," he replied a little sheepishly. "We're just finishing breakfast here and we will come to you then. Let's say about ten-thirty."

Nancy thought that he sounded as if he was arranging a round of golf instead of going to discuss his brother's mutilation and murder.

"They want to talk to both of us again," he said as he ended the call, and then added as if to ease the pressure, "It'll be an opportunity for us to find out when we might be able to plan a funeral."

Nancy merely looked at him in disbelief and then stood up to return to their room to ready herself for another uncomfortable round of questions.

37

McVeigh had phoned Alice after nine o'clock on Sunday morning to see if she would be able to be a support to Brenda and Jed who were coming in for more questioning at eleven-thirty that morning. He said he expected each interview to take approximately half an hour and they would have a short break between them. Constable Zara Pradić, a new member of the team, would accompany him.

Alice agreed to be there a little beforehand and phoned Brenda to see how she was.

"Oh Alice! You are so good to give up your time again. It makes everything so much less scary when you're there too. It feels like the bad thing can't happen when you're beside me."

Alice quietly accepted this as the ultimate in positive feedback to a witness-support person. She smiled. She could hear Jed clattering something very loudly in the background.

"Sorry about the racket, Alice. We're having occupational therapy here. Jed is making a wee bit of cooked breakfast for Martha and Brian before they head off back to Dublin. They'll be back in time for the Paddy's Day parade – my mam loves all that paddywhackery. There's no point in them hanging around here when we are so busy with the police that we can't even speak to them." She went quiet for a bit and then continued. "But we had a lovely walk at Helen's Bay yesterday with them. It was nice to be by the sea and it did us all good. Brian was great with Jed. He told him all about his difficulties growing up and how he got himself together and made a life for himself. Jed needs to hear those stories so that he realises he's more the norm than an exception."

They agreed to meet later on in the waiting area of the police station.

Alice had explained that sometimes the police like to do some prep work with witness-support workers so that the understanding of roles is clear. "It's a good thing," she'd explained. 'It means relationships are good and –"

There was another, more catastrophic bang in the background.

"Sorry, Alice! I'll have to go. Small crisis in the kitchen! See you later."

And she was gone.

Brenda's mood had been positive, Alice reflected as

she started to clear up her own kitchen mess from the previous evening. Her garlic prawns had won great favour, she mused contentedly as she threw the remnants in the bin and opened the windows to air the place. *Standards are slipping*, she internally parroted her father's frequent remark when systems around the house became relaxed and signs of a chaos he really dreaded began to emerge. He had certainly ensured that Alice was an extremely orderly person, an annoying trait that she was trying hard to eliminate from herself. Caroline was unwittingly helping her by example in that objective. She smiled as she noted the difference in the amounts of debris at Caroline's place at the table and her own. Alice thought she would have to try much harder if she was to become a really spontaneously messy person. At least now she had the perfect role model for that goal.

While Burrows and Paton questioned Nicholas Quinn, his wife Nancy sat in the waiting area, inattentively reading the Sunday papers. She marvelled at how life had a way of taking the most unexpected turns. There was no great sorrow in her response to the death of her brother-in-law whom she had never found one single reason to admire. He was an extreme version of all the negative qualities that her husband possessed with only a modest amount of his physical attraction. Of course she could see that the two brothers were alike. Their family ties were fully evident in their overall appearance but Mick's outer shell was tainted for Nancy by her knowledge of his real persona. The fact that he had entered the priesthood and used his role as a way of taking advantage of vulnerable young women really grated on her. And worst of all … that only too often he had implicated Nicholas and her in the resolution of his sordid affairs had left her with a sense of guilt and disgust that she had been unable to shed.

After the episode with Theresa who had worked for the Ganleys, she had called a halt to her participation in Mick's life, aside from the safety of family gatherings where the underbelly of his lifestyle would never be allowed to surface. He and Nicholas had remained close but she had removed herself from any proximity to him, his life or his work in the North Dublin parish. That must be nearly twenty years ago now.

While she was lost in a review of her past encounters with Father Michael Quinn the door was pushed open and a young man approached the reception desk uncertainly. Nancy, lips pressed closely together, sucked air through her nostrils and tried not to call out a totally misplaced greeting to the young man. He was the ghost of Nicholas past. Her smile at her own witticism quickly faded as she realised that this was Michael's son, her nephew. Of course if Mick was killed in the north there would be a connection made between him and his mother. Nancy hoped that she might avoid a meeting with Brenda just now in these circumstances. She raised the newspaper so that she was concealed behind it.

"I'm Jed Clinton," he said a little too gently for the man on the desk but Nancy knew what he had said, almost without hearing.

"Speak up a bit, son," the desk sergeant said kindly. "My ears are not what they used to be." Then he laughed at himself. "If that's not a very strange thing to say." He leant forward on his elbows towards Jed. "Give me the name again, please."

"My name is Jed Clinton," he said more forcefully. "My mother, Brenda, is already here and I am after her for questioning. She will be with Alice Fox and I will be too." His accent was flat and very Belfast, which confused Nancy who was expecting the soft South Dublin lilt of the young Nicholas that he so closely resembled in her mind.

Jed was directed to take a seat at the other end of the foyer from her and so she was spared the need of entering into conversation with him. He took a leaflet from a display about security in the home and began to study it closely. It was as if he was translating what he read from a language that he knew only slightly and was being careful not to miss the point. Behind the paper Nancy hoped that Jed would be taken in soon and that the meeting of Jed and Uncle Nick, or worse still Nick and Brenda, could be avoided for now.

Like an answer to prayer, if you believed in such things, Nancy thought, the doors to her right opened and grown-up Brenda Clinton and an impressive-looking tall, blonde woman came through, talking quietly.

"It will be fine, Brenda," the woman drawled in what sounded to Nancy like a Boston accent. "You go home and relax and leave Jed with me. I'll call by with him later and we can have a chat then. You did very well in there. Go home now and put your feet up."

And with her arm across Brenda's shoulder, the tall woman walked with her towards Jed and the three stood together and talked quietly for a few minutes. Then Brenda left and the other two went back through the double doors and all was quiet.

As the years shrank and expanded for Nancy she began to feel weary of this trip north and all it entailed. She hoped that they might finish here today and make the necessary arrangements to bring the prodigal back to Dublin and bury him. To get to that stage would be a job well done, she concluded as she folded the paper in her lap and closed her eyes.

38

On Sunday, DIs Paton and Hegarty caught up with each other after lunch, reviewed progress and agreed the next stages of the investigation. The telephone response in both areas had been steady and was still keeping the teams busy. The collated forms from each conversation were fed back to Zara Pradić who was able to wave some form of digital wand over them and get an overview of common factors, create ongoing lists of those that needed a callback and digest and analyse the stats from any number of perspectives. Zara had promised an "easily read report" for them by six that evening. This was as well as having become the second staffer in the morning interviews where Alice was involved and Caroline had excluded herself. It was as if Pradić could bend time, thought Caroline. This was what the digital revolution was bringing to the work of solving murder cases and Caroline wondered fleetingly if she could continue to be part of this innovation or if she should be looking for an early retirement package. She was taken aback by the very idea that she would consider leaving the police force that had been her whole life for so long. Future Caroline can take the time to think about that, she decided, and brought herself safely back to the present and Orla Hegarty's hearty praise for all things Pradić.

Zara Pradić had not stopped for lunch with the others. There was a lot going on in her area and, rather than go with them to the canteen, she had agreed that McVeigh would bring her a cheese roll and a coffee. She was an undemanding colleague, Caroline observed, as she wondered how they might best integrate her into the team. She really did shun attention that was not directly to do with the task in hand and there was a pleasing lack of pressure to make small talk. Caroline had given a small amount of praise to Pradić earlier that morning and the young woman had looked unimpressed and had announced curtly, "From each according to her or his ability ... I do my job as required." And without leaving space for further exchange she had secured her jade hair with an old-fashioned mother-of-pearl clip and continued on with manipulating her many screens that seemed to be crowded with data.

Over a late lunch the trio of Paton, Burrows and McVeigh had chatted about the morning's interviews and the contribution that having an extra pair of hands was making. Pradić had already won the favour of her two male colleagues. They liked her concentration on the facts and admired her skill at manipulating data.

"It's simple genius to have all the digital links embedded to recorded interviews and data sources," said Burrows. "It just saves so much time for us to do the face-to-face stuff if Zara can provide the evidence we need with such efficiency." His eyes seemed to open further in recognition of each of Pradić's new skills.

His interest in all things and people technological was reaching dizzying new heights, Caroline noticed.

"And she likes to explain things too," McVeigh enthused. "She doesn't like chat but she finds ways to share her know-how that even I can get the gist of – and that's pretty miraculous."

"By the sound of things we are going to be disappointed if she doesn't choose to stay," Caroline teased, having already observed the intensity of engagement Pradić was showing for her task. She knew that creatives needed that or they got easily bored and she reckoned that the great diversity of the murderous mind would keep Zara supplied with new material indefinitely. Unfortunately, she thought, that was the way of the world as she knew it.

After assisting at the interviews with Brenda and Jed, Alice spent the next few hours in the Divis Tower. She had been reminded of Jed's fragility during his interview when he had been asked about Father Michael Quinn. Of course the investigators needed to know if he had met Quinn beforehand or if there had been any contact between them. That would be one way of explaining Quinn's planned visit to Belfast. Jed could have been the motivation if he had managed to track his father down and asked to see him. Burrows had asked him if he had ever had any contact with his mother's siblings – his aunt and uncle. He had needed help with even getting to understand the question, never mind answering it. When it came, his response showed how he had yet to consider just exactly how extended his biological family could become.

"Even my nan, who actually had those other two babies – they never wanted to meet her, their mother. So why would they want to be bothered with the likes of me?"

The manner in which the phrase "the likes of me" signified Jed's view of himself was saddening for Alice. She found these verbal measures of the depth of harm some people absorbed and carried in their lives to be shocking each time she heard them. And in her line of work she heard this deeply buried pain far too often.

When Brenda had been interviewed there were echoes that resounded in the subsequent questioning of Jed. They were trying to identify if someone else associated with Brenda and Jed might have had reason to kill Michael Quinn. McVeigh had asked Brenda if she had met other people that Father Quinn had known. No one stood out in her memory, except once or twice she had met his brother and another time she had met his sister-in-law. Brenda recalled the woman telling her to "think about her future" which was hard when she was barely sixteen and the present filled her head so much. The woman had been quite posh but she hadn't put any pressure on Brenda who, despite her youth and vulnerability, had been sure the best choice for her was to make her own life, without Quinn, as best she could.

Towards the end of her interview Burrows had asked Brenda if she had kept in touch with others she'd met that summer. Did she know if Quinn had been involved with others after her? Did the name Theresa mean anything to her?

Brenda had not kept in touch with the others nor did she know what had become of Quinn. "Don't forget that I was very pregnant for the time after that and then I had a small baby to keep me busy. It was different then with no mobile phones and, anyway, I wanted to forget about Mick as much as that was ever possible." After a moment, she added, "Jed is like a thinner version of him."

Brenda became thoughtful and Alice wondered if maybe now the secret was out, she felt freer to think about the familial link between Jed and Quinn.

Burrows left Brenda a little time. And then he asked

if she had told Martha the story of her time with Quinn.

"Of course I did." She looked taken aback by Burrow's lack of understanding of her relationship with Martha. "When I met her, Jed was still a young fella and we talked all about me getting pregnant and deciding what to do." Those in the room could tell that Brenda was reliving a lot of that conversation with her mother. She had been so delighted to have a mother at all by that stage and then when it was kind and gentle Martha … "We had a lot in common, Mam and me, and we discovered that very quickly. She comes across as a bit gaga when you first meet her but then you realise that she's just quiet. She doesn't say too much but she thinks a lot and she is very wise." Her love and respect for Martha and all she had lived through was palpable when she talked about her. "Sure, of course I told her everything, except his name. I didn't tell her that because I didn't want her to be upset thinking about a real person, with a name, that she could meet some day – even accidentally."

As she walked over to the Tower Block with Jed later, Alice could hear that same deep appreciation in the way he spoke about his mother. Martha and Brenda and Jed were links in a chain that had become a family despite all the people and circumstances that might have kept them apart. And then there was Brian too. What was the story that he had shared with Jed? He had become another link in the Clinton chain but what gap did they fill in his life that had made that relationship so rock-solid in only five years?

By the time she was walking home to Botanic, along Great Victoria Street, Alice's mind was full of the stark reality for those who had lived through clerical and institutional abuse. She realised that Martha might well be in the Dublin survivors' centre where she was working with Tara on Tuesday. Brenda had explained that her mother attended several times a week and had discovered what she now called "her tribe" there. Alice hoped that she might get some time with her to ask about Brian's past and satisfy some questions that she had about the "Connemara man".

She knew from Brenda that in discussion with others, Martha had bit by bit learned the language to name her own experience. Until that point she had perhaps been shielded by the dearth of words with which to name her world. With that new truth came an emotional landslide as a host of events and experiences long repressed were unlocked and Martha felt their hurt as if for the first time. Preparation for her attendance at the National Inquiry into Institutional Abuse meant once again reliving her abuses so that her story could be recorded and become part of that awful collective history. As a comfort, alongside all the pain was the relief that she was one of many and that connection to her 'tribe' brought great comfort. The public discussion about abuse in the media in the South brought an additional solace when it became clear that the majority of people agreed that what was done to her, and others like her, had been wrong. So schooled was she in shame, guilt and silence that this series of major jolts to her view of things had only gradually allowed her some peace.

Eventually Martha had relaxed into the company of others that she met in the Phoenix. The centre provided a place to meet and socialise. There were endless cups of tea and biscuits and someone made sandwiches at lunchtime that were eaten in a social area where the stories of the past were rehearsed and retold and affirmed and even sometimes laid to rest.

The centre had been set up as part of the steps the Irish government put in place to make some reparation for the major detrimental impact that the industrial school system had caused. Provision was made for counselling for survivors and funds were put in place for education and other supports. Each day in the centre there were classes to help make up for survivors' atrocious schooling and these included basic literacy, anger management and a number of creative arts and drama.

As many children had been separated from siblings and lost touch, Barnardos set up a family tracing service that used government and church records to locate and reunite family members. Through this service, Martha finally realised that she could see if any of her biological children wanted to meet her and form a relationship. That was the year the final report had been published that told the whole world the horrors that they had lived in their lives. Brenda had told Alice that her mam often said that it was all worth it because she got to have Brenda and Jed in her life and Alice had wondered to herself how those checks and balances ever got worked out.

39

Mid-afternoon on Sunday, Zara Pradić's first report on the calls received in response to the press appeals dropped into the inboxes of investigation colleagues North and South. The report was, as she had promised, clear, concise and extremely useful.

Between the two jurisdictions, in a relatively small number of hours there had been almost a thousand calls and a similar number might come through in the next day or two. Of course, not all the calls had been pertinent to the case. There had been lengthy, generalised outpourings about the injustices that had been visited by religious people on defenseless children. Some wild speculations had been proffered about who might have decided it was time to seek retribution for decades of wrongs that had gone unpunished. Pradić had applied a cool and unbiased eye to each piece of information and given respectful attention to each viewpoint. Better a few wild goose chases than a missed opportunity, she thought.

Report (ZP1) on the breakdown of calls to police freephones and NGO helplines between Saturday 15 March at 1900 hours and midday 16 March (17 hour period)

Calls to NI Freephone number....................168
Calls to Garda Freephone number................492
Calls to survivor support line (NI)................. 47
Calls to survivor support line (ROI)..............205

Some callers spoke to both the police and NGO helplines. This is accounted for in the finer detail overleaf. One caller had knowledge of both victims.

There were a number of calls that voiced an opinion on or personal reaction to the death of the victim but gave no evidence that would enhance the profile of the deceased or otherwise aid the investigation. These callers' numbers were stored but no action is recommended at this stage. A number of exceptions (see over under follow-up) to this have been signalled where the callers' level of emotional response was extremely elevated and merits further investigation. (For deep analysis of callers: contact details, gender, age, location etc click here.)

Profile data re: Father Michael Quinn (numbers in brackets refer to number of instances an element is mentioned. These are also shown in graphs overleaf.)

Positive experience of victim as a youth worker in NI (84)
Negative experience of victim as a youth worker in NI (27)
Positive experience as a parishioner of the victim (135)
Negative experience as a parishioner of victim (106)
Victim reported as a heavy drinker (29)
Reported inappropriate relationships with youth club members (31)
Criticism of victim's relationship with money (28)
Allegation of inappropriate use of parish resources (7)
Miscellaneous (13)

Profile data re: Brother Francis Twomey

Allegation of physical cruelty (328)
Reports of psychological cruelty (289)
Specific allegations related to withholding food and/or water as punishment (176)
Positive testimonies (4)
Miscellaneous (3)

Victim profile report (ZP2) on the calls to police freephones and NGO helplines between Saturday 15 March at 1900 hours and midday 16 March (17 hour period)

Michael Quinn: He was well known in the coastal resort of Hilltown Bay as the organiser of a youth summer camp attached to the Guardian Angel parish. Some called to lament his murder and to speak positively about his service to disadvantaged youth. Numerous people from his latest Dublin post also called and praised his gregarious nature and his attention to older parishioners. Negative reports of Quinn are mostly related to his earlier role in the North although southern parishioners raised the issues of drinking and suspect requests for donations to the parish. His critics found him self-interested, narcissistic and unpriestly. Specific complaints related to Quinn's earlier post as youth worker when his excessive interest in young women was allegedly common knowledge. The driver of the youth club bus claims that Quinn used the back seat of the bus for trysts with young women. He was often asked to sit at the front and deter unwanted entrants. A woman from a local housing estate, who previously worked abroad, said that Quinn was custodian of her mother's house keys while the older woman was in hospital. Several neighbours had observed Quinn taking young women there at different times of the day and night. There were a number of miscellaneous reports detailing remarks and behaviours described as 'strange for a priest' – including his tendency to make sexualised comments, wear casual clothes and not identify himself clearly as a clergyman.

Francis Twomey: Calls were almost entirely related to his time in the industrial school in An Cuan, County Galway. He was responsible for the agricultural element of training including animal, crop and vegetable husbandry. There is no suggestion of sexual abuse but he reportedly physically and emotionally abused large numbers of children who worked on the farm over the years. Several callers noted Twomey's propensity to strip boys as a punishment that they now saw as a sexually motivated act. He was also associated with the refectory where meals were taken and often punished young people by withholding food and water. Several callers noted drinking water from lavatories. One man who had worked on the roads in England until he retired related a punishment that involved daisy chains that links directly to the postmortem image of Twomey. This call is available in text and audio (Click here). A few local people where Twomey lived in Wicklow found him to be reclusive but not unpleasant. They were most concerned about the violent event in their area and the impact on property value.

Those colleagues who read the report turned immediately to the full and detailed analyses of the data upon which the summary was based. There they learned that while all of those allegedly abused by Quinn were young women, Twomey's victims were all young boys of school age. Both men were abusers who were members of Roman Catholic religious communities but apart from that it was a strain to see what specifically they might have in common that would enrage one person to kill them both. It was always possible that they were chosen at random, as examples of what was most despicable in Church history but, for now, the search for a link to one individual killer continued. With this in mind, all immediately clicked on the details of the one person who had reported knowing both victims. This was disappointing in that it related to a survivor of the school in An Cuan who had indeed been abused by Twomey and who now happened to be in Quinn's parish in Dublin. As someone who gave up on religious faith after his school experiences, he had no dealings at all with Quinn but had truthfully answered that he knew both men.

Those who received Pradić's first report also accessed a version of the full story of the daisy-chain call. Colleagues that listened to the spoken recording were even more moved than those who kept to the written text, which did not fully capture the emotion of the teller's voice. At this point, details of the murder victims as they were found were not available in the public domain and this made the voluntary mention of a daisy chain all the more interesting. Until relatively recently, the man who had called the survivors helpline in the South had never before spoken to anyone other than his late wife, about what had happened to him.

The full details revealed that, as a boy, the man had

been placed in An Cuan because he had been caught playing truant from school and was therefore categorised as a delinquent. Although he was from Dublin, after 1954 the Christian Brothers decided to concentrate all those under twelve years of age who had broken the law into one industrial school in An Cuan, County Galway. While some boys learned a manual trade like wood or metal work, others laboured on the farm under the direction of Brother Francis Twomey, whom the boys had nicknamed "Smiler". Smiler had held his nickname, passed down through generations, since he first began to work there as a young brother aged twenty. His facial expression reportedly gave an impression of a smile even when he was being appallingly cruel.

Later that evening Burrows told the story of the flowers to his wife and they both wept at their own good fortune and for the misery that had been done to so many children in Ireland over the years. When he got home, McVeigh had looked at his baby sleeping peacefully in a room already full of toys and baby books and been aware of his son's life stretching ahead, full of affection and possibility and the story of those left to the mercies of the Christian Brothers seemed all the more disturbing by comparison.

As in the case of all the boys in An Cuan, a visit or a trip home was very rare indeed. Probably because of that, when the young 'daisy-chain boy' was allowed home to attend his mother's funeral, everything that happened during that time was firmly imprinted on his memory. On one of these home days, he sat on the grass in the municipal park with his older sister and she showed him how to make a daisy chain. As he tried out his new skill, she had made a perfect chain and put it around his neck and despite the sad context that moment had always remained one of his happiest life memories.

On returning to An Cuan after this brief, grief-ridden experience of life elsewhere, the boy was immediately put back to work. One of his tasks was to take two cows from the milking yard to the lower pasture. He set off with a stick in case the beasts needed encouragement and quickly shepherded them to their fresh pasture in a meadow that was full of wild flowers. Then he noticed a particularly abundant patch of daisies and, ignoring the passage of time, sat in the sunshine amidst the flowers and grasses and began to fashion a collection of daisy chains. In his mind he was going to distribute these jewels to his peers and gain their admiration for his newly acquired talent.

Time passed and Brother Twomey went to look for the two missing cows but failed to see the boy hidden in the long grasses. When hunger pangs finally reminded the boy that his evening meal might well be already in progress, he carefully gathered the daisy chains and ran back to the grim institutional building. Brother Twomey was waiting at the door to the empty refectory and his fury had reached full steam. He grabbed the boy by the ear and dragged him into the front hall of the building. This part of the building reflected the generosity of spirit of the original owners. The floor was made from brightly patterned cold tiles and there was coloured glass in the top of the glass panels around the door and in the big window over the staircase. Boys did not use this part of the house and all was eerily quiet. The man who called the freephone remembered the beauty of the evening light coming through some red glass above the door.

Brother Francis did not ask the boy why he was delayed. This had no bearing on the consequence, which was that he was gone missing and had not been present for the evening meal. The carefully made daisy chains were carelessly discarded on the ground. Then the Brother roughly stripped the skinny boy of his threadbare clothes and then with the same left hand that he used to beat the boys, in an equally forceful manner he shaved the boy's head so that his golden hair lay amongst the scattered daisies.

"You can stand there now until I tell you to move. Everyone who passes by the window will see what a miserable specimen you are. Believe me, boy, you will learn to be obedient and not to think you can go off dillydallying in the fields when there is work to be done."

And Brother Francis, in his long black soutane had

turned and swept away like some kind of departing bird of prey.

A few moments later, a small scrawny boy carrying a brush and a shovel came under orders to sweep up the mess left by the punishment. This was a local boy from a family that was destitute. When they had become homeless, the parents had placed their children in service wherever they could find an opening. This boy rescued the daisy chains from the debris on the shovel and put them carefully in the wide pocket at the front of the long servant's apron that he wore.

One of the southern team of investigators had subsequently had a follow-up conversation with the daisy-chain caller and his report posted in the documents on the shared drive told a sad but not unfamiliar story. The man was determined that he did not want to be named and opted for the pseudonym 'Dan'. He recalled that his mother had died when he was ten years old and so the incident with the daisy chains would have happened in 1956. Dan said that in 1960 when he left school, aged fourteen, he only wanted to put as much distance between himself and Ireland as he possibly could. He was by then a tall boy and may have looked older than his years but, in any case, he went unchallenged when he got the boat directly to England.

At first he had worked as a tea-boy and subsequently as a navvy for the company constructing a major road network around London. He reflected that he had grown up with these rough men. Some of the men had become his supportive adults and a kind of family to him. They had found him suitable lodgings, included him in their lives and celebrated his birthday and other milestones. Dan had fallen in love and married the daughter of one of the older men and stayed all his life on the outskirts of the English capital, until his wife died. He said that he had found intimacy difficult but she had been his angel and he had slowly learned with her not to be afraid of his body. Once she was gone, it was England that contained too many memories and so by then, retired and quite arthritic, he had moved back to Ireland.

Dan told the person who spoke to him that he had settled in Dublin and eventually tracked down a sister that he had not seen for half a century. He also found the Phoenix Centre for survivors in Dublin and began to really come to terms with his past. Counselling helped with this, as did days spent listening to others talk about childhood experiences that resembled his own. The caller had told his daisy-chain story to his fellow survivors and it was added to the catalogue of historic abuses stored in the heads of those whose childhood resembled his own. His account became well known by those in the centre whose attention it grasped and where it gained a poignant, symbolic status in terms of the cruelty done to innocent children. Those who now knew his story were too numerous to count and needle and haystack were mentioned quite often in this regard. While he had merited some follow-up, the member of the southern investigation team concluded that although some might think he had just cause, on the grounds of his age and infirmity it was very unlikely that he was the killer of Brother Francis or anyone else. The man known as Dan had said he never heard of Father Michael Quinn until the recent news of his killing and he had never been north of the border.

When asked about the young boy from the local area who worked for the Brothers in exchange for his keep, Dan recalled that the boy was his own age. He didn't remember his name but he remembered that he had sandy red hair and slipped silently, almost covertly, about the building doing his chores. In the strange hierarchical world that they all inhabited, those whom the State had placed in care were seen as a cut above those given into service by their pauper families. A boy labelled delinquent might still have some family at home, some hope however distant. The boy given away by his family because they couldn't afford to feed him had nothing left.

That boy, Dan commented, would also be sixty-four years old now, if he had survived this long. He said he often wondered what had become of him, after such an impoverished beginning.

40

On Tuesday morning, just before seven o'clock, Alice
Fox boarded the Enterprise train heading from Belfast
Central to Dublin's Connolly Station. It was still dark
when she took her seat at a window on the left-hand
side of the carriage where she hoped she would catch
some glimpse of the countryside as daylight crept above
the horizon. A young man and woman, who were
evidently business colleagues, occupied the two places
opposite her. They were preparing their pitch to a new
prospective customer in Dublin and Alice quickly put
on her noise-excluding earphones to ensure that she
didn't have to listen to their enthusiastic exchanges. She
closed her eyes and let her recorded cello concert
soothe away any irritation. She wanted to have a clear
head when she met Tara at the station. They would go
somewhere for coffee and Tara would bring her up to

date with the agenda for the focus group with survivors in the Phoenix. Alice hoped to be able to stay around a bit afterwards and meet some of those who attended the day centre, particularly anyone who had been in An Cuan and who may have known Brother Francis Twomey.

Connolly Station at nine o'clock was a heaving mass of commuters and day-trippers weaving their way slowly towards the exits or train platforms at the limited pace that the sheer volume of other travellers permitted. A man with long grey hair and a leather jacket was playing a brightly painted upright piano, set off to the side of the main throughway. A small backpack sat by his feet and he was making a fairly good job of playing and singing the Beatles' classic, "Hey Jude". Some passersby clapped appreciatively on their way past and there was a general air of good-natured camaraderie. As Alice watched out for Tara who was meeting her by a small kiosk selling coffee and pastries, the pianist finished with a bit of a flourish and headed off towards the intercity platforms. A young Asian woman took his place. She immediately began to play some haunting traditional air that transformed the atmosphere into something more subdued.

Tara tapped Alice's shoulder and interrupted her fascination about the role that a simple piano could have on a public space. The two women hugged and headed for the exit and the moving staircase that led to street level.

Sipping mugs of coffee and warmly ensconced by the coal fire in a nearby hotel lounge, Tara explained the purpose of this morning's focus group to Alice. The survivors in the South were greatly in advance of those in the North in their access to financial redress and an opportunity to make a record of their experience of abuse in a whole range of State-sanctioned institutions. All but a very small number had been run by the Catholic Church and funded by the State on a per capita basis. The scathing national report published several years previously had made a number of recommendations about reforms needed to State services to meet survivors' ongoing needs. Today's focus group was to gather people's impressions of how well those reforms were going and what else they felt was needed to support them into the future. Tara explained that for those with no family network, the future was much more daunting than for those with extended family who were ready to help with life's day-to-day challenges. She would gather survivors' accounts and formulate those into a set of recommendations to put to government. This was one in a number of such pieces of work and Tara had earned the trust of the groups' organisers and the individual participants that she had worked with on a number of occasions. She said she was careful to check back on her suggestions with the survivors and guard against straying away from their wishes. At the other end of the process she worked with government officials to make sure things happened and that her reports didn't just gather dust on someone's desk. It was a great example of how social research could really be of benefit to those who had experienced social harm.

At a little before ten o'clock they walked briskly to the Phoenix Centre and were buzzed into a building that looked for all the world like a city-centre office block. Once inside the main door on the second floor the office comparison ended. There was a reception desk where entrants were welcomed and recorded by a middle-aged woman who exuded warmth and cheerfulness. While they waited their turn behind a number of people at the desk, Alice glanced around and noted that people had organised themselves in circles of comfortable chairs. Mugs of tea and coffee and plates of biscuits were carried from a kitchen area and there were newspapers and magazines on the tables along the side of the room. All around the walls were examples of people's artwork and creative writing. Photographs of group celebrations and outings were there too and it was clear that the Phoenix filled the role of a family for those who hadn't had the chance to make one of their own.

There was a range of ages from those who might be in their early forties to those with white hair, some with walking aids, who were considerably older. A group that was mostly women was busy knitting and crocheting as they chatted. There were rooms off the main space where it seemed that educational classes were taking place. A large handwritten timetable stuck to one of the windows out onto a smoking area announced the activities of the day – Art, Anger Management, Basic English, and Focus Group meeting – and indicated their location.

The woman behind the desk welcomed Tara and told her the meeting room number for the research session. Tara introduced Alice and the woman shook her hand enthusiastically across the desk and told her to make herself at home. "I'm Sonia," she said. "If Tara has brought you we know we can trust you, Alice Fox, so you are most welcome. This is an adult learning centre but it is also a home for those that need it to be that. We try to meet all needs as best we can."

As they moved towards the room where they were to work, Tara was greeted by a number of people in the various groups. Alice didn't pick up all the words as there was another whole range of thick accents here with a totally different melody to the northern ones to which she had now become attuned.

Then she was surprised to hear her own name called out and turned to see Martha standing at the door to one of the classrooms. "I'm going in to my English class now but I'll see you after, Alice," she said as she playfully slapped Alice's shoulder. She was more at ease here with her tribe than Alice had seen her even with her family in the North. Perhaps she was different when Brian wasn't about, Alice speculated. His attention to her was certainly fulsome but only now did it cross Alice's mind that it might also be stifling of Martha's individualism in some ways.

"Talk to you later, Martha," she said and observed the older woman's pleasure at having a connection to this stranger in the place where, unusually, Martha was the one on familiar ground.

41

Back in Grosvenor Road police barracks, the day had begun with a case review. Of course they had continued their work on the Bank Holiday Monday but this had mostly involved wading through reports on follow-up calls that resulted from the freephone response to media coverage. Caroline and her southern counterpart had an early call that morning and agreed their priorities for the next stage of the inquiry. Burrows and McVeigh and their new colleague Zara Pradić had been waiting in the meeting room when she finished her call with DI Orla Hegarty. Caroline observed the ease with which the three got along together and was grateful her hunch about expanding the team had worked out so well.

"Morning, team," she announced as she joined them and was glad to see that Eileen had been around with the breakfast Danish and some fresh coffee.

She took her seat and noted the file waiting at her place. Pradić had really sharpened up their organisational capacities but Caroline wanted to be sure that didn't mean that they became complacent about the spontaneous elements of their detection. This was their major strength and she needed to make sure it wasn't overshadowed by impressive paperwork. There was a yellow Post-it stuck to the cover of the folder that said that Johnny Power's workplace had confirmed his presence there on the previous Tuesday and Wednesday from eight until four-thirty. She tapped it and nodded to show that she had absorbed the implications. It had seemed too easy at the time but sometimes life was not as complicated as one expected.

"I'd like to start with a check-in," she began as she filled her mug with steaming coffee and slipped a chocolate Danish onto her plate. "Let me begin by saying that I am heartened at the developments in our capacities since Constable Pradić has joined us." She acknowledged Pradić with a nod but the woman made no response. "I know we are only talking about a few days but already we have garnered a lot of praise from the Dublin Squad for our contribution to the joint investigation." At this she paused and glanced around the group. "Any comments anyone wants to make or issues that have arisen in terms of our expansion?" Smiling, she dipped her Danish in her mug of coffee, narrowed her eyes and placed it in her mouth with conspicuous satisfaction.

The healthy-living spell was definitely over, Burrows thought happily. He raised his eyebrows and made it clear he would speak next.

"I'd like to say I think that the arrival of Zara has positively added to how we work. Of course an extra pair of hands can lighten the load but another person who isn't clued in to what we are about here could also be an impediment."

While Burrows was speaking Zara Pradić sat expressionless and yet seemingly quite relaxed. She was a very interesting woman, Caroline decided.

"Ian and I already have discovered that Zara doesn't like to chat. She likes to get on with the work and we respect that." He laughed kindly. "In fact we are quite relieved about that and we are already learning a lot about how working in a digitally friendly way might support us in solving murder cases." He nodded to show he was emphatic about this view.

McVeigh held his pen aloft to claim the next speaking position. "I agree wholeheartedly with what you have said, ma'am, and also what Sergeant Burrows has said. I hope and believe that we will be better at what we do for the skills that Constable Pradić brings to us. As you say, ma'am, it's very early days but for the moment everything is looking good."

Caroline noted his unusual emphasis on rank and realised that with the arrival of Pradić he was no longer the most junior member of the Squad. He appeared to like that development and Caroline smiled at the predictability of things.

"Zara?" Caroline met Pradić's open expression. "This is when you get the chance to say, briefly of course, how things are going for you in the moment." She realised that not all her colleagues managed their teams in this egalitarian manner.

Pradić's gaze did not falter. There was no discomfort or timidity here.

What a relief, thought Caroline, who didn't like to have to coax words out of her team.

"I am entirely happy with my work, DI Paton," Pradić said slowly and thoughtfully. "My colleagues have made clear to me what will be useful to the work and I am using my skills to deliver on that. I am also busy with all the data that is coming in and I like that a lot." She ran her hand through her gleaming jade hair and made it clear that she had said her piece.

They already knew that this was a lengthy utterance by Pradić standards but they appreciated the sparseness of what she said which had covered all the essential ground in very few words. For a small moment in time everyone around the table was smiling.

"Good!" said Caroline. "Let's see where we are with these murders. I've had the usual full briefing with DI Hegarty this morning and I'm thinking we need to move things forward in the next few days. Apart from anything else, I have committed to another meeting with the ladies and gentlemen of the press this evening and they, and the Super, will be wanting to hear about progress. So let me begin by bringing you up to date on the developments in Dublin and then we will look at the issues."

There was an encouraging sense of solidarity around the table as they listened to her account of her call with DI Hegarty.

"The southern forensics team didn't turn up anything useful in Quinn's rooms. Seems that only he and the housekeeper who cleans the room weekly have left any trace there. The detectives who gave it a thorough search found nothing either. So, our close look at his belongings retrieved on Friday shows that he had been in touch with the Family Tracing Service but had traced Brenda and Jed through some other means. Possibly he had used his clerical position to track them through Social Services or some such. I'd say he was an accomplished blagueur."

"Once you have a name you can manage a lot on the internet without ever having to resort to contacting the authorities," Burrows said thoughtfully.

"The team there had also talked to Quinn's parish priest, housekeeper and some parish volunteers that he worked with on some of his social projects with older people and people with disabilities. Seems he was purposely kept away from young women. We can assume that his reputation preceded him when he was moved from the north. Burrows you might follow up on that with the Church authorities here and just make sure that there was nothing else that would be of interest to us in his list of misdemeanours." Caroline crossed something off her list. "In fact, I think that it would be useful if tomorrow both of you," she nodded to Burrows and McVeigh, "arranged a series of meetings in the Hilltown Bay area." She looked at them inquisitively. "What are the possibilities, do you think?"

McVeigh tapped his notebook. "Well, we have drawn up a list already that includes the youth-club bus driver who is still associated with the parish. He has a daughter who is the same age as Brenda and might have some useful recollections."

Burrows added to this from his own iPad notes. "While we're there we thought we might arrange to follow up with some of those who phoned in with comments on Saturday evening and yesterday. Zara has compiled a list with contact numbers and we can set those interviews up today. We also want to check if anyone has been asking questions about Father Quinn, or indeed Brenda Clinton recently or in the area around St Oliver's. Some detailed planning went into these killings and, in the case of our victim, the subsequent placing of the body. We'll get the local community police to check back with the caretaker, local pubs and cafes and such like." Burrows waited for Caroline to nod agreement to these suggestions and then continued.

"We have been talking about the need to check in with the local survivor network as well and all the issues that raises in terms of taking account of people's fragilities. We don't want to come in heavy-handed and distress people. We wondered if given the fact that Dr Fox is already linked in with the Clintons she might be able to attend the Wednesday meeting in Amnesty. There's bound to be a lot of discussion of the murders in that forum."

"Good idea, Bill. Alice Fox is meeting with southern survivors today and that would be a good extension of that work. You get in touch with her, and see if you can organise that and see what she comes up with." She was pleased that for now she didn't need to make any of these connections. She pursued the line of thinking a little further. "We clearly need to probe carefully into the all-island survivor's network and see what we can find out there. And you're right, Bill, that we need to be delicate in the way we do that. Zara, can you see what you can find out about survivors with any kind of record of violent assault, or membership of the British or Irish armed forces. The differently abusive nature of both our victims suggests that to be a key factor. Our perp, and I do think there is just one, knows about what happened in An Cuan and also about a seemingly disconnected series of clerical abuses of young women ... I'll say more about that anon when we discuss the messages left with the two bodies. First, let's finish with the report from the South and any other immediate follow-ups we need to consider. Our trawl through CCTV has shown nothing so far but there are so many ways to cross the border that's probably not surprising. There are not many cameras in the wilds of the Dublin Mountains either so I'm not hopeful about that. We'll stick with it anyway just in case. It would help if we had a steer on the perp's vehicle."

The team signalled their assent.

"There are just two other immediate findings to report, both of which are interesting in terms of understanding how these killings were orchestrated. Firstly, in a follow-up interview with the woman who cleaned and shopped for Twomey, one of DI Hegarty's team learned that Twomey had received a phone call the previous week. The caller had informed him that he had been registered for the Meals on Wheels service and would be receiving a warm meal several days a week starting on the Tuesday that we now know he was murdered. The woman said that he had been delighted and told her that he was looking forward to getting some really tasty food delivered." Now that was clearly a scam and it seemed like a particularly cruel way to taunt an elderly man, she thought. "From what we know of how he treated boys in An Cuan about food, it's not such a surprising detail."

The team received that snippet in silence.

"The second item is," continued Caroline, "that Quinn's car has been located in the car park of a pub

285

on the north side of Dublin off the M1 motorway exit towards Rush and Donabate. These are two small seaside places where a lot of people would have second homes or mobile homes and are now established commuter towns. Some of the southern team are going to follow up with the bar staff and see what they can remember about Quinn's visit there. Did he meet someone and can they provide a description, or better still some CCTV images from the car park? If we had a vehicle registration for the potential perp we would be really getting lucky."

"I wonder did Quinn also receive a preparatory phone call," mused McVeigh. "Almost all the other detail is the same in these cases so maybe the phone call is also common to both. I'll chat to my counterpart and get them to check that out with the housekeeper or one of the other priests. He may have been lured there and then on to somewhere else where he was killed before being brought to St Oliver's."

Caroline felt they were slowly edging closer to their killer. She sensed that familiar moment when the identity of the killer begins to take shape and it's as if the discernible scent of the prey suddenly makes hunting them easier.

"OK. Now I want to tell you the result of my review of all the elements of the crime staging and signature. Let's take them individually first and then we can consider them together. Then we'll agree what we do next."

42

When the focus group was successfully accomplished, Tara Donnelly had to rush back to South Dublin University where she had a pressing meeting about the need to generate external funding. Alice was booked on the late afternoon train back to Belfast and Tara had arranged with the Phoenix Centre staff that she could wait there and chat to the survivors who were available in the social area. It was lunchtime now and there were lots of people milling about and exchanging greetings and joking remarks in that whole range of accents that Alice didn't easily understand. There were plates of salad and cheese sandwiches sitting on all the tables. In the kitchen area, yet more plates piled with biscuits were ready to be handed around and steaming mugs of strong tea filled the air with a sense of comfort.

Alice could see that food played a big part in the

activities of the Centre. It was a tangible expression of care for those who knew all about its absence from their earlier lives. Aside from the nourishment, there was the camaraderie and the way that everyone seemed to be looking after themselves but also everyone else. She had seen in her own work back home this capacity of food to bring a group together and tighten their bond.

Martha waved to Alice from the centre of a group of women who were chatting and eating enthusiastically.

"This is a friend of my daughter and her son," she announced proudly as Alice made her way over to the table. "She's from the United States, aren't you, love?"

"I am. I'm from Lowell, Massacheusetts." Alice waved to the women who had paused in their chat and nodded and smiled at this newcomer. Then, as if reactivated, they continued with their animated discussion.

Martha beckoned to Alice to lean down and whispered loudly in her ear. "I'm going into my English class in a bit but I'll be finished at three o'clock. Brian meets me in the café on the corner and he said to bring you along too. He'll treat us to some coffee and nice cake."

"I'll be right there, Martha." Alice indicated one of the tables where there were two men, sitting apart and quietly looking at the day's paper.

They had both been in the focus group earlier that morning and nodded to her when she approached and sat down.

"Have a sandwich, Alice," an older man called

Vince said, pushing the plate in her direction. She took a salad on white bread and placed her water bottle on the table beside it. She knew that she didn't need to ask any questions. She could hear that the killing of the Brother from An Cuan was being talked about around the room in different groups. She had chosen these men because they were of an age that meant they were most likely to have been in State care during Twomey's time working in the west. She hoped that she would be lucky and get to talk to someone who knew him.

As if reading her thoughts, Vince commented. "Quite a few of us here would have been in the Smiler's loving care," he said sardonically with an expression of near disgust. "You'll note there are no tears at his passing." He looked at others who were having animated discussions about the killing and shrugged his shoulders. "The big question is, Alice, is there ever such a thing as a just killing?"

The other man at the table lowered his newspaper and met Vince's inquiring gaze straight on. "In my opinion ... as someone who was never in An Cuan but met my own shower of unchristian bastards in Artane ... I'd say that murder is too good for any of them. Did he deserve to be killed? Would that be a wise thing to do? Those are two different questions. He's dead now so we won't worry too much about whether he deserved to die or not. The second question is the interesting one. In terms of the wisdom of giving him his marching orders into eternity, in my opinion it would not be a good idea. We all did our time already when we were kids and you'd have to be mad to be prepared to do more time for killing one of those boyos. The Smiler must have been half dead already. You might be happy he got what he deserved but where would the satisfaction be if you were the one being punished afterwards?"

"Listen to Aristotle, will ye?" Vince spoke with that lilting accent that Alice could hear now and identify as coming from the west of the country. "Not everyone is of your philosophical frame of mind, Ollie." The exchange was good-humoured. "I could list you a page of names of men that were boys back then and wouldn't take the time to think once, never mind twice, before finishing the Smiler off, if they got the chance. I'm not saying it would be right and I'm certainly not saying it would be wrong either. That's one that would take a brain better than mine to work out."

"Well, what's certain is that whoever did it thought about it a good deal," said the man called Ollie sagely and left the statement hanging.

Vince did not respond to the tease but Alice wanted to hear more.

"What do you mean, Ollie?"

Another man who had been listening on the sideline sat down and joined in the chat.

"I'm Fra," he said to Alice.

"I'm Alice."

He quickly turned his attention back to Ollie and waited for a response.

"Well, it seems as if there have been two men of the cloth killed in a very short space of time ... nearly a week ago. For now there's no talk of any arrest so whoever did it is smart enough not to get caught." He waited to see if anyone would argue the point with him but he was unchallenged. "Then," he said "there's the logistics of leaving two bodies at quite the distance from each other and in two different jurisdictions. Was that part of the plan to delay the detection work and make things more complicated for the forces of law and order? We know the north-south cooperation is great in theory but not always pursued with the same enthusiasm in practice."

"You're making a lot of sense, Ollie!" said Fra.

Vince was reserving judgment but listening with close interest.

Ollie was warming to his topic and others were gathering to listen.

"What connects these two deaths?" asked a younger man with a shock of ginger hair. "I know they are both religious and probably abusers but An Cuan is one thing ... I don't see how it connects to a priest that the papers say had a liking for young girls. I don't get it."

Ollie was ready with his analysis. "Your right, young man. The connection is one of the very interesting

291

things to think about. The killer might be someone who just doesn't like religious bucks and decided to kill a few at random. Let's remember that Ireland is a small place. It may be our executioner was in An Cuan and had a female family member who fell foul of the other fella in the North. Or again it could be the other way round. Maybe the killer is a woman who was abused by the priest and was close to one of Twomey's legions of victims. And those are only a few possibilities."

"I get you, Ollie, but how would that all work out in terms of ages? The papers said the priest was in his early sixties and we know well that the Smiler would be over eighty by now." This query came from a frighteningly thin man with a fragile voice and a worried expression. "I, for one, am glad the bastard was got by somebody and I hope they never get caught."

Ollie nodded slowly. "You won't be alone in that view, Jim, and we all know you have good reason to feel like that." He held the man in a kindly regard for a moment and nodded slowly several times so as to acknowledge the depth of the damage the man had suffered. "But let's think about the age question." He looked around and quipped, "Where's the numeracy tutor when you need them?"

This got a laugh from the small group now gathered around the table.

Alice watched the range of reactions carefully and thought that these men were not vicious enough to kill anyone. They were too harmed by their abusers to retaliate with the self-assurance needed to commit a double murder. They would be unlikely to have the resources needed to cover the ground between the two murder sites, never mind plan and set up the killings.

Ollie was doing the maths. "You're right to say we are talking about two different generations of abusers but let's stick with the one we know most about. An Cuan closed in seventy-four, forty years ago, so that is one natural cut-off point. Let's say that Smiler was in his early to mid-twenties in 1960 ... then we are talking about a period of fourteen years – from 1960 to 1974 during which our killer might have been an inmate. In other words our fella would now be aged somewhere between his mid-fifties at the youngest and mid-sixties if he was there during the earlier period." He looked at the man across the table from him and smiled wryly. "What were you doing last week, Vince, for example?"

There was a mix of laughter and muttering around the group as people speculated about the points Ollie had made.

"Do you think the gardaí will be interested in An Cuan men, Ollie?" The speaker was the younger man with red hair.

"Well, you're safe enough, young fella, but the detectives have quite a job ahead of them. It's not even certain it's someone who was in An Cuan but if it was then there are fourteen or so years of ex-inmates to consider. I'm sure there are some who left Ireland and never came back and some that have died young because of their poor start in life but even with that we're looking at several hundred potential suspects. That's just for starters."

People started to drift away towards classes and the conversation petered out for the moment. Ollie went back to his newspaper and Alice Fox turned to Vince sitting beside her. He had not been drawn into the conversation even when Ollie had pointed out that he was likely to be within the right age group he had calculated to be of interest.

"What sort of place was An Cuan, Vince? I know it was in a remote part of County Galway but that's all. And of course if you don't want to talk about it just say and I'll fully understand."

"No, you're all right, Alice. We spend a lot of time here talking about the past and trying to make sense of it. The counsellors say it's part of our healing process so I'm happy to tell you my story."

Alice nodded. Vince had a calmness that she liked. Both now and earlier in the focus group, it was clear he had been through a lot in his life and learned plenty.

"I remember arriving there as a small boy from quite a big town and being awestruck by the emptiness of the landscape. Nowadays Connemara is famous for its beautiful countryside but I suppose my beholder's eye has never been able to see it. I could see it was beautiful in some way when I was small but also shockingly empty." He paused and nodded as if he had just realised something for the first time. "I'm sure I was already quite empty myself having lost the only relative I had, in my mother. That makes me think that I was layering one void on another. This was just too much emptiness and my small mind was afraid of it all."

His almost poetic use of language caught Alice's imagination and she had a clear picture of the type of landscape he was describing.

'I'll bet, Vince," Alice said wholeheartedly. "Seems as if you were right in your first impressions too."

"Oh, indeed I was. It was a living hell and much of it engineered by the Smiler, as we called him. Even in his facial expression he was misleading us. When we knew by his words and his actions that he was in a foul temper, his face was still smiling. Such an evil, twisted and violent man." He was lost in the past for a few moments then continued thoughtfully. He rolled back one of his sleeves and showed Alice a series of scars where the skin was raised over welts that were white and shining as if overstretched. "These are just some of my mementos of the Smiler. My body is quite the map of his efforts to make me a better human being. And mine is only one of many such maps that chart the Smiler's zeal for punishing us."

Alice remained silent and attentive as the extent of this teacher's perverse testament was re-concealed beneath this gentle man's sweater sleeve. His sadness as he spoke was profound.

"People always associate working the land or with animals as being good for the spirit but the Smiler made sure that none of us will ever make that association. Even now, all those decades later, I'd much rather be inside and away from all vegetation and pets. The very smell of the countryside makes me feel anxious." He smiled faintly at Alice. "I am not a violent man, Alice, but when I heard that Twomey had been killed my first thought was relief that justice had finally been done. I'm sure I wasn't alone in that reaction."

43

Back in Belfast, with the images of the two victims side by side on the large screen, Caroline had outlined her findings about the staging of the bodies and the killer's distinctive signature.

She had talked in confidence to a behavioural psychologist who specialised in the aftermath of physical and sexual childhood abuse and had gained some useful insights. They had worked through the way the two bodies had been posed and the direct and indirect messages that seemed to be left there. The fact that the killer had significantly detailed knowledge of the two contexts of abuse, possibly decades apart, would be important in identifying him. Both murders were about settling old scores and punishing supposedly religious men who had separately abused boy children and young women. The psychologist had said the messages were there to articulate the killer's anger and his justification for making the men pay for their past misdemeanours. But the signature elements of the murders were also clearly designed to prompt analysis that would reveal what angered the killer in the victims' behaviours.

Quinn, the sexual abuser, was maimed and made to suffer the indignity of swallowing his own penis. The part of his body seen as central to the abuse was removed and used to symbolically silence him once and for all. Quinn's body had then been transported to St Oliver's, possibly from the other side of the border, and placed in a confessional. The implications of the confession box may have been his lack of suitability to listen to the sins of others when the killer found Quinn's behaviour totally reprehensible. Or it may have been the murderer's sense of irony, which the trauma expert thought was particularly evident in the way all the messages were framed. St Oliver's had a long association with a Mother and Baby home further up the Ormeau Road and, given the priests propensity for getting young women pregnant, that may be what prompted the killer to select that location. Caroline said that she wondered how they might go about determining a suspect's sense of irony but they could deal with that when the time came.

The psychologist felt that there was a possible crossover in the messages left on the two bodies that made it clear that one killer had committed both murders. The priest's arms were crossed in a posture of innocence that was well known to those who had heard accounts of childhood abuse in state and religious institutions. Boy children recounted being made to sleep with their hands in this position, or on top of the covers to ensure that they were not lured into the temptation of masturbation. Paradoxically, the same adults who would use these children for their own sexual gratification had created this sanctimonious regulation. Crossed arms seemed to the trauma expert to be more closely linked to institutional control and repression and she was inclined to think that this was the primary source of the murderer's deepest personal hurt.

Then there were the Beatitudes. Again, the typed messages were in capitals that implied the force with which they were articulated. The statement affixed to Quinn sounded sardonic to the expert and written to highlight Quinn's lack of humility. It may also have referred to the priest's victims whom the killer wanted to elevate above reproach. It is they who were 'meek' and would 'inherit the earth' while their abuser would suffer the final ignominy of public exposure and humiliation.

As a result of the phone call that outlined the daisy-chain incident, reading the killer's messages about Brother Francis Twomey had become somewhat easier. The victim's left hand had been removed, indicating that the offensive body part for Twomey was the hand with which he used to severely beat the boys in his care. The expert made the point that the extremes of physical abuse in industrial schools were not devoid of a sexual element, particularly when boys were stripped naked and left exposed for long periods of time. The added cruelty of this was to be found in the testimony of those who phoned the freephone number. A sizeable number of them pointed out that Twomey freely used his left hand to abuse them while they were repeatedly physically punished and verbally abused if they attempted to write with their left hand. Using a left hand in the classroom caused them to be accused of unnatural and even demonic behaviour.

Callers also identified that Twomey used deprivation of food as a way of reprimanding children who had incurred his displeasure. This was one of his favoured ways of wielding power over those dependent on him for satisfaction of their most basic needs. The bread placed in the dead man's mouth and the beatitude that referred to those who "hunger and thirst after righteousness" again used irony to highlight the man's torturous behaviour. Twomey had been killed where he lived after the taunting promise of a wholesome meal. The added visual reference to his nickname confirmed that his killer wished the Smiler to pay the ultimate price for his ill treatment of the boys in his care.

Caroline ended this input by stating that forensics had

reported that the paper, font, ink and safety pins used were identical but not remarkable in any way. The pins were possibly another reference to the ill-treatment of young babies placed in residential institutions where they received no care or affection but some of these messages left by the killer might never be deciphered by anyone other than him. She looked at her three colleagues and asked if she had overlooked anything in terms of what the killer had communicated with the remains of his victims.

Pradić had been looking intently at the images in front of her. Now she spoke slowly and carefully. "Perhaps we can deduce from the unusual direction of the safety pins that our killer was also left-handed."

Caroline reproved herself silently for missing this clue. In the midst of crime scenes that were laden with messages they had all overlooked something important.

"You're right, Zara," declared McVeigh, "and that would probably be one more reason for his fury against Brother Twomey."

"Well spotted, Zara." Paton looked sternly at Burrows and McVeigh. "The rest of us need to sharpen our game if we are not to miss essential details in the evidence." And she beat her breast with her clenched fist to include herself in the admonishment.

Burrows and McVeigh looked suitably cowed at having incurred Paton's criticism. She rowed back from the negative mood.

"Let's look on the bright side. Thank you, Zara. We

are becoming clearer about the perpetrator profile. Perhaps, Zara, you could draw together all the data we have in that regard and we'll come together later to consider that. In the meantime we have plenty to get on with. Also, Ian, can you look at who we've questioned who may be left-handed."

They spent some time agreeing their next steps. As well as accumulating all they had from both jurisdictions on the perpetrator profile, Pradić said she would do some online searches about records from An Cuan. If there were school registers or census data accessible she would cross-reference them with the names of callers to the helplines and see what that produced.

Burrows was looking perplexed and the others were waiting to see what he wanted to say. "I was going to say that it might be useful to include names of those in the survivors' groups North and South to see what that yields. I think, as we said earlier, it has been becoming clearer that we need to be engaging with the communities of survivors of abuse both North and South. I know it sounds invasive as an approach and I'm not even sure how we could do that but in terms of motive it seems that they are an obvious cohort." He was choosing his words carefully and demonstrating even more than his usual degree of sensitivity. "And of course we need to find ways of doing that where we are not adding to the pain and distress that they have already experienced in their lives."

McVeigh nodded in agreement. "Maybe it's about asking for their help rather than approaching them as possible suspects ... but then again the survivors may well think both these guys got their fair comeuppance. Why would they be speaking out against someone who had delivered what they might see as these guys getting their just deserts?"

Caroline could see this thread was likely to become more and more tangled if they continued to try to follow it at this point in time. "Let's continue to go at this step by step, guys, and not try to rush ahead. You made your point about survivor sensitivities earlier, Bill, and we may need more advice on that one but for the moment let's continue to dig into the other leads we have. Let's see what your trip to Hilltown Bay turns up tomorrow and I'm sure DI Hegarty will be back to us soon about the follow-up on Quinn's car."

This case investigation could easily become a sprawling mess, she thought to herself, but there was no way she was going to allow that to happen.

"Lunch, anyone, before we get started on the next steps?"

All three of her colleagues followed her through the door in the direction of the canteen. Caroline smiled to herself as she observed that Pradić was going to take the risk of eating with them.

* * *

Two detectives from the southern investigation team drew into the car park of the Lonely Duck public house just after eleven. They reviewed the cameras in the car park and then made their way to the office where they were to meet the owner and the barman who had been on duty when Quinn was there. The owner had done his homework and reviewed the CCTV from the previous Tuesday when Quinn's car was left in his car park. The cleric is seen arriving and making his way into the bar but there is no camera inside the premises so there is no visual evidence of the man he meets. He does not exit into the same car park, which suggests that the person he met was parked along the minor road to the front of the premises. At this entrance the camera is focused on the doorway where any altercations tend to take place at closing time and there is only a brief blurred image of the two men leaving around half past two that afternoon.

The barman was an anxious young guy whose right leg was hopping in perpetual motion. He was from the locality and said that he had never seen either man before. Quinn had been wearing a scarf and so he had not realised that he was a priest until he had seen his picture in the paper. He recalled that the priest had two large whiskies while they were there and the other man had mineral water. Neither ate anything and he got the impression they were on their way somewhere else. They had talked for almost an hour and then left together by the front door. He wasn't able to say for certain but assumed they had gone in the direction of the coast. The road led directly to a number of small seaside resorts popular with Dublin people.

The barman was vague about the description of the second man. When he had recognised the priest from the Sunday paper he contacted his boss to report the car to the gardaí. The other man had not removed his baseball cap during his time in the pub so his face was constantly in shadow. The bar was busy with lunchtime customers including a community group who were booked into the function room for a morning meeting followed by lunch. If he was pressed he said he would say the guy was not young … maybe late fifties, early sixties. Of an age with the priest really, he thought. He was quietly spoken, maybe with a country accent, and when he arrived he had shaken hands with the priest in such a way that he gave the impression they were meeting for the first time. He was a good bit smaller than the priest and wore a black leather jacket and jeans.

The detectives took the details of the local community group so that they could check if any of them might have been able to add to the description of the man who had now become of prime interest. When the Irish detectives left they took the road out to the coast so that they could get the lie of the land and check in on some of the holiday parks in the area before heading back into the city centre.

44

Just after three, Martha emerged from one of the teaching rooms in the Phoenix Centre and tapped Alice on the shoulder. "Are you ready for a cuppa, Alice?"

Alice's conversation with Vince and Ollie had continued after the others had moved away to join in classes or other conversations but Alice was happy to spend some time with Martha now. She said her goodbyes and thanked the men for sharing their stories with her.

On her way past the reception desk she stopped to let the woman know she was leaving and how grateful she was for all she had learned.

Martha led the way to the corner café, linking Alice's arm amicably and telling her about her English class. They had been discussing a poem about a woman who said she was going to wear purple clothes when she was old and drink brandy.

"My teacher says that when you get old you don't have to be well-behaved any more." She laughed at the very idea of it. "She says that we need to think about how to get better at being silly!"

Alice knew the poem that she was talking about and said she thought Martha's teacher was a very wise woman and the two of them skipped down the road, laughing and getting out of breath.

Their mood shifted abruptly as they arrived into the café and saw Brian sitting at a table for four and looking very downcast.

"What's wrong, love?" Martha immediately sat beside him and hugged his arm as if he might otherwise escape from her.

"Sit down and we'll order our coffee and cake, Martha, and I'll tell you what's on my mind." And he waved to the waiter who was busy arranging a display of brightly coloured doughnuts behind the counter.

Alice noted that Brian's complexion had retained a pallor she had previously construed as fatigue and wondered now if he might in fact be ill. She thought too about Martha's devotion to him and indeed her reliance on him in so many ways but stopped herself short of imposing her own fears about the fragility of life on the circumstances of others.

He was tenderly asking Martha about her day and what type of cake she wanted and, as if to endorse Alice's observations about their relationship, Martha's reply was, "You choose for me, Brian. You always get those things just right."

Brian ordered for himself and Martha and Alice ordered an americano and passed on the cake.

When they were served and settled at the table Martha looked inquisitively at Brian. "Well, go on then. Tell me what was making you look so worried when we came in."

"Well, the first thing to say is that I'm glad you're both here." He nodded meaningfully at Alice. "OK so … this morning, a good while after you had gone into the Phoenix, I was round in your place having a look at that leak under the bathroom sink and there was a knock at the door. They always wait until you're in a tight corner to call, don't they?" He smiled at Alice who nodded in agreement at his wit. "Anyway it was two detectives who had called to talk to you, Martha." He looked warily at his partner, gauging her response to this, and seemed relieved that she wasn't obviously concerned.

"Did you ask them what they wanted?" She had a large piece of cake in her mouth and was only vaguely concerned with his answer.

At the same time Brian's anxiety was clear to Alice and she saw in that moment that as well as the practical ways in which he cared for her there was a sizeable emotional burden for which he also assumed responsibility. Martha was protected to some extent by her lack of engagement with the complexities of life.

Alice was sure that this wasn't a conscious choice on Martha's part but a lifestyle response that had resulted from years of having little understanding about how things worked in the world. Martha's educational neglect had also in many ways cushioned her against some of the harsher elements of being an adult.

"They wanted to ask you some questions about what happened to that priest in Belfast," he went on. "When they went through his papers they discovered that your name was also there, as well as Brenda and Jed. Apparently he had done some checks into Brenda's background and your name had come up as her birth mother. That makes you a person of interest to their inquiry, they said."

Martha was now giving more of her attention to Brian's news.

"I'm sure I won't know the answer to their questions. Will you be able to come with me, Brian?" She began to worry as the prospect of speaking to the police became clearer.

"I said I would bring you to Harcourt Street Station this afternoon and then I phoned Brenda. She suggested that Alice would be the best person to go with you, as she knew how these things worked." He looked at Alice now to see if she was willing to play the role that was on offer.

She looked at her watch and then took out her phone.

"I'll just need to check that my going along with Martha fits with the PSNI strategy. I don't want to ruffle feathers there." And she smiled to herself at the image that suggested.

There were several missed calls from DS Burrows and a message to say that she was required to accompany a vulnerable witness in Dublin later in the afternoon if that worked in terms of her schedule. She texted him back to say that she was able to do that and would phone him from the train later that evening. Then she looked at Brian and Martha who were looking expectantly at her.

"Well, folks," she said good-humouredly, "it looks as if we have a date in Harcourt Street. We'll need to move swiftly now if I'm to be able to catch the later train."

Brian went to settle the bill and Martha took Alice's arm as they headed for the door. "This feels like a very busy day, Alice Fox, doesn't it?" And she smiled quite happily. "I feel like I should be wearing something purple," she said and laughed impishly at the younger woman beside her.

On the seven o'clock evening train from Dublin's Connolly Station to Belfast, Alice had a sizeable amount of space to herself in her carriage. It was a pleasant change from the stiflingly busy morning journey. Burrow's phone went directly to answering machine and she texted him to say – **Mission** accomplished. **Talk when you're free** – then she settled down to read a paper Tara had brought her about a social harm perspective on the Irish industrial school system. She felt she had already had quite a day full of immersion into that sad history but before the introduction was finished she was fully engaged in the article and the journey time passed by virtually unnoticed.

Emerging through the barrier at Belfast's Central Station, Alice was surprised to see Caroline waving at her in welcome. "I always think it's very lonely not to be met off a train or a flight," she said as she enveloped Alice in a warm hug.

"You know just how to surprise a woman, DI Paton. I was wondering if I had the energy left in my body to walk up to Botanic. It must be all of twenty minutes!" She mimed exaggerated tiredness and took her partner's arm. "There's nothing else for it, officer. I need a little light sustenance and then I need to be put straight to bed."

Caroline laughed heartily. 'For once we are totally in agreement, Doctor Fox. Just put yourself in my hands and, before you know it, everything will be just tickety-boo."

"I'm not completely familiar with the local dialect, DI Paton, but I'm hoping that I accurately get your drift about the direction the evening is taking."

And they happily made their way arm in arm to the car park on the lower level.

* * *

Alice and Caroline lay peacefully side by side in the back bedroom in the solid Victorian house just off Botanic Avenue. It was a quiet room spared the worst excesses of late-night student activity by its solid walls, additional insulation and double-glazing. The bedside light glowed amber and made mountainous shadows of the duvet that they had pushed back because of the heat.

Alice had considered whether or not to raise the issue of Caroline's childhood spectres and decided that it was better to make sure her lover wasn't dealing with her issues in solitude.

"Caro ..." she began as she pushed herself onto her elbow so as to make eye contact with her partner. She moved her other hand to cradle her lover's face and smiled at the sense of contentment they shared at the end of their busy day. "I just want to check that you're not too haunted by your recollections of your uncle's abuse. I don't want to reopen that issue but I want to be sure that you're at peace for the moment."

Caroline smiled at Alice's fearless approach to life's difficulties. She wasn't one to run away from monsters and Caroline was glad to be under her protective wing.

"No, Alice. I'm not tortured at all, thanks to your early intervention. In fact, I'm planning on taking some overdue holidays when this case is wrapped up and thought that would be a good time to find a counsellor who will allow me to lay the whole business to rest." She put her hand behind her head and turned slightly towards Alice. "Actually, my psychic one, I'm meeting a second expert psychologist tomorrow to talk about our perp and thought I might ask her if she knows any good people in this line of work." She shivered a little and pulled the duvet around them. "But I'm managing to keep the personal stuff in its place for now. Thank you for asking." And she reached upwards to put a gentle kiss on Alice's nose.

"I've been thinking a lot today about my time in Dublin ... is it OK to talk a little bit about work?"

Caroline nodded. "Go ahead."

"I feel like I had an immersion in the survivor's world and it has stayed with me and got me wondering about the question of 'why now?' I mean it was clear to me talking to the men in the Phoenix and then later with Martha ... the reality of their history is always very close to the surface for them. It never fades. There are so many reminders ... especially when it's in the news like now ... or so often in TV dramas and soaps. Sometimes it seems like every branch of the media is saturated with stories of childhood abuse."

"I know, Alice. Sometimes it seems inescapable."

"What I mean is the currency of the topic is not new. It's ongoing. So what has prompted our killer to act now? My conclusion is that perhaps the change is not in the wider social context but rather in the circumstances of the individual. What has happened that means that the inhibitors that were in place for decades have now been removed? The men in the Phoenix were doing the math yesterday. Assuming that the person was actually an inmate of An Cuan, he'll have finished there at the latest in 1974 when it closed. That being forty years ago the killer may be in his mid-fifties or older. Has something happened to him personally that means he no longer fears the opprobrium of killing or the consequences in his life? I think those who have been incarcerated, particularly as children, would not easily forfeit their freedom. Why take that risk now?"

Caroline sat up and pulled the duvet up under her chin. "It's an interesting question, Alice. Our killer has been very clever and very careful but of course we are edging closer and he will know that. He must have links to the survivors' community and be aware of our focus closing in. He may even have been there yesterday when you were in the Phoenix ... " She grimaced and said, "I hope that you're not putting yourself in any danger, Alice." She paused and then smiled wryly. "Or maybe I should be worried for the wellbeing of our killer after your last encounter with one of our murder suspects."

And they both were drawn back to a previous case,

where Alice's proficiency in Tae Kwon Do had meant she very much got the upper hand when she was confronted in the dark by a very unpleasant individual.

"Don't worry unnecessarily, Caro. I'm able to look after myself, and anyway this killer has some very precise targets and I do not fit the bill." She could see Caroline was struggling to stay awake. "Let's get some sleep now. I want to get going a bit earlier tomorrow as I have the meeting in the evening and then I have a lot of writing to catch up on. I need to fit some time for my research into the week as well. You'll have to make lying in bed with you a little less alluring or I'm going to be in bother with my supervisor!" And she laughed playfully and switched off the light. "Good night, lovely Caro, and sweet dreams."

Caroline merely murmured something indistinguishable and was already asleep.

45

DS Bill Burrows called Alice at eight the next morning as she was just heading out for a run along the river, a little later than usual. Caroline had just left fifteen minutes before the phone rang and Alice consciously tried to erase all memory of her as she listened to the Murder Squad second-in-command at the other end of the phone. Burrows wanted to meet as early as possible as he and McVeigh had interviews scheduled outside the city for most of the day.

When he heard that she planned to be in her office in DePRec by ten o'clock, he said he would call and see her then. "We're heading to Hilltown Bay so we can go directly from the college," he said as he planned his route aloud. He explained that he wanted to get her feedback about her day in Dublin and talk to her about making links with the Squad's new digital wizard. He also wanted to discuss with her the possibility of her taking on another meeting with a survivors' group, on behalf of the investigation team.

Although she wasn't fully briefed on the developments in the case, Alice was forming her own views and was pleased to be able to talk them through with Bill Burrows whom she found to be a sensitive and astute detective.

At five to ten Alice bounded up the stairs to her fifth-floor office. From the corridor outside she heard Mairéad Walsh, the departmental manager's infectious gurgling laugh that she reserved for her special callers.

DS Burrows was relaxed in a comfortable chair and clearly enjoying the older woman's witty conversation. He stood up and assumed a serious expression when Alice appeared.

"Good morning, Dr Fox," he greeted her. "Thank you for agreeing to see me so promptly. I will be as speedy as I can and let you get on with your day's work." And he followed Alice into her office.

Mairéad made one of her dramatic faces behind Burrows' back and winked conspiratorially at Alice.

Once Alice and Burrows were seated, she briefed him about her day in Dublin. Firstly there was the background information she had gleaned from her time with the survivors she had met. Alice told Burrows that she had gained considerable insight both into the treatment of children in An Cuan and other institutions and how this had impacted on them subsequently throughout their lives. Brother Twomey, or Smiler as the men called him, was not being mourned by anyone with whom she had talked. He had abused all of them to a greater or lesser extent and any one of them might have a motive to seek revenge for their ill treatment. Alice shared her view that the men she had met did not appear to have the temperament to carry out two killings within a short time span and in different parts of the country. Given the number of boys that had been through An Cuan, the logistics of tracking down someone with a motive to murder Twomey were hard to quantify. She could imagine that anyone who had been in An Cuan until its closure in 1974 could potentially be angry enough to kill. You were talking about hundreds of possible perpetrators at least, so the connection to Quinn would have to be the defining variable she suggested. Who had a connection to both abusers and at the same time had the capacity and resources to plan and implement the murders?

Then there was Martha's interview with the gardaí. Despite having appeared unconcerned at the prospect of the interview, when in situ the woman had become distressed at having to be in the Garda Station, never mind answering questions. She had regressed to the default position of frightened, powerless child and it had taken all Alice's mediation skill to coax the gardaí to allow Martha the space to feel comfortable enough to understand and answer their questions. Alice explained to Burrows that Martha was used to her partner, Brian, relieving the pressure of difficult situations for her and without his support she could quickly flounder. Anyway Martha was clear that she didn't know anything about a Christian Brother called Twomey and she had only heard the priest's name for the first time during the past weekend. She knew that a priest had taken advantage of Brenda but Brenda had never told her his name.

Alice told Burrows that she had made some reflective notes on the train and she would email them to him when she had tidied them up a bit. She hoped they might just make some sense to him and help him make a useful connection.

Burrows reached forward and placed a business card on Alice's desk. "DC Zara Pradić is coordinating a lot of the information we're processing for this inquiry including from the southern colleagues. Send your notes to Zara as well, please, and if you think of something that might be of use from your conversations with the survivors' groups then contact her directly. She knows to expect your call."

Alice added Pradić's number to her phone.

Then Burrows raised the issue of Alice attending the survivors' meeting in the Belfast Amnesty International offices with Brenda Clinton that evening. She told him that she already planned to go along but that she would let the organisers know in advance that she was associated with the police murder inquiry in her capacity as a support worker for vulnerable witnesses. She didn't want there to be any hint of duplicity in her role.

She knew that the interests of the Murder Squad and individual witnesses might well be conflicting and she thought it best to forewarn him. "It hasn't happened yet, Sergeant Burrows, but I can see a time when our collaboration may be in conflict with my conscience."

Burrows seemed unconcerned.

"I'd say, Dr Fox, we'll find a way to deal with that when the time comes." He placed both palms flat on his sizeable tummy and smiled at her. "As you can see … I'm not one for running back and forward across bridges unnecessarily. Best to cross them when the time is right."

They both nodded in agreement at the wisdom of this approach to life and arranged to talk again that evening after the Amnesty meeting.

Alice's jottings from the previous day took a little longer to organise than she expected. She realised that to be useful she needed to share them in a logical form. In actual fact, she decided not long into the exercise that what she was doing was taking on an investigator role herself. She smiled to herself at the powerful allure that detection had for her. The thought processes involved were those she was deploying daily in her academic work and she understood clearly why the transition into a criminal inquiry was pretty seamless. What had she really learned the previous day in the Phoenix Centre? She began her list.

1. Survivors in the South are ahead of those in the North in every stage of addressing the legacy of childhood abuse ... did that mean they were more likely to be killers or not? Had they greater closure? Had they had more time to plan a complicated murder?

2. Experiences and impacts of abuse are the same across the island and so the killer could be from either place ... but the An Cuan connection is very strong and suggests a killer from the South ... possibly the west of Ireland.

3. It's possible that institutional and clerical abuse cause irreparable damage. There was no sign that the pain went away. Like a chronic disease, their abuse baggage was a central element of people's daily lives. There is a link here to motivation but not necessarily agency.

4. All who had been in his care universally disliked Brother Francis Twomey. No sadness (aside from by association) was occasioned by his death. In fact it was clear that for some his killing had delivered a sense of justice.

5. Anyone in a large number of survivors of An Cuan (and every other such school) would arguably

have a motive for Twomey's murder either on their own behalf or because of the wrongs against the collective. How does Quinn fit alongside this? He had no apparent links to industrial schools either north or south.

6. No evidence in the Centre of crossover between the two contexts of the killings. Those in the Phoenix did not appear concerned to any degree with the death of Father Quinn … Finding someone with a link to both victims is a key element to this case.

7. There is a gender dimension too. An Cuan was an entirely male institution while Quinn's targets were all young women … Somehow those issues come together for the perpetrator. Someone who has come to see abuse as something that happens to all genders; someone who has first-hand experience/accounts of abuse of both boys and young women. Might youth be a salient factor?

8. The killer is clever, well organised and clear about the messages he leaves. He knows how to apply a chokehold and has access to transport that allows him to move a dead body. That all suggests a certain level of physical strength and determination. Unless someone is covering for him, he is independent enough to murder twice without attracting too much attention or questioning from others around him.

And then Alice was halted by another thought altogether. It wasn't completely clear just this moment but some disparate pieces of the current situation had just slotted unexpectedly together and she was halted in her tracks. Before she could grasp the picture clearly, her phone rang and Brenda Clinton's name flashed onto the screen.

"I was just thinking about your mum, Brenda. I'm sure you heard about our spell with the gardaí. She was going to talk to you yesterday evening after they left me off at the station in Dublin. Your mum was an absolute trooper!"

"She told me you were sure she was able for it – and so she knew that must be right." Brenda laughed. "She's so open to trust – even after all that's happened in her life. She never fails to give me hope!"

And Alice wondered when it would become clear why Brenda had called her. She didn't have to wait long.

"Alice, I want to ask you a big favour."

She waited and Alice responded with an open mind. "OK."

"Jed and I have been talking here and he wants to go to his father's funeral on Friday, in Dublin. We'll meet up with Mam and Brian afterwards at least. I think Brian has something he has to do at the same time as the funeral. It's some regular Friday thing that he can't miss. Mum isn't sure about going without Brian but I feel it would be good for us to be a family, with Jed like, when he meets all his father's ones after the funeral Mass."

"I see," said Alice, becoming clearer about what the forthcoming request might be.

"Will you come with us, Alice? You know you've kind of got yourself a job as our social secretary." Brenda feigned helplessness. "We can only meet other people if you come with us," she pleaded, half laughing.

"I'm soon going to need a season ticket for that Dublin train," Alice quipped. "And of course I'd be happy to come along, Brenda. In fact I was going to call you about going to the northern survivors' meeting this evening. I'd be gathering some learning about the group for the local PSNI and of course I'm interested myself anyway. They don't think it would be appropriate for them to weigh into a meeting. A little heavy maybe … I think they're right of course and if they had lots of time I'm sure they would ease in gently but just right now … Do I sound like I'm over-justifying this, Brenda?"

"Maybe." The other woman laughed. "But I'm not going to be Norma Nitpicky. Why don't you phone Amnesty and say you'll be coming? It's an open meeting anyway but it would be better, I think. I don't like secrets … as I'm sure you'll understand."

"I'll see you there this evening and we'll grab five minutes afterwards to agree the times for Friday."

Alice was glad she would be about for Jed on Friday when he would come face to face with the paternal part of his human heritage. She was also hoping to put part of her budding theory about this case to the test. For now, she turned her mind back to her list of yesterday's learning that she wanted to send to Burrows before lunchtime. She added some insights about the perpetrator that she had gained from her day in Dublin and sent the list in an email to Burrows and copied Pradić. She had a few clear hours now when she could finally get on with some of her overdue paperwork before heading west to the EXIT group for a chat with Hugo about this evening's session which she was going to miss.

46

On the northern side of the border, further up the coast from the area explored by the Irish detectives the previous day, Burrows and McVeigh were immersed in a series of interviews with local people who had known Father Quinn during his time in their parish. They had begun their inquiries in the comfortable home of the Ganley family with whom Theresa de Paor, first mentioned by Nancy Quinn, had been in service as a young girl. Mrs Ganley had contacted the police helpline in response to the request for information from those who had known Michael Quinn during his time in the town. She was keen to point out that it was only long after the event that her family had heard locally that Theresa had been associated with the murdered priest. She said that they had been appalled at the discovery but that it had explained why the young woman had left so unexpectedly, claiming that she had found work in England and would not be coming back. At the time they had contacted the nuns who had originally provided Theresa as a home help but they had been far from helpful and did not seem interested in the girl's fate. As far as the Ganleys knew, Theresa had no family and they had long ago forgotten about her. Now they wondered what had become of Theresa and what her relationship with the dead priest had actually been.

From Ganleys' detached coastal splendour they had called to the modest home of Gerry Bailey, the youth club bus driver. He admitted to being shaken by the news of the priest's murder.

"I worked very closely with Father Quinn over the years," he said. "We drove the youth club members to Lourdes every summer to work with the pilgrims and then down to Spain for a week's break. He always treated me well and he was good company. He liked his drink and we had some great laughs together." Bailey seemed to remember then that his duties had not all been innocent fun and he dropped his head as if the shame were his by association. "When he asked me to sit guard inside, at the front of the bus I didn't think too much about it. I was a bit slow. I thought he wanted to talk to the girls privately and my job was to stop them being disturbed. When the penny dropped, I was a bit surprised at his behaviour but I didn't think it was my place to criticise the priest. You're talking over twenty years ago. Different times. I honestly never thought of it as abuse, ye know. But I can see now that it wasn't right."

Burrows looked at this man and thought he was punishing himself enough for his collusion and didn't need them to add to the weight on his conscience.

"You had a daughter in the youth club, Mr Bailey. Was she aware of what was going on between the priest and some of the girls?"

Bailey looked horrified. "You don't think I would have allowed that to happen to my own daughter, do you?"

A chasm opened between the two men and Burrows hoped that he had prepared his children well enough to be good people in this strange world. At least he hoped they would be indiscriminately kind.

"I didn't imagine that would be the case," Burrows said pointedly. "I just wondered if she might have noticed anything from her perspective. We have arranged to talk to her when we finish here."

Bailey just nodded in a defeated manner as Burrows asked a final question.

"Mr Bailey, have you been aware of anyone asking about Father Quinn recently. Maybe someone from another part of the country, asking questions perhaps or trying to start a discussion about former times."

Bailey just shook his head and muttered, "Sorry. No. Sorry."

* * *

Burrows and McVeigh had soup and sandwiches in the local pub. They took the chance to question the barman and a few locals installed on high stools at the bar about anyone asking questions in the recent past about Quinn and his time in the town. The barman was from Moldova and only recently recruited to the job and the men at the bar were disinterested and unhelpful. It only struck him later that if he'd bought them a drink they might have been more talkative.

Laura Bailey taught at the local primary school and they had arranged to talk to her there at two o'clock when the younger children had gone home. When they arrived, the school working day was still in full swing for the older years that didn't stop until three o'clock. Miss Bailey's classroom was a testament to someone who was skilled and devoted to her job. It was bright and every surface was covered with some carefully presented stimulus to satisfy the inquiring young mind. McVeigh was struck by the contrast of their investigation now taking them into this place of innocence. He felt he needed to keep his voice low so as not to allow his questions to pollute the environment. Laura Bailey told them that back in the day everybody did not know about Father Quinn's activities but that some of the more savvy girls had noticed that he paid special attention to those who had no family behind them. Personally she had known Brenda only a little but she knew Theresa better because she lived in the area all the year round.

"Theresa was a very gentle girl who had spent all her time in care and working in the homes of richer people. You'd have thought she was younger than she actually was. She had a hard time with the nuns. They were mad into Irish language and all the girls were given the Irish version of their names. De Paor sounded quite exotic to us back then!" McVeigh took notes and Burrows tried to bring Laura back to the focus on time around Theresa's disappearance.

"Can you remember how she got drawn into a relationship with Father Quinn, Laura?"

"She was grateful for any attention and I could see that Quinn was specially interested in her. He was flattered by her interest in him ... and she was very pretty in her own way." She stopped to gather her thoughts and then continued. "I knew when she was pregnant because she got into a complete panic and told me herself. I think she had a brother and she thought he was somewhere in the south. They had lost contact as small children and she was trying to contact him but I'm not sure she ever succeeded. In the end, I remember that Quinn's family paid for her to have an abortion in England and she said she would never come back. She promised she would send me a contact when she got settled but I never heard from her again. That's over twenty years ago now and she could be dead and buried for all I know."

After some brief and unproductive calls with freephone contacts, Burrows and McVeigh had made their final visit in the home of the elderly parish priest who remembered Quinn clearly.

"We couldn't have him here any longer," he said without any of the dissimulation often present in such conversations about errant clerics. He grimaced when he spoke. "I certainly don't want to speak ill of the dead but Father Quinn was not able to live a celibate life and this parish is too small to keep that type of behaviour from getting out and causing trouble. He had to go. I told the Bishop that enough was enough and that he had to be moved from here immediately." The older man made no attempt to make the issue one of morality rather than social acceptability and the conversation was not extended any further. The Church had moved the problem away rather than acknowledging or dealing with the wrongdoing and it was left to others to deal with the immediate and longer-term consequences. It was a depressing and familiar story that numbed the spirit of these seasoned investigators. Strangely, the two detectives felt relieved to be driving away from the beautiful coastal town and back to Murder Squad HQ in Belfast.

When they arrived back in the office DI Paton came out to meet them. "Just in case you think your day by the sea is finished, guys, we have some interesting stuff in from forensics on the oil and other deposits on the nun's jacket and in the downstairs loo in St Oliver's."

Burrows made an exaggerated dramatised scene of being overwhelmed and needing to sit down and mop his brow. Paton couldn't help but laugh. Burrows' occasional Bette Davis moments never failed to take her unawares. "OK! Here it is!" and she fluttered some single sheets at him with the Forensics' distinctive logo on the top. "The oil is one most frequently used in farm machinery or vintage motor cycle maintenance. And … the soil that may be from the perp's shoes, and found in both murder locations, has ingredients – minerals, pesticides and such like, that match an intensive vegetable farming area along the coast in North Dublin."

"How very curious indeed!" responded Burrows, suddenly reverting to his serious self. "Perhaps one of Brother Twomey's students became a vegetable farmer, despite a rough apprenticeship in An Cuan."

"That's a bit of a leap, Bill, but it does fit with the area where Quinn's car turned up and suggests that is a location of significant interest for our colleagues in the south. I'll talk to DI Hegarty this evening but I think it may be a good moment to have a full staff joint review of where we all are at this point, a full week into the investigation. I'll speak to DI Hegarty later and see when suits." She was headed to her office but remembered something else and turned back towards her three colleagues. "I've been thinking that we might use the Press Conference slot tomorrow evening to gather in some more public support. Our killer has a lot of public sympathy for his actions but we need to get another narrative out there that doesn't demonise survivors of abuse but also stops the idea that murder can equate to some kind of civic justice."

Before Caroline had time to return to her office again, Pradić swung her chair around from where she had been engrossed in her multiple screens and addressed her colleagues.

"Might I ask that we have a meeting ourselves before speaking to the larger investigation team. I may have some things to share, about which I need the advice of the team."

This was unexpected from the woman who had become well known in the force for her solitary work style and Caroline saw it as just another positive sign that Pradić was finding a niche in the Murder Squad with which she was comfortable.

"Good idea, Pradić. Might tomorrow early afternoon be good? I'll hold off with DI Hegarty for the time being. We have plenty to be getting on with in the meantime. Let us know as soon as you're ready for a confab." And she returned to her office and rang through to Eileen in the canteen to see what fuel she might provide for her busy workers.

Alice had a brief but relaxing time with Hugo and brought him up to date with the events in Jed's life. She withheld her suspicions about the identity of Jed's father's killer until she could discuss them with the Murder Squad and be sure the back-up evidence was there.

"Just as well you're here," Hugo said earnestly. "I can't imagine how I would have been able to cope without you. Jed would not have got all the support you're giving if it had been down to me alone." He looked lost in thought for a moment and then fixed Alice with an unusually serious expression. "I think we have shown over the past six months that there is at least a part time position here in EXIT for another worker. Would you be interested in that as a paid proposition, Alice?" His expression was equal parts enthusiasm and fear.

She realised he was afraid she would turn down his offer and was careful in her response.

"Hugo! That's a very interesting idea for sure." She smiled at him and his shoulders dropped several inches in relief. She raised a hand to stop him rushing ahead. "I don't think I am allowed to take on paid work while I'm on a post-doc scholarship and so I can't change that status until August at the earliest, when my place in DePRec comes to an end."

"But you haven't said no, Alice, and that's encouraging. Might you consider staying on in Ireland?" He raised his eyebrows roguishly. "Say you'll think about it and I'll do some lobbying and see what the funding possibilities are. You could write your book and do some work here and I'm sure DePRec would take you on for some lecturing hours. They'd be mad not to."

Alice's head began to buzz with the permutations and possibilities he was presenting. "I promise I will think carefully about all that, Hugo. I need to think about the folks at home who are expecting me back. Right now I'm on my way to the survivors' meeting in Amnesty with Brenda so I need to park this topic for now." She didn't want him to think she wasn't appreciative. "To be continued. I promise, Hugo."

And she collected her bike from the alcove and headed of into the murky Belfast evening and another meeting with survivors harmed while in the care of the State.

Alice had reported to Burrows on her way home from the Amnesty meeting with Brenda and been invited by him to join their meeting the following afternoon.

"You have a unique insight now into the survivors' world, Alice," he had said "and we are not in a position to weigh in there and probably just upset people. We need you to be our eyes and ears."

She hadn't made any comment in response to that. Something about the idea displeased her. It sounded covert and underhand and not a quality she wanted to add to her repertoire.

During the night, Alice was tortured by the idea that

she should have reported her hunch about the killer's identity to the team the previous day but had decided to keep it for the meeting. She told herself that she needed to take the time to become clearer about her position. Survivors of institutional and clerical abuse needed support, understanding and redress, she thought. But if they decide to kill their childhood aggressors, or those who have mindlessly hurt others, was that justifiable? She was clear that the criminal justice system was flawed and it was a travesty that those who harmed fragile children and young women rarely had to answer for their actions. And yet, was it tolerable for anyone to take on the role of executioner? She really didn't think so even though she absolutely understood why that might happen.

47

Late on Wednesday night/Thursday morning, an email from Detective Constable Zara Pradić arrived, which was '**copied in confidence**' to Alice Fox. Over an early coffee the following morning at the kitchen table, Alice consulted the detail and watched Caroline do the same, without comment.

"I'm assuming, Caroline, that you feel more comfortable if we don't discuss the case in our private time ..." and she closely observed her lover's reaction.

The senior detective met her earnest gaze and smiled. "Well, I am conscious of boundaries and how easily they can be breached and then how quickly that in turn can impact negatively on other working relationships." She raised her eyebrows and waited to gauge Alice's level of agreement.

Alice remained quiet.

"I think your collaboration with Burrows and McVeigh is working quite well and I think it's logical that you receive some useful info – like this profile for example. Burrows is going to suggest that you join a pivotal case review that we plan to have today when Pradić is ready. Your exchange of info with Burrows is fine but there are always things that are picked up that don't make it into the notes … better if you are there in person. I know Burrows has told you to make contact directly with DC Pradić if there is something you want her to check. She is cross-referencing lists of names from institutional records, UK and Irish army recruits, violent assault convictions and lists of registered martial arts participants. Maybe you heard something in one of the survivors' centres that you could pass on to her. If you can give her a steer about anything, don't hold back."

"That's all fine with me for now, Caro, but I want it to be clear that I am not keen on secrets, especially when they border on deception. People who have been kept in the dark about something can see it as a slight… a failure to trust their ability to cope with the truth … or maybe even a sense of shame about a relationship. How would you deal with our situation if it was a heterosexual relationship?"

There was no rancour in Alice's response and Caroline nodded in acceptance.

"I know everything you say is right, Alice. I tell

myself that I don't want to derail this investigation by
introducing a distraction that could upset everyone's
focus on the facts ... but maybe I'm just afraid of
changing how I'm perceived."

Alice reached across and covered Caroline's hand
with hers. "No pressure from me. I know there's a
timing issue about us hanging around in the ether too.
Why come out at work when I might be gone in a few
months? I'm happy enough that we keep the topic on
the agenda and see what the future brings." And she
flashed her lover a sideways smile that put things back
on an even keel and delayed the difficult issue of their
future prospects for another while.

First thing on Thursday morning the two Murder
Squad DIs had a more than usually detailed discussion
about the findings that had emerged from the previous
day's inquiry. The southern team had worked their way
through all the follow-ups from the freephone and had
called at all the caravan parks in a twenty-kilometre
area along the eastern coast in both directions from the
Lonely Duck. They discovered that these places were a
haven for Dublin families, retirees and the occasional
couple looking for a few hours privacy away from the
public eye. Out of the holiday season there was little
surveillance in place and those with keys to caravans or
mobile homes came and went unchecked. No one had
seen two men there on the previous Tuesday and they

had left without making the hoped for breakthrough. Orla Hegarty had admitted to Caroline that without something more solid to go on they were running out of definite lines of inquiry.

Before she hung up, Caroline made some encouraging noises and then sat back and reviewed the progress in the northern element of the investigation. She did not have the same sense of frustration and she could see that her team was continuing to edge forward meticulously through the evidence they had amassed. Zara Pradić was busily typing on her keyboard and closely reading the data in front of her. From her office Caroline could see her jade hair sparkling in the light of her many screens. The young woman's absorption in her work was impressive, the DI thought. Her team had been impressive before but now she felt they were ready for a whole new era of solving murder cases. She turned back to Burrows' and McVeigh's reports from their day on the County Down coast. They had covered a lot of ground and she needed to get on top of all the detail.

Burrows and McVeigh had written up their reports and they had mostly served to confirm the evidence given by freephone callers and Nancy Quinn about her brother-in-law's activities while in the parish there. They now had a surname for the other woman who Father Michael Quinn had got pregnant. As a long shot, they had asked Pradić to see if she could find any online presence for Theresa de Paor who would now be in her mid-forties. If Nancy Quinn was right the woman would have had a termination several decades beforehand and possibly settled in England after that. During the night Pradić had sent an email to Nancy Quinn to see if she could help narrow down the date and the clinic that she had arranged for Theresa to visit. She was still waiting for a response.

It was a crisp morning with an ice-blue sky and Alice was aware of the fragile shimmer of green that was becoming visible on the trees along the river path. The cumulative effect of the budding trees gave her a surge of hope every year after the long winter. This daily route that Alice took allowed her to note the small gradual changes that the seasons wrought in the landscape and she felt attuned to these shifts in a way that was far bigger than just her perception of them.

As she rhythmically ran she mentally reviewed Zara Pradić's emailed profile of the perpetrator of the two recent murders. The killer had old scores to settle with two men of the church – one on his own behalf if the psychologist's intuition was correct and another motivated by the experience of a younger woman that he knew and cared about. These were historic debts that despite decades of inaction had become more imperative of late. It was likely that as a child he (or someone close to him) had spent some time in An Cuan industrial school in Connemara. He knew Brother

341

Francis Twomey to be a violent, abusive man who punished children with brutal beatings and by withholding their most basic nourishment.

The killer, like many others, was familiar with the physical abuse and public humiliation of a particular boy whose mother had recently died and whose crime was to make daisy chains and miss his evening meal. Although not the man called 'Dan', who was too disabled by arthritis, this was someone who had perhaps witnessed these acts of brutality and kept a daisy chain as a reminder. This was a man who was knowledgeable about how to administer a chokehold and despite his age (between mid-fifties and mid-sixties) had sufficient strength to manipulate Quinn's hefty body into a wheelchair and from there into a confessional. Perhaps he practiced martial arts or had been in the Defence Forces. The killer was computer literate, had access to Diazepam, was probably left-handed and well attuned to noticing and possibly commenting on life's ironies. He was well organised, strategic and had great patience. He had stored his considerable anger and resentment against these two men for decades without acting upon it. Perhaps something in his life circumstances had changed recently that meant he no longer felt any restraint in punishing the wrongs that he attributed to his victims. For some reason, the fact that their crimes had remained unpunished or generally unremarked was an injustice he now needed to rectify.

Perhaps his time was limited, Alice thought. And then it all began to become clear to her. Small pieces slipped into place and she stopped as if physically winded. She leaned forward and breathed deeply into her lungs and straightened. She looked at her watch. Then she took her phone from the zip pocket in her jacket and called Zara Pradić.

By the time she had completed her morning run Alice had tested her theory from a range of angles and was sure it held up. She just wasn't sure about how she felt about contributing to this killer's ultimate capture and punishment. She had taken Vince's question the previous day to heart: "Is there ever such a thing as a just killing?" As she pounded the Lagan towpath earlier she had considered this perplexing problem. Yes, of course it was accepted as just to kill in self-defence ... but even in that case there were limits. It was defensible to harm or even kill someone who is attacking you, your family or your property. But the acceptance of "just cause" didn't extend to all cases. A woman who kills her daughter's rapist or her own abusive partner while he sleeps, so as to avoid a violent struggle, may well be incarcerated for causing bodily harm or murder. From her father's generation, she knew that it was legally acceptable to wipe out entire villages in Vietnam as part of US involvement in that war. But for someone to decide to punish a member of the clergy who had systematically harmed hundreds of children and offended against the laws of humanity and the state would undoubtedly be classed as murder.

In all of this she was faced with consideration of her own role in supporting the police to track down the person who had taken the life of Father Quinn and Brother Twomey. She wasn't sure how she felt about that final objective of the work. It was one thing accompanying a vulnerable witness to an interview and helping them to ensure their rights were respected. It was a very different role to be facilitating the detection and capture of someone, himself maybe a victim, who had decided to punish acts that had incurred little or no punishment inside the legal system. Did that reluctance within the system to bring these abusers to book make it okay for someone to take the law into their own hands? Should those who are wronged be expected to behave more morally than their leaders?

Fundamentally Alice did not really agree with resorting to violence to solve problems. She liked the idea that most things could be resolved through non-violent means. In the projects in the poor areas where she worked, violence was everywhere and although she understood some of the frustration that lay behind it, she didn't condone it. She and Hugo had several times discussed the rights and wrongs of the different waves of the republican armed struggle against what he saw as British colonialism in Ireland. It was widely accepted now that the peace process was a good outcome to the most recent Troubles but Hugo's point was that might never have come about without the civil unrest and the bombing campaign that preceded the peace talks. These were arguments familiar in DePRec. Perhaps she needed to talk to some of those proponents of peace and reconciliation studies and become a little clearer on her own views. Yet another thing to add to a very long list of things she wanted to do during her time in Ireland.

Perhaps some of these thoughts resulted in her decision to call to Brenda later that morning. She remembered when she was almost there that this was Brenda's weekly shopping day but she wanted to check in with Jed anyway so she kept going.

On the tenth floor of the Divis Tower Block she waited at the door and was relieved to hear some movement inside and then the door opened by Jed, who had a pen in his hand.

Alice greeted him cheerily and to his obvious pleasure remarked, "Hey, Jed. I hope I'm not interrupting your writing."

He flushed with pride at this statement of his new identity.

"It's OK," he accepted coolly. "I was just finishing for today."

Jed's wide smile allowed Alice to know that things were all well in Flat 10B. He was relaxed and confident and went directly to put on the kettle without asking her what she'd like.

"I was just going to make a pot of Relax Tea, Alice – if you'd like to join me?"

"That would be just perfect, Jed." She delighted in his good humour and hesitated momentarily about introducing any negativity. "I was wondering how you are feeling about the funeral on Friday and if you'd like to have a bit of a chat about all that before we all head off to Dublin tomorrow."

"Well," he said, putting two mugs on a tray and two herbal tea bags in the teapot, "Mam and I have talked it through so that there won't be too many surprises. It will be as much of a shock for my father's family to have to take Mam and me on board as it will be for us seeing them all together for the first time … and him dead like." He looked at Alice as if to show that he had a fair grasp of what the practicalities would be.

She wondered if he could ever be prepared for the emotional surprises that might be in store but said nothing. She would be there on the day and would discreetly keep an eye on all that.

"I wanted to go because it's almost like I don't want to miss my chance to learn a little bit about him … like … it's sort of like the last minute." He poured the boiling water into the teapot and continued. "I want to be there for my mam as well. It's a last chance for both of us really to be with him before he's buried." He looked at Alice as if to gauge her view of that concession. "Mam has been talking to Nancy, his sister-in-law, my aunt I suppose. Apparently they liked each other back in the day and Nancy phoned Mam to ask if we wanted to attend the funeral. It made Mam, and me too, feel that we were recognised as part of the family in some way."

"And Brenda wanted Martha to be there too," Alice prompted, as she hadn't heard the outcome of that discussion as yet.

"Yeah. She did. I did too because it's almost like we get strength from each other and if she isn't there that would be missing. My gran doesn't come across as very sharp but she makes us feel safer when she is there. Does that make any sense?"

"Well, yes." Alice was sure Jed was right about that. "Martha loves you and Brenda unconditionally. You are family and when you are going into unknown territory, like meeting your father's relations that will make you feel stronger for sure. I get it, Jed."

He smiled to know that he had made sense of his feelings and carried the tray of tea and biscuits into the living-room area.

"And what about Brian?" Alice asked. "Your mum said he couldn't be there and that made Martha less comfortable about going."

Jed pushed a cup of steaming tea towards Alice and nodded. "Yeah. He has some appointment that he goes to on a Friday morning and he says he can't miss it. It's a bit of a mystery really but Martha has agreed to come along if we collect her." He seemed pleased to be the custodian of the plan. "My nan lives in a place called The Ranch. No – no horses and Stetsons. "It's not a bit like what it sounds. Just small flats inside a fenced-off area." He checked Alice was keeping up. "You and me and my mam will get a taxi there from the station tomorrow and then go over to the funeral home when it's time for the coffin to be closed. After that, we'll head to the chapel for the Mass." He hesitated and then continued a little awkwardly. "It makes a big difference that you'll be there too, Alice." He held her gaze and blushed a little.

"I'm happy to be of any use I can, Jed. And I'm glad Martha is going too. It will make a big difference for you and your mum."

"Mam gets annoyed a bit that Gran won't do stuff without Brian but I get that she likes him about the place. He looks after everything like – and he knows a lot about things, you know? He's not all talk. He's actually pulled himself up after a really awful childhood. Much worse than mine." Jed looked at Alice and seemed to decide to continue. "He doesn't like to talk about it and I'm not supposed to tell either but I know that you are good at respecting people's privacy ..."

He paused and Alice smiled encouragingly. She was eager to hear this story but didn't want that to be too apparent.

"When I was feeling really bad about my father and

all he talked to me about his own childhood and said that I was lucky to be loved by so many people. He said I could use the hard things to make me strong."

"Good advice," Alice replied, ensuring that she put no pressure on him to elaborate.

The young man was silent for a moment and then continued. "Brian's family was very, very poor. He used the word 'destitute', which I think means that they were as poor as could be. They lived in west Galway in Connemara."

Alice remembered Brian's words to her in the Felons Club: "I'm a Connemara man." She had not realised that Connemara was an area located in the county of Galway and had missed an important message there. Now things began to really fall into place. She kept her face calm and open and waited for Jed to continue.

"When he was a boy his parents couldn't afford to keep him and his brothers and sisters and so some were given to relatives and his father took him to An Cuan and left him there. It was a time when Ireland was a very poor country without supports for people who fell on hard times. They only had charity. His parents and some of his brothers and sisters died of TB and others emigrated and never made any contact after that."

Jed had remembered Brian's story well and Alice could hear the older man's influence in his retelling.

"Brian worked as a servant and only got very little education. He was like me in that. When he left he went into the army and studied in the evenings to better himself. He told me the army became his family. He was fed and given clothes and a warm bed and he said he grew up there. He never made any contact with his own family. I guess that's why he and Martha are so close and why he is kind of part of our family now."

Alice absorbed the full significance of Brian's story without letting Jed see how his words had impacted on her. She sipped her tea and was relieved to hear Brenda coming in through the front door, struggling with her bags of shopping and calling out to Jed to help her.

As she stood to lend a hand, Alice was dealing with the tragic possibility that Brian Mulgrew had killed Jed's biological father.

48

At a little before midday Alice stopped her bike to answer her phone which was buzzing in her pocket.

"I am Zara Pradić," the caller announced formally and asked Alice would she be able to call to the Murder Squad offices. They were due to have a meeting later that afternoon but she wanted to work through something with Alice beforehand. "I have followed up the idea you gave me this morning and I have some successes but it will be better if you are here to progress your idea."

Alice reviewed her position on Great Victoria Street. "Actually, I can be there in five minutes," she replied and hung up.

The Murder Squad offices were a hive of silent industry. Alice stood outside the glass doors and observed the scene within. The light glowed through the half-closed venetian blinds in Caroline's inside office space and DC Pradić sat in a gloomy corner illuminated by the light from at least four computer screens. Burrows and McVeigh were in a huddle in front of a sheet of paper that seemed to contain a list of names and other details. They were discussing each entry and crossing things off according to some criteria they had worked out. Alice was able to deduce that this was the outcome of Pradić's elaborate cross-referencing exercise. They had produced a list of those who might fit the killer's profile and were scrutinising them for opportunity and means.

As she pushed through the doors, the men turned to see who had come in, nodded a welcome to her and returned to their task.

Alice headed toward Pradić's workstation where an extra chair was already in place to the woman's left. Caroline's door was closed but Alice could hear her lover's distinctive voice from within. There was a press conference that evening and Caro would be under pressure to make sure her Chief was fully briefed. Being an all-island inquiry and the need to keep abreast of progress in both jurisdictions complicated the whole process but Alice could see the team ethos of moving steadily forwards was forcefully in action here.

Pradić patted the chair beside her without looking away from her screens. "I have done as you suggested, Dr Fox, and just managed to track down the additional data you alerted me to."

The paper that Tara had given Alice to read on the

train home from Dublin had alluded to difficulties in compiling complete data sets for those who had been in Irish industrial schools. Details of those referred through court orders and local authorities were mostly accurate but children voluntarily put into these institutions by destitute parents were less meticulously listed. Often they were either unrecorded or named separately from the main body of residents. When it came to redress procedures some survivors had found that there was no evidence of their ever having been incarcerated and as such they were denied compensation. The scholarly paper had suggested that the national census returns should have provided a full list of those present in places such as An Cuan and copies of this data set was subsequently made available to the Redress Board. Alice had asked Zara Pradić to include this additional data source in her searches and it transpired that a new name had emerged.

Alice looked now as Brian Mulgrew's name blinked at her from Pradić's main screen. There was an ID photo from his army records that showed an earnest, youthful Brian with sandy hair and freckles.

"Can you check what vehicles and properties are registered in his name?"

Zara's fingers leapt into action across the keyboard.

Alice knew that her hunch had been accurate and tried to stop herself rushing forward with the distressing consequences for Brenda and Jed. They were due to travel to Dublin by train the following day and collect Martha to attend Michael Quinn's funeral. It was hard to imagine what that journey would be like now that yet one final shocking element had been added into the mix.

The screen showed Land Registry records of a field along the North County Dublin coast in the name of Brian Joseph Mulgrew. It mentioned permissions for the presence of a mobile home and a temporary corrugated metal workshop with electricity and plumbing. Vehicle registration detailed a relatively new hybrid car and a vintage motorcycle with sidecar.

Alice smiled at the man's ingenuity. "So that's how he did it!" She could see it clearly now – Brian on the motor cycle and Quinn in the sidecar en route for St Oliver's and his final confession.

Pradić was already sending details of the motorcycle to those involved in CCTV searches North and South. Their job would be straightforward now.

"We had better tell the team," she said and went over to Burrows and McVeigh.

When she returned to her seat, Alice remarked ,"I'm wondering if this is the first time they'll have had a murder victim driven to the ultimate crime scene in a motorcycle sidecar. Such a clever plan for one who was given a very poor start in life!" She was sure that the woman understood her meaning completely.

Burrows had immediately gone and tapped on Caroline's door and soon they were all there standing around Pradić's desk, looking very pleased. However, while they were happy to have solved the puzzle, neither Alice nor Pradić were joyful about the consequences for Brian Mulgrew.

Zara Pradić scraped her green hair back and fixed it in place with her mother-of-pearl clip.

"I will let Alice explain," she said. "I have only done what she asked."

And so Alice explained how she had little by little come to fix her attention on Brian Mulgrew as someone who had a connection to Connemara and a close relationship to generations of women who had been abused at the hands of members of religious orders, including Father Michael Quinn. Her reading about the background to An Cuan and other such schools had let her know that the records were not always fully up to date. She had asked Pradić to track the recorded census detail for An Cuan in the sixties and seventies. Although the Census itself was not available, the copies of submissions made by the school authorities were recorded and available in the Christian Brothers' archive. This had shown that in 1960, Brian Joseph Mulgrew, then aged seven, had been voluntarily admitted to An Cuan by his father who had declared himself destitute and unable to keep him.

"*Yes!*" said Caroline as she punched the air. "I'll get on to DI Hegarty with that detail and we'll see if Mr Mulgrew can be brought in by the gardaí for questioning. Zara, forward the details you have to me, please, and let's see if we can get all we need to copper-fasten this, preferably before this evening's press conference. Really good work, everybody. We'll meet at two o'clock as planned."

And, smiling triumphantly, she turned and made her way back to her office.

McVeigh took orders and went to the canteen to get sandwiches and coffee for everyone and they settled down to finish the tasks they'd been working on. This wasn't the moment to let some details slip.

Alice took a moment and phoned Hugo and told him there was a further development in the murder investigation that would impact on Brenda and Jed. She suggested they call to the Divis Tower later that afternoon. Brenda would be home from work shortly after four o'clock and they could see what help they could offer them with processing this latest development in their family saga. Then she returned to her place beside Pradić and watched as the final stages of the inquiry fell into place.

Pradić was googling the name 'de Paor'. "I thought this name that Burrows sent me was French but now I see that it is Irish for the surname 'Power' and that is very interesting indeed. This is also the name of Johnny Power who was part of our investigation."

Alice nodded and hoped silently that this might be a glimmer of good news emerging from this whole business. She sat beside the DC as she contacted the abortion clinic that Nancy Quinn had booked for Theresa de Paor just over twenty years ago. The historic records had been digitised and showed that Theresa had not kept her appointment. It seemed she had taken the money provided by Nicholas Quinn for the termination and disappeared into the English ether.

"Check the records of UK births and deaths, Zara." Alice lightly touched the woman's arm to remind her she was there. "She was pregnant and it seems she may have decided to keep the baby."

And so the tracking of Theresa proceeded until they had a photograph, an email address and a mobile phone number. Mary Theresa Power from Connemara, thanks to the nun's insistence on Irish surnames, had segued into Theresa de Paor, a live-in maid in County Down, Northern Ireland. From there she had discreetly begun a new life with her son Jonathan, Jed Clinton's younger half-brother. It seemed that Brenda and Johnny were about to have more in common than they could ever have envisaged.

"What now?" asked Zara Pradić.

"I think we can discuss this at the meeting and maybe the team could agree to my giving this information to Johnny later and allowing him to gently renew his relationship with his sister and nephew, in their own time." Alice looked speculative.

Pradić nodded agreement and with an emotionless

expression turned to silently accept her cheese sandwich from McVeigh.

Alice emphasised her point. "This has no further bearing on the investigation and I am sure everyone will be happy that there is a potentially happy ending to this small branch of the story of Michael Quinn."

She sat back and sipped her awful canteen coffee and waited for the clock to get around to the time for the meeting to begin.

At five to two they all moved around the large table at the other end of the room. Caroline sat at the head of the table and seemed in buoyant mood.

"Hearty congratulations from our southern colleagues and from our own very happy Chief Super." She smiled broadly at them all. "DI Hegarty was beating herself up about not picking up on Mulgrew when they interviewed Martha Clinton. I told her that we had gone along a similar path and there would be time enough for evaluating things when everything is done and dusted." She reached across the table and took a small chocolate bar in hand. "They have gone to both Mulgrew's addresses, and to Martha Clinton's but he is not there so there's a full search on for him now. In his Dublin flat they found medical appointments for weekly chemotherapy, every Friday in a Dublin Clinic. Our perp is terminally ill and that no doubt was the catalyst that prompted his revenge killings."

She paused then for a moment as if deciding what to

say next and then she fixed her gaze on Alice and smiled.

"It would be remiss of me not to acknowledge how well the collaboration with Alice has contributed to this successful outcome. We all play our part, differently but significantly to the work of the Squad but the additional insight, that having a witness support person brought, has been invaluable. Thank you, Alice, for your innumerable skills." And she raised her eyebrows mischievously and quite explicitly licked her lips.

No one else seemed to notice and so Alice nodded in modest acceptance of the praise, which the others endorsed with nods and smiles.

They worked their way forensically through the detail of their case and then were interrupted by the DI's phone buzzing insistently.

"I'll take this. It's DI Hegarty."

She walked into her office and closed the door.

Several minutes later she emerged holding a bundle of faxed sheets.

"*Curiouser and curiouser* ... as another Alice once remarked. In Brian Mulgrew's mobile home they turned up Michael Quinn's wallet and a letter addressed to Dr Alice Fox. I took the liberty of asking them to open it and fax us the contents. And here they are." She held the pages aloft, looked at Alice and formed a question with her eyebrows.

"Be my guests," Alice responded with a magnanimous wave of her arm. "It's all evidence now, isn't it?"

49

Dear Alice,

By the time you read this I will probably be already dead or damned near it anyway. I will be washed up in the tide some day and that will finish the story once and for all. I have no desire to be a trophy in a police investigation nor do I want to linger and experience months of pain. I particularly do not want Martha, Brenda and Jed to be the witnesses of any of that. They have suffered enough in life through the actions of egotistical men and I do not want to be another name on that list. I have explained to Martha that I am ill and have no choice but to leave her. I think she is assured of my love for her and I have told her that I will stay as close to her as death allows. None of us can know what comes next, if anything, but she will take comfort from my promise and that is what matters. I know that

Brenda and Jed will look after her and she has friends in The Ranch who will look out for her too. She has more money than she will ever need and I have left all I have to Brenda and Jed so that they will be able to have the choices they deserve in life.

If, or when I am finally discovered to be the killer of Quinn and Twomey, I know that it will be because of your intervention, Alice. When I was making my plans, I could not have anticipated your involvement with Jed and then with Brenda. That exposed me to your very eagle eye, Alice. I knew the night in the Felons Club when I told you that I was a Connemara man that I had made my first error in what I think were two well planned and implemented executions. I don't think I would ever have come to the attention of the police if not for you and your getting close to Jed and Brenda.

I am not really the killing type but those men would otherwise never have faced any kind of punishment for their torture of young boys and exploitation of disadvantaged young women. It was a personal matter but also much bigger than just me and Martha. I had hoped that the system would eventually show some justice to those it allowed to be cruelly harmed and neglected but as time passed it looked less and less likely.

When I learned last year that I was terminally ill, I realised that freed me to act where others had failed to do so and I began to make my plan. I saw a picture of Twomey in the paper one day with a few of the remaining Brothers and it was easy enough to track him down. It is amazing how easily you can convince those boyos that you are on their side. It is absolutely what they expect. I said I wanted to volunteer to support elderly religious who no longer had a community to live in and sure I was welcomed with open arms. They gave me names and contact details and suggestions for how I might help. Meals on Wheels for the Smiler was too good an opportunity to miss.

The State did me no favours as a child and later in the army it was the same State that taught me to kill even though, ironically, my role was that of peacekeeper. I like to think that they unwittingly provided me with the skills to get some justice ... or maybe I mean revenge, for generations of boys and young women abused at the hands of supposedly religious people. Even with my meager experience of a family I knew that what passed as normal daily life in An Cuan was not right. Life was meant to be another, better way. I had only seven years with my parents and siblings before we became destitute and my family could no longer stay together. I then spent a lot of my childhood watching the treatment that Twomey and his likes handed out to poor and defenseless children. Mostly I watched but on occasions I also experienced my own fair share of beatings and buggery. Those were hard lessons for a small boy to learn. Once I swept up after he had shaved a young boy's head and humiliated *him for making a daisy chain and that was only days after the boy's mother had died. I had an old envelope where I kept those daisies and other small treasures, like big safety pins, for all these years. They served as a reminder of the wrongs done to that gentle boy and others like him by the Smiler and his likes.*

I was lucky in a way that I was the lowest of the low in An Cuan – beneath everyone else. I was a slave who was only required to follow orders. I learned very quickly to remain invisible and to perform my tasks in such a way that they rarely gave me a second glance. I'm like you in that respect, Alice, in that I learned how to wait quietly on the sidelines without drawing attention to myself. I've seen how you operate and, like me, you know there's a great freedom in not being noticed.

When I went to his Wicklow home, Twomey had no idea who I was and yet I had committed to memory his every action all those decades ago. Perhaps that's the difference between the powerful and the weak. Power does not need to remember those it dominates but we, the powerless, only survive by developing a detailed understanding of the people that try to control us. That is our ultimate survival technique – to know their ways and what to expect, so we can protect ourselves.

Oh, the absolute irony of the Smiler! He actually thought I was coming to bring him a hot meal! His sense of entitlement got a rude awakening when I explained that my purpose was to end his appetite

363

forever. By way of excuse, he told me he punished boys for their own good, so that they would learn to better know their place in the world. That response made my task a whole lot easier. There was no need for second thoughts, no softening of my resolve. He demonstrated that he had learned nothing from all the enquiries and public discussion that took place about child abuse in Ireland. His sense of his own righteousness remained utterly unshaken by the Ryan Report, by any of the survivors' testimonies and by all that media criticism. No regrets for Brother Twomey. He even smiled his way into the hereafter.

Michael Quinn was a different kettle of fish although just as deadly in his own way for those he set his sights on. I think you know, Alice that I was totally devoted to Martha. She is such an angel – really utterly goodness itself. For all the generations of harm done to her mother, to her, and to her daughter, she was completely without bitterness. I never met a kinder more good-natured person. And she was the best fun to be with. She loves a pint of beer and a singsong and any excuse for a party. People who think she's slow-witted often judge her harshly but she judges nobody and wishes nobody any harm.

I had one of the Sisters that had charge of her in the orphanage on my list of potential victims too but when I got wind that Quinn was trying to track down Brenda and Jed I realised that was a more urgent priority. The nun got lucky that day. You see, I was the person who answered all Martha's correspondence. I realised that the boy's father was trying to find them and I wasn't going to allow that to happen. No way. That was never going to be a happy ever after of that sort for anyone I cared about. As I said to Brenda when she was debating about telling Jed his history, 'He doesn't need a scumbag like that in his life.' I think that she heard me and was holding off telling Jed about his father... but then the bastard was on his own mission and I had to stop him.

How did I know who was Jed's father? It couldn't have been easier. I knew where Brenda had been working during that summer when she got pregnant. She had talked to me about Hilltown Bay and the Youth Club for poor kids and I knew that it was someone there who had abused her and got her pregnant. I went there and followed up with the parish office. I said that I was trying to track down the person who was running the youth group twenty-three years beforehand. It was easy to find Quinn's name and his new parish and the chat in the local pub let me know he had a reputation with young girls. Still I couldn't be sure so I consulted some photos and the family relationship was clear as daylight. Jed was very obviously his father's son.

Quinn was totally self-indulgent. I saw his weaknesses and how easy it would be to fan his ego. I arranged to meet him and told him someone from his past wanted to catch up with him. Someone that he had been close to wanted to meet up with him again. I brought him to my place up the coast telling him I had photos of the woman. I told him she was nearly forty and had a son of twenty-three now and I could see him doing the calculations and taking the bait. I gave him whiskey with some of Martha's Diazepam in it and he conked out soon enough. I had dealt with Twomey in the morning so I had worked out a bit of a routine. Chokehold and then in Quinn's case I cut off his dick and I got him into the sidecar of my old bike that Brenda and I used occasionally for fun. I had recently serviced it so it was running well. I brought everything I needed for setting up the body and after dark I took the back road to the border and then staying clear of the main roads I made my way to Belfast and the Ormeau Road. Now that you know that the evidence will be easy to find.

Why bother to take Quinn all the way to the North when I could have put him in any number of places nearer home? He wasn't the most attractive or sweet-smelling travelling companion and I thought long and hard about that decision. I knew from Brenda that the survivors in the North had to fight very hard to get even a fraction of the support and recognition that the ones in the south had... and that was unfair and needed to be set right. I wanted Quinn's death to provoke a public discussion and I thought that leaving him in Belfast, beside the old Magdalene laundry, was one way to show that this is an all-island issue.

The back gate of St Oliver's was open all the time but I had made sure Peadar, the janitor, would be in the pub and the side door of the church would be open. I had met him by chance one night in the Felons and he was far gone with the drink. He told me he should be locking up the chapel but sure what would it matter if it was open all night? Wouldn't God look after his own? That made me laugh I can tell you. I knew then what I would do with Father Michael Quinn and it was as simple as that.

I wonder if you might have found my treatment of these men unnecessarily harsh, Alice. You are a gentle soul. Why did I cut them? Was that a step too far? Well, first of all I'm not sure they deserved any just treatment but even so, I waited until they had been quickly and painlessly killed before doing any removal of body parts. It was less about making them suffer and more about making a public statement. Murder attracts attention and questions get asked. I wanted to be very clear what their offences had been and how they had broken their own rules ... repeatedly. They and their likes had caused so much pain in so many lives. I left my messages so that people would have to search for answers to explain the particular arrangement of each body and the words that best captured their hypocrisy.

I honestly didn't feel that I was doing something wrong, Alice. I felt that they both deserved to be exposed and punished for all the people whose lives they had messed up. I know it wouldn't work if everyone settled their own scores like that but just once, when my number is up anyway, I thought it was worth putting my message out there. What does it matter now anyway? What's done is done and others will judge me as they see fit. I'm pretty sure that there will be none of the old boys of An Cuan who will be finding fault with my actions. In lots of ways I'm sorry that I didn't act sooner in my life but maybe I had too much to lose then. Prison would have been one institution too many for me and as long as I had Martha in my life I wouldn't risk losing her. Interesting how knowing the Grim Reaper is at the door will bring things sharply into focus.

Why am I telling you all this, Alice Fox? Good question. I am really unconcerned about how I am to be judged but I guess I had an inkling that you might understand that I saw the chance to get a small bit of justice before my time was up. Even a small bit of justice is better than none, I reckon.

Yours truly
Brian Mulgrew

50

On the train home from Michael Quinn's funeral, Brenda, Jed and Alice made a quiet trio. Martha had refused the offers that she should come with them to Belfast for a while until it became clearer what had become of Brian. For the moment he had disappeared without trace but Alice was sure that he had ended his life and that his remains would materialise eventually. In the meantime Martha had accepted his preparatory messages and just kept saying, "I know he's close by." She seemed sad but at peace with that.

The rhythmic sound of the train soothed them in a way and the silence allowed them to weigh the entirety of the events of the past ten days. Each had a version of the same script in his or her head that no one else would ever fully understand. Jed had been calm and dignified at the service in the chapel. He walked between his mum and his gran, wearing a dark suit borrowed from Gary and one of Hugo's ties. His Quinn family genes were obvious as he stood beside his uncle and cousins outside the church. Nancy had decided not to make things more complicated than necessary and introduced him without apology as Mick's son. She had promised to stay in touch with his mum and he guessed that might mean there would be some small link between him and his father into the future.

Brenda had somehow managed to sleep the previous night despite Alice and Hugo delivering the bombshell about Brian and then the visit from Johnny. He had told them about his first conversation with his sister in over thirty-five years. His nephew, another of Michael Quinn's progeny was a few years younger than Jed but the physical resemblance between them was remarkable. Johnny's presence made even her anxieties about her mam and Brian seem less burdensome. Brian had acted to try and right an unrightable wrong, she thought. She knew why, but she thought that if he had asked her what she wanted it wouldn't have been anything like the path he had chosen for them all. She didn't need Mick Quinn killed and castrated to know that he had wronged her and made her life harder than it needed to be. She wondered how Brian had allowed himself to do such dreadful things when he had been such a gentle and caring man with Martha. Now there was another whole new reality for her and Jed and she knew that they would be fine. They would make the best of what they had as they had always done and their solid love would make a space for the new people that would claim a spot in their lives.

Alice had watched as the story of the two killings and Brian's choreography of it all had come to light in Flat 10B in Divis Tower. She and Hugo had continued their double act of assuring Jed and Brenda that they would stay close through all these upheavals. Alice saw herself becoming more and more connected to this new life in Ireland and wondered where it was all leading. There were options for sure and she would have to make decisions about all of them before too long.

She and Caroline had managed a few hours' sleep before she had to head off on Friday's train journey.

The satisfaction with the inquiry outcome had led to some Murder Squad celebrations the previous evening and Caroline had been quite merry on her return to Botanic. She made an effusive drama of how pleased she was with the outcome of the day. In particular the Chief Superintendent had wished to pass on his acknowledgement of Alice's significant role in the inquiry. "I'll swear he winked at me when he said 'significant role'. He was very nearly saucy." She made a revolted expression that looked as if her features were melting. "I don't want any more close encounters like that I can tell you, Dr Alice Fox." And she laughed heartily and announced that she now wished to show her full appreciation to Alice, in a horizontal position. In the real world, she had been asleep as soon as her head touched the pillow.

Throughout the day in Dublin, Alice had stayed unobtrusively alongside Jed and Brenda and watched how well they had looked after each other and Martha. They were quietly dignified beside some of the brash Quinn men and Alice was filled with certainty that the Clinton family would manage life very well in the future. She doubted that there would be many family reunions. Nancy Quinn would get drawn back into her middle-class life and concerns about the misfortunes caused to the Clintons by her brother-in-law would cease to be a priority.

"Thanks for everything, Alice." Brenda hugged Alice as they stood in line waiting to come out the gate from the Dublin train. "Johnny's collecting us. Can we give you a lift home?"

Alice declined and promised she would keep in touch.

Standing a little to the side of the railing's Alice could see Caro waiting, smiling broadly. She was on holiday now for two weeks and second on her 'to do' list after starting counselling was organising an Easter break for them in the Catalonian sun. Apparently Caroline had the idyllic place for them to go and the best small hotel where the slogan was '*Fet amb love*' – a mix of Catalan and English that meant 'made with love'. Right now they didn't need to look any further ahead than that.

Endword

Whether you read this as an eBook or in paperback copy and enjoyed the experience, please take the time to post a short review on <bookdepository.com> or <amazon.co.uk> or <amazon.com>. This reader feedback has become one of the main measures of the success of a book ... to the extent that it is possible to buy a batch of favourable reviews and thereby boost ratings. I prefer to hope that reader response will be the honest judge of whether *Just Killings* has merit as a murder mystery. Thank you for supporting me in this.

Acknowledgements

The writing of this second book in the Alice Fox series was completely influenced by extensive ethnographic research that I did some years ago and that was published by Tufnell Press in 2014 – *Learning care lessons: Literacy love, care and solidarity*. These were the accounts of real lives that made a deep impact on me. *Just Killings* is entirely a work of fiction and none of the characters, apart from small details that I have borrowed in my story-making, are reflective of the real people with whom I worked. They inspired me with their courage, kindness and resilience and I continue to draw daily on those lessons.

Both *Murder in the Academy* and *Just Killings* are based on imaginary scenarios that would occur if those who behaved abusively incurred the ultimate punishment of losing their life. It is interesting to me that this type of retribution is rarely put into practice in real life. The law does not allow such retaliatory actions but their infrequency perhaps illustrates a hopeful dimension of human nature: that in the face of rampant injustice (outside of war and gangland culture) most people do not see killing as a fair or useful response.

I am grateful to my critical readers: John Baker, Ursula Barry, Vesna Jankovic and Petrena Williams, all of whom helped shape the final draft of this book. Michelle Page and Trina Barr kept me right about police procedures and protocols and Paula Campbell and David Prendergast of Poolbeg were an invaluable support. Gaye Shortland has again performed her editorial miracle and polished my rough draft into a more presentable story. I am most appreciative of the gift that her skilful work bestows on my efforts.

Margaret Ward is a knowledgeable writer and constant friend who deserves recognition for her daily encouragement of my efforts and of course, nothing at all would happen without the judicious reading, honest comments and bountiful love of Ann Hegarty. I am so lucky!

Printed in Germany
by Amazon Distribution
GmbH, Leipzig

27771406R00227